Lara

her mo...   ...t adventure

Please return / renew this item by the last date shown above
Dychwelwch / Adnewyddwch erbyn y dyddiad olaf y nodir yma

Discover more at millsandboon.co.uk.

THE LORD'S INCONVENIENT VOW

Lara Temple

MILLS & BOON

First Published in Great Britain 2019
by Mills & Boon, an imprint of HarperCollins*Publishers*
1 London Bridge Street, London, SE1 9GF

© 2019 Ilana Treston

ISBN: 978-0-263-26942-0

MIX
Paper from
responsible sources
FSC
www.fsc.org
FSC® C007454

This book is produced from independently certified FSC™ paper
to ensure responsible forest management.
For more information visit www.harpercollins.co.uk/green.

Printed and bound in Spain
by CPI, Barcelona

To Lucas and Chase and Sam—
I've lived with you and loved with you
and now I have to let you go.

Prologue

'The Hidden City isn't truly invisible, Gabriel. Most people are blind to what threatens their world. Life is easier thus.'
—The Sprite Queen,
Desert Boy Book One

Qetara, Egypt—1814

'For heaven's sake, Lady Samantha, come down before you fall down.'

'Oh, go away, Sir Stay-Away-from-the-Edge.'

'Stop calling me that.'

'Well, Mama says I mustn't call you Edge any longer because now that I am eighteen it is no longer proper. But I refuse to call you Lord Edward Edgerton; that is even stuffier than you are.'

He burst into laughter. He didn't often laugh freely, but it always surprised her how it transformed his face, softening the sharp-cut lines on either side of his mouth and between his overly straight brows. With his serious grey-green eyes and hair as dark as any of her Venetian cousins he'd always appeared so adult. Or perhaps it was his insistence on dressing so properly even in the heat of the Egyptian desert.

Next to him her brothers looked like heathens or corporeal manifestations of the gods etched on the temple walls where her mother's cousin Huxley spent all his waking hours working with Edge's uncle Poppy. Once those two were caught in the web of their historical weaving, everyone else faded into nothingness—more ghosts in a landscape of ghosts and far less interesting.

He stopped laughing and frowned even more awfully, as if he needed to compensate for his moment of levity.

'Proper. You have no idea what that means.'

'Yes, I do. It means doing nothing enjoyable at all.'

'No, it means showing respect. And it means not climbing on the antiquities.'

'If this sphinx survived two thousand years, it will survive me.'

'It is not a sphinx but a ram and Poppy says it is likely at least three thousand years old based on references in…never mind. In any case it should not have to suffer the indignity of being climbed upon. And barefoot, too. One day you will step on a scorpion and that will be the end of it.'

'You have my permission to dance a jig on my grave if it is, Lord Hedgehog.'

He ignored her latest variation on his name.

'Don't be a fool, Sam. Besides, I hate dancing. Why the…why are you up there anyway?'

'Come see.'

She turned away and waited. He might be as dry as a mummy, but he had his uncle's curiosity. She wondered if he realised he'd reverted to calling her Sam as he once had. Probably not.

It took five minutes. She heard the scrape of his boots and a muffled curse. Probably something like 'drat' or 'bother'; despite being such good friends with Lucas and Chase, he never participated in their cursing contests. Since his uncle and aunt had brought him to Egypt when he was only six years old he spoke Arabic better than all of them, but he rarely indulged in the very colourful epithets Lucas and Chase mined from the locals, at least not in her hearing. In fact, she sometimes wondered why he and her brothers were so close.

She waited for him to say something unpleasant about her occupation, but though he cast a shadow over her sketchpad he said nothing. She twisted to look at him, but all she could see was a dark shape haloed by the sun.

'Not bad. You're improving.'

The temptation to give his legs a shove and send him tumbling off the sphinx…off the *ram*… was powerful, but she resisted. He had a point—

she was now eighteen and perhaps it was time to resist such puerile urges. Still, she smiled at the image, taking some pleasure in cutting him down to size in her mind. When she answered, her voice was dignified.

'Cousin Huxley believes I am very gifted. He says some of the Sinclairs possess artistic skills. Like my Aunt Celia.'

She spoke her aunt's name defiantly, waiting for him to attack that as well. But no doubt the scandal of Lady Stanton's elopement with a spy and their subsequent demise was too much for him to even consider because he merely sat beside her.

'May I?'

'Sit? You may. This is not my ram, after all.'

'No, may I see your sketches?'

He took her sketchpad with all the care he gave to the shards and remains his uncle excavated. She tried not to squirm as he lingered over a sketch of a wall painting from the temple below the cliffs and one of a funerary urn bearing the head of Bastet, the feline god.

'You've a good eye for detail. There is not one mistake here. Very strange.'

She gritted her teeth, but as he turned she saw the wavering at the corner of his mouth and relaxed a little. She could never tell when his peculiar sense of humour would surface. She'd forgotten that about him—under his granite shell there was another Edge, the one who was endlessly considerate of Poppy and Janet and her mother, and who she often suspected was laughing even when he was doing his very best to scold her.

'Most amusing. You would not be smiling if you know how close you came to being shoved off on to your posterior.'

He frowned.

'That is most definitely not a proper word in mixed company.'

'Posterior? It is a perfectly innocuous word.'

'The word might be innocuous, but its…what it alludes to…'

'Your behind?'

'Sam! Will you ever grow up?'

'I *am* grown up. In a couple of months I shall make my debut in Venetian society, be crammed into a frilly dress and have no choice but to behave like a simpering simpleton. But I am not there yet and I see nothing wrong with speaking of something completely natural. You and Lucas and Chase did it often enough when in your cups——I distinctly remember you once discussing the attributes of a certain *ghawazi* dancer in rather off-putting detail.'

He groaned.

'You are impossible.'

'And you're stiff-necked, stuffy and stodgy bundled together and tied with a neat little bow and dipped in vinegar.'

'Not little. I take offence at that.'

She couldn't stop her smile. Somehow he always managed to pull the rug of her annoyance out from under her.

'No, not little. Is being a great big bore preferable to being a little one?'

'As long as I am great at something.'

She shifted, turning more fully to him and shielding her eyes from the sun.

'Do you wish to be great at something, Edge?'

'Doesn't everyone?'

'I don't know. Probably in some vague way, but not in actuality because it means they must invest effort in it. What do you wish to be great at?'

Even under the glare of the sun and the warmth of his tanned skin she could see the rise of colour in his lean cheeks. He moved his leg as if to slide off the statue and she caught his sleeve.

'Wait. I won't press if you don't wish to talk of it. Is your arm better?'

He rolled his left shoulder.

'Better. But it was infuriating to be invalided out just before Napoleon abdicated. Have you heard from Lucas or Chase?'

'They sent word they are to remain in France. Something to do with my uncle. I haven't seen them in…far too long.'

She clasped her hands, hoping he didn't notice them shaking. Moving so often meant her only home was her family—Lucas, Chase and her mother in the inner core, and Cousin Huxley and the Carmichaels directly after them. And Edge. Beyond them she had no home, no roots, no anchor. If something happened to Lucas or Chase... It would be unbearable.

'I miss them.' The words burst from her. 'Even with the war ended everything is uncertain. Even now they might not be alive and it could be weeks before I know.'

He placed his hand on hers, warm and firm, but he didn't try to reassure her. She wished he would break with his nature and offer comfort, even lie to her, but it wasn't Edge's way. Talking with him always felt like approaching an island patrolled by a wary navy—being allowed ashore was an arduous process. Perhaps it was because he came to live with the Carmichaels when he was six. She'd never dared ask why. All she knew was that Poppy and Janet loved him deeply and absolutely and were never wary of showing that love, even now he was grown. They'd cried when he arrived and even Huxley and her mother had looked a little damp. In fact, only Edge remained calm during the reunion, though he'd looked different than her memory—familiar but a stranger. Or perhaps *she* was different, grown up. She didn't want to be, but everyone told her she was.

She resisted the urge to lean into his strength, searching for something to say.

'I would like to see London again one day. My mother swore never to return so I have not been since I was a child. Did you visit the British Museum? That would be top of my list if I ever return.'

He withdrew his hand and clasped his arms round his knees.

'One day you will. Your mother's decisions after your father's scandal are her own, Sam, not yours. From what Poppy and Huxley said, he was merely a good man who made a mistake while he was far away from his family.'

'It is not like you to varnish the truth, Edge. An affair with an engaged woman and a duel with her cuckolded betrothed is a rather serious mistake,' she scoffed.

'True, but it is still sad when an otherwise good man's memory is reduced to his worst action. And remember that your father's death does not reflect on you in any way.'

'According to society, it does.'

He looked out at the horizon, his voice shifting again, turning stiffer and more hesitant. 'Society is strange. People separately can be...pleasant, but sometimes together... They are like a mythical many-headed beast guarding a kingdom, full of suspicion and even exultation when one fails to solve the riddle that allows you in.'

She turned to him, concern overcoming her pain.

'Did they say things about you when you were in London, Edge?'

'There is always gossip.'

'But you're perfect,' she blurted out and even before he laughed she turned as red as a sunset and hotter than the Nubian Desert in midday.

'I did not mean you are *perfect*...' she said crossly.

'I know that.' He was still laughing. 'You meant I was so boring there could be nothing to gossip about.'

'I did not mean that either. But truly I cannot see what they could object to.'

'Thank you for that, Sam. But anything outside the ordinary is suspect to a closed group.'

'Do you mean because Poppy and Janet raised you instead of your parents? Why *were* you sent to live with them, Edge?' It was the most daring thing she'd ever asked him and she waited for his usual dismissal, but he merely stared at the horizon, his profile sharp against the sky. She knew him almost as well as her brothers, but she was not certain she knew him at all. Perhaps that was why those people were suspicious of him.

'I don't remember. I don't remember anything of those first six years at all. No... I remember snow and grey, that is all. But if it was anything like what I saw these past months then I'm glad I don't. My parents... I spent time with my mother because of my sister's debut. My father thankfully does not leave Greybourne because he could make a funeral procession feel like a fête. They are utterly unlike Poppy and Janet. My mother is very cold and condescending and my father is…rigidly pious.' He glanced at her. 'Go ahead, say something about the apple not falling far from the tree.'

There was almost a snarl in his words which also wasn't like him and she shook her head.

'I shan't say what I don't think. I never saw you condescend to anyone, no matter their choice of gods or their place in society. And as for cold…' She paused as his frown deepened—she could almost feel him haul up the drawbridge and she realised with surprise that her words mattered to him. She'd never thought that before. 'I think you do your best to build battlements of ice, but they keep melting because you aren't really cold. Poppy and Janet could never have loved you so deeply if you were.'

Her words surprised her as much as they appeared to embarrass him. His high cheekbones turned dark beneath his sun-warmed skin and he planted his hands on the stone as if ready to push to his feet. She almost took his hand and asked him to stay, but his embarrassment spread to her and she waited for him to make his excuses and leave.

He sighed, his hand relaxing a little on the stone.

'If I didn't know how honest you are, Sam, I'd suspect you of trying to butter me up for some reason or another. Did you happen to topple some precious antiquity while I wasn't looking by any chance?'

She smiled in relief.

'The fallen Colossi of Memnon? That was I.'

He laughed and she relaxed a little further.

'I hope you do come to London soon, Sam. When you do, I shall take you to the Museum. There is a statue there that made me think of you, a bust of a girl staring at the sky like you do when you make believe you haven't heard your mother when she summons you to supper.'

She laughed as well, embarrassed but peculiarly flattered to be compared to a statue and that anything made him think of her at all, let alone fondly. It was so very unlike Edge to say anything remotely nice to her. She smoothed her grubby skirts over her thighs, suddenly wishing she wasn't dressed in this dusty jumble of eastern and western garb.

'What else did you do in London? Aside from being forced into the company of your unworthy parents,' she prompted, not wanting him to stop talking. He smiled and the strange lightness about him struck her again. He'd changed so much since his last visit to Egypt two years previously. Or she had. Or both of them.

'I had to attend endless balls and assemblies for Anne's debut. You would have enjoyed watching me squirm.'

'No, I wouldn't. Was it terrible?'

'Sometimes. Other times I actually enjoyed myself...' He brushed some sand from the stone between them, a frown drawing his brows together. 'It pulls you in, that world. Everything appears so...easy. We barely survived the war and yet they are all so gay, so full of life. It tips the scales back a little; washes away the blood and dirt and pain and you can begin to believe London is the truth, not...everything else. That you are who they see.' He hesitated, gathering back the sand he'd scattered into a little mound. 'Everyone calls me Edward or Lord Edward there.'

'Well, those are your names.'

'I know, but... I have been called Edge for years. Ever since a certain annoying six-year-old on her first visit to Qetara decreed I didn't look like an Edward or Lord Edward Edgerton and rechristened me Edge.'

Sam flushed again.

'I still don't think you look like an Edward, and Lord Edward Edgerton sounds like a particularly pompous character from a morality play, but I hardly forced anyone to call you Edge, they did that all on their own.'

'Yes, well, you had a way of dragging people along with you. And I didn't object. I liked that it was uncommon. Edward is my father's name.'

'Oh.'

'Yes. Edward Raphael something something.

The two monikers bestowed upon the first two Edgerton males.'

'If you don't like them calling you Edward, tell them so. I've certainly told you often enough not to call me Samantha.'

He frowned. 'As you said, that is my name. It is who I am.'

Sam didn't understand what he was trying to say, if anything at all—Poppy and Janet and everyone still called him Edge and he had not objected. Absently she traced a little pyramid in the sand he'd gathered between them and he added a crescent of a moon.

'Deep in the desert, by the light of a silver sliver of a moon...' he intoned and she smiled. One of Edge's redeeming features was how well he read aloud. There was little entertainment in Qetara and their small group did their best with the material at hand, from cards to charades to books. Since childhood she'd loved the moment someone handed Edge a book to read aloud. It wasn't merely the depth and timbre of his voice, but how it would shift and change with the tale. She would close her eyes and see every word he spoke, more vivid than a dream. It was the one quality for which she was willing to excuse all his lectures about her lack of decorum and his ability to ignore her absolutely when she annoyed him. Someone with such an ability to bring a tale to life could not be wholly humdrum.

'No,' she corrected. 'You are telling a different tale—deep in the heart of London, by the light of a hundred chandeliers, they danced that night away…'

He brushed the sand away completely and re-clasped his hands around his knees.

'Three chandeliers, but enormous. I think each one held a hundred candles. At least it looked that way. I kept worrying the hot wax would drop on the dance floor and we would skid and waltz into a wall.'

She laughed, but something in his voice caught her attention.

'We?'

He turned his head and then she heard it as well.

'Daoud's horn. Come before the flies win the battle for luncheon.'

'I thought climbing that poor ram yesterday was mad enough, Sam. I should have known you would outdo yourself. Couldn't you at least wait until they cleared the sand off the rest of the temple before you set claim to it?'

'Why do you even bother becoming annoyed with me? You know it makes not one iota of a difference,' Sam said as she looked down at Edge from her perch on the lintel of the temple.

'Only too well. One day you will fall and crack that thick head of yours.'

'I shall do my best to land on top of you; you are so stuffed with pomp it will be a soft landing.'

His grin flashed lighter in the shadow.

'How did you get up there?'

She indicated the enormous twin sphinxes that flanked the sides of the temple. They were still mostly buried in sand, but there was enough accessible to climb from them to the temple roof.

'I climbed that statue's arse,' she said and Edge visibly winced.

'Sam!'

'Well, you objected to my saying posterior yesterday.'

'I admit defeat.'

'You keep saying that and yet you persevere. Go away, the sun is sinking and I want to finish this today.'

He walked away and she felt the silence around her more keenly. Contrarily she wished he had stayed. Then she heard a grunt and the slither of sand and smiled to herself. He sat beside her again and she noticed a small fresh scratch along the edge of this right hand where he braced it on the roof beside her and she resisted the urge to reach out.

'You scratched your hand,' she said instead and he raised his hand, inspecting it.

'So?'

'So nothing. It was merely an observation. Or an opening so you can berate me for that as well.'

'I can hardly blame you for my clumsiness.'

'It would not be the first time. Remember Saqqara, two years ago?'

His frown fled before another of his surprising smiles.

'Good Lord, yes. Well, that *was* your fault. What the deuce did you think you would find clambering over those piles of rubble?'

'I thought I would make a great discovery. I did not expect to fall into a tomb and be attacked by bats.' She shuddered at the memory.

'Of course not. Why would bats congregate in a dark, dank tomb and, even more surprising, why would they take alarm when someone tumbled into their lair and swamped it with daylight?'

'I did not know there was a shaft entrance hidden under the rubble!'

'Well, if you had not climbed there, you would not have fallen through and dragged me into it as well.'

'I apologised. Several times.'

'So you did. So you should have.'

'You still hardly spoke to me for the rest of your stay.'

'I am certain you regarded that as a reward, not a punishment. And since anything I said might have led to a bout of fisticuffs with your brothers, it is good I held my peace. You were a menace, Sam.'

'Were?'

'You have mellowed with age, apparently. Despite your tendency to climb the antiquities, nothing horrible has happened since my arrival and, with only a couple days remaining before my departure to England, we might yet scrape through without any disasters.'

He spoke lightly, but there was a peculiar note to his voice and she shivered, as if she was back in that tomb, huddled in a corner while he shielded her from the swooping bats and told her precisely what he thought of her. She'd known he was leaving, but somehow she had managed not to absorb that fact. Now it was unavoidable and so was an equally unwelcome realisation.

She did not want him to go.

Somewhere inside her a pit opened wide. Her cheeks tingled with heat and she closed her sketchbook carefully. She felt she was dangling over a ledge, a little dizzy, a little queasy. What was wrong with her?

She stared at the line of the hill, the sweep and dip and then the ragged collapse into the valley. Though the colours were monotone once the sun rose fully, trapped in shades of pale brown and yellow against a stark blue sky, it was a landscape of contrasts and surprises. Not all of them pleasant.

'But you were in England only a couple of months ago.'

'So?'

'But… I thought you would be joining your uncle on the expedition to Abu Simbel next week.'

'Not this year. Next year I will likely return with Dora.'

'Dora?' The pit yawned wider.

'Miss Theodora Wadham. I met her in London and we are to be married in June. I've asked Poppy and Janet not to discuss it because she is still in mourning over her father's death, but I'm surprised your eavesdropping abilities haven't ferreted out the information yet. It hardly matters now since we will announce our betrothal as soon as I return to London. She is looking forward to seeing Egypt. I have told her all about it and she finds it fascinating.'

Dora.

June.

Married.

Edge?

The dizziness was clearing, revealing sharp, distinct quills of anger and pain. She had not even realised she *liked* Edge. He was annoying and opinionated and always so *right* one simply itched to kick him. Certainly it made no sense for her whole body to ache like this because he was to be married. No sense at all.

As the silence stretched he took her sketchpad, leafing through it again.

'You really are very good. I like the way you capture the heat over the valley here. I don't know how it shows that, but it does. This one I like in particular. That is a strange angle… Don't tell me you climbed the statue of Horus to sketch that?' He laughed again. 'You are bound to break your head; do you know that? This is what comes of growing up tagging around your brothers. I told them you would get into trouble one day.'

'And what did they tell you?' she asked dully.

'To mind my own business.' He smiled and the pit became a great big chasm with a swamp at the bottom, sludgy and sucking.

'So why don't you?'

'Did I upset you, Sam? I didn't mean to. Is it because I spoke to your brothers? You needn't worry, they are loyal to you before anything. Sometimes I think your brothers minded you more than they ever did their commanders during the war. But you really must grow up at some point, you know. You can't wander around for ever in local robes with your hair down your back. I never understood… I mean, your mother is always so smartly dressed and—' He broke off at her glare. 'Anyway. It is no concern of mine, but…perhaps when Dora comes here, if you are here with your uncle next year, she can go with you to Cairo. She has impeccable taste and would probably be glad of a friend here. You will like her; she is very dashing.'

I shall hate her. She had best not climb any statues with me because I shall be tempted to push her off. I hate you.

She stood, shaking out her cotton skirts, suddenly all too aware of her dusty, crumpled state, the hair clinging to her sweaty cheeks and forehead, the scuffs on her hands and the ink stains on her fingers.

Idiot. She hadn't known she liked Edge this morning and she was damned if she would like him by evening. She would climb the Howling Cliffs and rid herself of this stupid, pointless liking for this stupid, tedious boy. He might think he was a man, but he was only a boy and Dashing Dora was more than welcome to him. She would find someone dashing of her own to like. She would go to Venice and find the handsomest and most charming man of them all and fall desperately in love with him and he would give her a home and a family and they would live happily ever after and...

'I'm going back,' she announced, walking across the roof. She heard the scratching of his boots following her and wished he would leave her be.

'Wait, I shall help you down. That is quite a drop. Careful.' He shifted past her on to the statue and leapt nimbly down on to the sand.

'I don't need your help.'

'Nonsense. Here, give me your hand.'

If she had not been so upset, she probably would have complied, but she didn't want him touching her so she began descending as she always did—she jumped. Unfortunately, he reached up to take her arm and her agile leap became a stumble, her bare feet sliding on the sandy surface, and she fell headlong on to him, flattening him on to the sand, her chin hitting his ribs and his chin cracking her forehead.

'Damnation!'

'Yina'al abuk!' Her own curse was muffled as she struggled to untangle herself, but the skirts of her cotton robe were snagged under his leg and all she could manage was to raise herself on to one elbow, her hair falling in a tangle over her face. She shoved it away and glared at him and the annoyance and surprise on his face transformed into a grin.

'I told you you would fall off one day. Did it have to be on to me?'

'I would not have fallen if you hadn't got in my way so it is only proper that you cushioned my fall. Now move your leg so I can...'

She gave her skirt a tug, shifting a little on to her side and nudging his leg aside with her knee. She heard his breath drag in and stopped, glancing up in concern.

'Are you hurt? Edge? Oh, no, did I hurt you? I didn't mean to. Where are you hurt?' She planted her hand by his side, raising herself as best she could to see where he might be wounded, but his arms were still around her and they tightened.

'Stop moving,' he growled in a voice utterly

unlike any she had heard him use so she froze, worried and unsure.

This was her fault. In her stubbornness and pique she'd ignored his gentlemanly gesture and now he might be seriously injured. Perhaps she had even broken his back. She had seen what happened to a worker who fell from a cliff and broke his back—he'd died in agony a day later. She hardly dared breath, staring at the handsome face beneath her, all her energy focused on willing him to be unhurt.

His eyes narrowed into slits of water green, his lips a little parted. His breath was warm and swift against her neck and she wanted to sink against him and feel her chest pressed to his once more. Underneath her shock her body was avidly mapping the feel of his legs clamped tightly about hers, the muscular force of his thigh pressed against an area between her legs she'd never even thought as a source of pleasure…

'What are you wearing under that *kamisa*?' His question was so unconnected she was certain she misheard. As her mind arranged the words into order, she wondered if perhaps his head had sustained the injury. Certainly he looked strange— his high cheekbones were hot with colour, his nostrils finely drawn.

'What?'

'You're not wearing anything under it.' This time he spoke through his teeth.

'Of course not, it is hot and I...'

He closed his eyes and growled again.

'Definitely grown up,' he muttered. 'Get off me.'

'But where are you hurt?'

'I am not hurt. Get *off* me.'

'I'm trying. You must move your leg for me to...' She reached between his legs to grasp as much of her skirt as possible and gave it a tug.

This time he groaned, his arms tightening even further, and her supporting arm buckled. She managed to turn her head in time not to slam her chin into his chest once again, but this was worse. Her mouth was just an inch from his neck, she could smell his warmth, a musky scent that made her think of an oasis, green and lush, cool water pouring from a spring. She wanted to taste his skin the way a woman dying of thirst might want to fling herself into that cool water.

Her fantasy shattered as he heaved, rolling her off him, but his leg was still caught in the skirt of her robe and it remained between her legs, a hard, warm, welcome presence. She clung to his shirt as if she was being dangled over an abyss. He was again a dark shape over her, just his narrowed eyes touched with shards of light.

'I always knew you were trouble.' The words barely made their way out between his gritted teeth. 'I just didn't know how m...'

The word was stifled as she raised herself

on her elbow and pressed her mouth to his. She hadn't meant to do it, it just happened.

It wasn't what she expected. His mouth was smooth and warm like a polished marble statue out in the sun. But it was pliant, it pulsed with life, and she couldn't help shifting her lips against it, tucking her lower lip into the parting, drawn by the warmth of his breath until she reached the moist inner curve.

It felt so...perfect.

She could stay just like that while dynasties rose and fell, her lips defined by the contours of his, his breath replacing hers. She sighed and without thinking her tongue came to explore the parting of his, sending a shock of tingling heat through her body and utterly destroying the lethargic beauty of the moment.

The whole embrace could not have lasted more than several breaths but it felt like an eternity, until with a sharp tug he all but ripped her skirt from about his leg, shoved himself to his feet and was striding swiftly down the path.

Sam stood on the veranda that connected Bab el-Nur's breakfast room to the gardens. The scent of honeysuckle and the first wisps of orange blossom were wrapped around her by the evening breeze that came down from the hills. Beneath it she could smell the Nile, murky and mysterious; could almost feel the dark rush of its waters just a few dozen yards away, night prowlers moving among the reeds.

She shivered and not because of the breeze or the crocodiles.

She had not seen Edge for two years and then she hadn't even liked him—he'd been a thorn in her side ever since she was a child, even if he'd saved her from coming to grief far too many times.

She didn't understand how it had all changed. How had Edge shifted in her map of constellations from a large but annoying star to the very centre, a sun warming and tugging all towards it? This rearrangement made no sense at all. Surely the stars would realign?

She wished more than ever that Lucas and Chase were there. She needed them to tell her it would go away. That this was merely an infatuation like the time Chase became all silly over Signora Bertolli when he was sixteen and wrote her poems and rowed his gondola past her palazzo in the middle of the night until her husband lost patience and threw a statue out the window, sinking the gondola and almost starting a feud between the Bertollis and the Montillios. The dousing cured Chase and a month later he was already enjoying the favours of a far more dashing and very scandalous widow.

That was what she would do. In a matter of weeks Huxley would be escorting her and her

mother back to Venice where she would be introduced to society and meet all the charming Venetian men she'd heard gossip about. She might even
meet Lord Byron and make him fall hopelessly in
love with her since he seemed to be completely
undiscriminating as he went from one Venetian
lady to another as if they were sugar-coated *cast-
agnoles*. That would certainly show Edge she was
not a silly child.

Her defiance flared and faded. She had so
looked forward to coming to Egypt for these
months. To celebrate becoming a woman here,
where she was most herself. Where she was Sam,
not Lady Samantha Sinclair.

Now it was ruined.

Because of him.

He must have sensed her malevolent stare because he turned. They had ignored each other all
evening, but instead of turning away as he had
each time their eyes happened to meet, he squared
his shoulders and came outside.

Her heart made a fool of her again, squash-
ing itself down to the size of a pebble and then
bursting in a spray of hot honey. She turned away
to stare at the wisteria vines Poppy Carmichael
tended with such love. When they flowered fully
it was one of the loveliest sights imaginable, but
she did not want to be here to see it. She never
wanted to come to Qetara again.

Because of him.

He looked at her across the mosaic-covered table, his hand spread over the small tiles. He had large but fine-boned hands and now she knew what they felt like on her. It was a strange thought and it made her shiver.

'I wanted to apologise,' she said, keeping her gaze on the floor. 'I didn't mean to…by the statues…that was wrong.'

'Yes.' The single word was sharp and she flinched. Before she could continue he spoke again, the words rushed and harsh. 'It was my fault, too. Everyone takes you for granted and treats you like you are a child who can do as you will and I did the same… I mean, Dora is nineteen, but it never occurred to me… I should have known better than to even be alone with you. That was my mistake, but I never imagined…'

He ran around, looking thoroughly miserable, and she stood rooted, ashamed to the depth of her soul, hating him and hating herself even more. She could think of nothing to say, either to fight back or regain her dignity. She had never been so humiliated in her life and he was not even trying to humiliate her.

'I don't mean to upset you,' he said, his voice almost pleading and in such contrast with his usual matter-of-fact approach a small part of her released enough tension to feel a little sorry for him as well. 'I only want you to understand, for your own sake, that it is time you grow up.'

What is the point? she thought, holding back from giving the table leg a kick. It was too late.

'I don't want to grow up. I know I will have no choice, but I don't want to. Bad things happen when you do, like Lucas and Chase and you going to war or even worse things like my father being a fool and getting himself killed and my mother still mourning him and...'

And you marrying. You should not.

'What is so wonderful about growing up?' she demanded as he remained silent. He looked older. Not serious Edge poring over his books and artefacts, but the man she had felt against her.

'It is not meant to be wonderful. It just is. There are things in life you do because you have no choice and you make the best of them. That is growing up.'

She covered her face with her hands, blocking it out, blocking him out.

'Then I want none of it. I am sorry I offended you, but that does not give you the right to lecture me.'

'You did not...never mind. Whether you want it or not, it has already happened. Your family and upbringing may not be typical among our class, but you are a Sinclair and very wealthy and that means you will be courted by some and regarded with suspicion by others. People will expect the worst of you because they do not know you as we do and if you behave as you did today...' His voice dropped as he spoke, from smoke to gravel. 'Whatever you think, I do not wish you to be hurt.'

She turned away. At least it was dark so he could not see the ruin she was becoming under his words.

He took a step nearer and stopped.

'I don't wish to hurt you, truly. I only want you to understand…oh, hell.' He took another step and stopped again. Then he reached out, tracing a line by her brow.

'You are bruised here. Is that my fault?' He sounded so bruised himself she tried to force herself to smile.

'No, I think we already established it was all my fault. It doesn't hurt. At least it didn't until you touched it.'

His hand dropped into a fist by his side and she wished she'd kept her mouth shut. Perhaps if she'd learned that valuable skill long ago she might have…what? Stolen Edge from the woman he loved?

'I am sorry, Sa—Lady Samantha.'

Lady Samantha. She moved past him.

'Goodbye, Lord Edward.'

'Wait.' He grasped her arm. 'Please don't be angry with me.'

'What does it matter if I am angry? You have been crystal clear as always, Lord Edward. If it makes you feel any better, your arrows have sunk home. They are deep in my posterior.'

His laugh was a little strangled.

'Blast you, Sam.'

'That is at least your third curse today in my presence, Lord Edward Edgerton. You should keep your distance from me henceforth, I am clearly a bad influence.'

He grasped her other arm and for a moment they stood there. Inside she could hear Poppy on the pianoforte and her mother singing. Familiar and horrible. Nothing would ever be the same.

'Yes,' Edge said at last. 'Yes, you are. I am leaving for Cairo at dawn tomorrow. I shan't see you again. I wish you happy, Sam. Will you wish me the same?'

'Always.' That was the truth, whatever the pain.

'God in heaven, how…' He actively strangled the words, his fingers pressing into the flesh of her upper arms. There was such confusion in his voice she sank her fingers into his immaculate coat, crushing the lapels as if she could knead the very fabric of time and space and force it to her will. She rose on tiptoes and touched her lips to his cheek. He had not shaved and the stubble caught on her lips and this sign of imperfection filled her with such need she gave a little cry, a puff of a wail against his flesh. He turned his head, just catching it briefly with his mouth, his lips covering hers, drawing her breath from her.

His mouth fit perfectly, she thought. Two pieces of a warm, tingling puzzle. It was so *right*…

And then she was free again.

She forced herself to speak the dreaded words, proper at last. 'My congratulations on your up-coming nuptials. Godspeed.'

This time he didn't answer as she left the ve-randa and made her way back to her room. In the morning he was gone as he had said.

But then Edge had always been a man of his word.

Chapter One

━━━━━━━━━━ ∾∾∾ ━━━━━━━━━━

*'No one passes through the Valley of the
Moon and emerges unscathed.'*
　　　　—*Lost in the Valley of the Moon,*
　　　　　　　Desert Boy Book Three

Qetara, Egypt—eight years later

Sam stopped at the rim of the Howling Cliffs
above Qetara. Below lay the ragged rock-strewn
valley and beyond was the gleam of the Nile, a
grey-brown ribbon nestled between green swathes
of reeds. The sun was hanging low and already
tinting the hills beyond the Nile in orange and
mauve and touching the white building of Bab
el-Nur with pink. She could just make out the
edge of the garden where the trees shielded her
mother's grave.

　　Could it possibly be three years since her
mother's death sent her back to Sinclair Hall in

England? The last three months here in Egypt felt more substantial than those three years. More substantial even than the long years that had passed since she married Ricki. As if she'd not truly been awake from the moment she returned to Venice and set out on a quest to mend her tattered heart and pride by finding herself a home.

Not that she knew what a home was. Living on sufferance with her mother's family in Venice or even as a valued and loved guest at Bab el-Nur with the Carmichaels did not constitute a home. Perhaps those two years in Burford in England when she'd been barely six—she remembered a vague feeling of being safe. Sometimes she wondered if she'd chosen Ricki from all her suitors because she'd discovered his father had a property near Burford, as if that created some magical link between him and her last memories of carefree happiness. They'd both expected the other to be something they weren't—no wonder they'd both been disappointed.

If only they had been older they might have weathered that disappointment and perhaps even built something on its ashes. And then poor little Maria might still be alive. She would be almost ten years old now had she not drowned. Sam rubbed her face wearily, trying to chase away the dank taste of the canal water. Thoughts of Maria always brought back pain.

She scuffed at the pebbles with the tip of her

boot, kicking a few over the ledge and hearing them snap against the stone as they bounced into the valley below.

Egypt wasn't her home, but she loved it here. Thank goodness Chase and Lucas had all but forced her to return. It had woken her and the thought of slipping back into the half-existence she'd fallen into since her marriage to Ricki was unacceptable. She'd made a terrible mistake marrying him, but she was older and wiser now. Poppy and Janet knew many people in London with ties to Egypt. It was not in the realm of the fantastical that among them she might find someone who would wish to wed her and yet be a good, kind man and father. Someone who would watch the world transform from one magic to another with her. Perhaps even agree to howl with her.

How many times had she and Lucas and Chase and Edge scrambled up these cliffs as children, imitating the night yowling of the jackals? Well, not that Edge howled with them, he had always been too aloof for that, but he'd come none the less. Then they would watch the hills across the Nile turn from ochre to orange to purple and then fade into the indigo of night.

She tilted her head, baring her throat to the rising breeze, and breathed deeply, trying to chase away the murky taste of the canal waters of Venice that always followed thoughts of Ricki.

She chased away all those ghosts, even her

own. She was no longer Lady Carruthers. Not
even Lady Samantha Sinclair. Only Sam.

I am Sam.

She raised her arms to the world, tipped back
her head and told the world that truth at the top
of her lungs.

'I am Sam!'

Edge was viciously thirsty. His heart was beating and his legs burned from the climb, but none
of the many physical discomforts concerned him
as much at the moment as what he would see when
he crested the sandstone cliff.

If he was wrong, if he'd made a single mistake
on the crisscrossing camel and goat paths from
Zarqa, there would be nothing but more desert—
an endless, taunting ochre grin. Even the faint but
distinct scent of the Nile could be nothing more
than a *sarab*, a desert illusion like the shimmering trees and water that danced on the horizons
until they were sucked under as he approached.

If he was wrong, he might end up like the jackal's carcass he'd passed hours ago. He should have
taken into consideration that eight-year-old memories of terrain were not necessarily reliable. He
was older, slower, less alert. But the path had
looked so very familiar…

He stumbled a little as he crested the cliff, pebbles skittering under his feet. He stopped, narrowing his burning eyes against the glints that

splintered along the broad green scar of the Nile. But it wasn't the Nile that held his gaze. Or the sprawling city of Qetara on the far side of the bank. It was the green gardens of Bab el-Nur tucked below the cliffs.

Home.

The word shivered in the air like a *sarab* threatening to disappear. Home. Not any more and not for many years since he'd tried and failed to build his own. They said third time lucky, but he didn't believe in sayings. Or in anything much any more.

He closed his eyes and heard nothing but air moving up the cliff below him, a distinctive hollow presaging the rise of the afternoon winds. He'd once loved this time of day when the sun finally showed signs of exhaustion from its brutal assault and the desert began changing, all kinds of new forces entering its stark stage. New colours, new animals, new sounds.

It had been so long since he'd just…listened. Absorbed. It had been so long since he'd felt like listening. Since he'd felt anything much at all.

He didn't know if this was a good sign. He liked not feeling.

At least he'd finally made it. More or less in one piece.

A very tired, aching piece.

Edge glanced up at the keening of a bird swooping in and out of tiny indentations on the cliff face and winced as the glare of the sun made his head pound. He'd finished the last of his water some hours ago, a miscalculation on his part. The hiss of the wind cooled the perspiration on his forehead and nape and he smiled at how good it felt now that he no longer feared for his life. His smile itself felt like a crack in the cliff face, sharp and threatening, but he allowed it to linger.

The sound struck him as harshly as if he had fallen off the cliff and hit the ground.

'Aimsa!'

It carried out over the valley and for a mad second he was willing to consider he had been wrong about his disbelief in all matters supernatural. But somehow he doubted an ancient Egyptian spirit would be yelling at the tops of its lungs. He hurried as best he could on his stiff legs along the cliff and stopped.

The image was worthy of any of the locals' tales: carved into a sky ignited into a blaze of orange and mauve by the setting sun was a figure cloaked in a pale billowing gown that snapped and surged under the evening wind as if being pulled towards the lip of the crater by desert furies. Then the figure raised its arms and the wind seemed to carry it upwards, as if preparing to hurl it over the cliff like a leaf.

Edge didn't stop to think, just vaulted over the boulders and ran towards it, his mind already anticipating the image of this woman casting herself off the cliff.

'Don't!' he called in Arabic. *'Laa! Tawaqfi!'*

The figure whirled, one hand outflung as if to hold him back.

They stood facing each other in mutual shock.

His breathing was harsh from the fear of what he had expected to witness and the need to stop it. But his mind was already rushing ahead with a series of realisations—that the woman who had just keened like a vengeful *houri* at the top of her lungs into the desert air was neither a local nor a hallucination of his, but something far worse.

Egypt had taught him to always expect the unexpected. Especially when it came to Sam Sinclair.

She was dressed in local dress, and local male dress at that, a cream-coloured *gibbeh* tied with a red cotton sash around her waist over a simple muslin gown. She was still staring at him, her blue-grey eyes wide and far away, but then the pupils dilated as recognition settled in and with it wariness. For a moment he wondered whether he was mistaken. After all, almost a decade had passed and this was no child. She looked very much like Sam and yet she did not.

Well, she wasn't Sam any more. She was Lady Carruthers, wasn't she?

'I thought you were about to jump,' he said, his breath still short and her eyes focused even further as she glanced from him to the cliff.

'Why on earth did you think that?'

'Perhaps because you were standing on a cliff, screaming?'

'I did not scream, I howled. These are, after all, the Howling Cliffs. I didn't expect anyone to be listening. I came here to be private.'

Anger was proving to be a wonderful antidote to fear and shock.

'I am so dreadfully sorry to have intruded, Lady Carruthers.'

His sarcasm kicked up the corners of her mouth, but they fell almost immediately.

'And I am sorry I frightened you, Lord Edward. I thought it safe to do so since no one dares come here. These cliffs are haunted, you know.'

'I do now.'

The smile threatened again, but again failed to materialise. Perhaps this really wasn't Sam at all. Or perhaps marriage had finally succeeded in taming her where all else failed. If so, it was nothing short of a miracle.

'Not by madwomen,' she corrected. 'But by the protectors of Hatshepsut. Poppy was telling us they think that is probably her temple down there.'

She pointed to the structure at the foot of the cliffs. It and the flanking sphinxes were now completely uncovered as was a broad gravel pathway leading towards a jetty. It looked very small and inconsequential from where they stood, nothing like the sand-covered temple where he'd sat with this woman eight years ago…

A lifetime ago.

He scrubbed a hand over his face. It felt raw and rough with sand.

'You are staying with Poppy?'

'Of course. Why else would I be in Qetara?'

Why indeed. His wits had clearly gone begging. Her gaze moved over him again and for the first time he realised how he must look. Filthy, for one. He hadn't shaved in days, or was it a week now?

'Where did you come from?' She looked around, frowning. 'I would have seen you if you came up from Bab el-Nur.'

'I haven't been there yet. I came from Zarqa.'

Her eyes widened, managing to look both surprised and suspicious.

'You'd best fetch your donkey or camel and come down. It will be dark soon.'

'I don't have a mount. I walked.'

Surprise turned to shock and then to outrage. He'd forgotten how expressive her face was.

'You walked from Zarqa. On foot. *On your own.*'

'Yes, on all counts. Is that an offence?'

'Only against good sense! And what on earth were you doing up here? The desert path leads directly through the valley to the Nile, not to the Howling Cliffs. Were you lost?'

'I wanted to see the view first.'

Her lips closed firmly on whatever was straining to be said. Then she gave her skirts a slight shake, as if dislodging something distasteful.

'Well, it's your hide if you wish to risk it. But I suggest you abandon this romantic conceit and make your way down before dark or you'll find yourself at the bottom of the cliff more rapidly and painfully than you would like.'

She set off down the path and he followed. The reversal of scolding roles was as peculiar as everything else about his return to Egypt. She was right, though. He'd been tempting the fates walking from Zarqa in the first place and going along the cliff path in his present state was...

Romantic conceit. No one had ever accused him of being romantic. Conceited, yes. Romantic—he'd only been romantic once in his life and that had cost him dearly. He sighed. The path which he'd climbed and descended hundreds of times in his youth felt endless and his legs were a mixture of wool and fire when they finally reached the gate in the high whitewashed walls.

'It has changed a little since you were here last,' Sam said as she secured the gate behind them and he forced himself to look up.

She was right. Bab el-Nur used to be a sprawling but modest whitewashed structure surrounded by neat gardens, but Poppy had constructed a second storey and the gardens were a lush jungle of trees and flowering bushes surrounded by high mudbrick walls.

'Good God, he's constructed a fortress!' he exclaimed as the house came fully into view.

She laughed over her shoulder, her face transforming, and for the first time the cool woman from the cliff and the girl in his memory connected.

'It is even more amazing inside and Janet has made a marvel out of the gardens. I have been sketching…' She paused and shrugged and it was like watching a flower furl its leaves as night fell, a physical and spiritual diminishment.

They continued through the garden, scents and memories engulfing him. It was already dark and the palm trees were weaving above them in their evening dance. The packed earth of the path gave way to the stone floor of the veranda and suddenly there was a flurry of movement.

'Good heavens, Sam, who is…?'

Edge looked up and his uncle's question melted away.

'Edge. Dear Lord. *My boy!*'

Poppy wasn't quite as tall as he, but he was a burly man and his embrace was powerful, his arms catching Edge in a vice, his bushy grey hair surprisingly soft against his cheek. For a moment Edge just stood there in shock. It had been so long since he'd seen this man, though he'd been closer than a father to him. How had he allowed so much time to pass?

'Edge…' The one word was a cracked whim-

per, then he was suddenly thrust away, his shoulders grabbed in Poppy's considerable paws. 'What have you done to yourself, boy? You look disgraceful! And why did you not tell me you were in Egypt? Janet! Edge is here!'

The last words were a bellow worthy of a call to prayer from the minarets and their effect was immediate. A plump figure hurtled into the room followed by others and Edge found himself being handed around like a parcel, embraced, scolded, questioned. He tried to keep his feet steady as he greeted everyone, but the room was beginning to move around him and suddenly a pair of blue-grey eyes were in front of him and he felt his hands clasped in a cool, strong grip.

'When did you last eat, Edge?'

Eat?

'This morning.'

His answer set off another bustle of activity, but at least it was away from him. Within moments a glass of tea infused with mint was shoved into his hand. It was so sweet it made him wince, but he drank and when they brought him food he ate and when they led him off to be bathed he went meekly.

It was very strange, being home.

'The poor fellow is still asleep,' Poppy announced as he entered the breakfast parlour and sat beside Janet.

'I know,' Janet said as she handed him a small porcelain cup of bitter coffee. 'I couldn't resist and peeked. He looks better now he's washed and shaved, but he's too thin, Poppy. You could cut stone with his cheekbones. I've told Ayisha to prepare the lamb stew he loved as a boy.'

'Don't fuss, Janet. You know he hates it.'

'I never fuss.'

Sam smiled to herself at how Edge's appearance had transformed her hosts. She'd forgotten how deeply they loved Edge. Janet was lit from within, her movements sharper but more abstracted, and after his heartbreaking show of love when he'd embraced Edge, Poppy now appeared taller, more resolute.

'He isn't ill?' Sam tried not to sound worried. He'd looked so haggard yesterday she'd lain awake a long time, waiting for the sounds of a household bustling around a sickroom. She knew desert fevers could be deadly.

'No, child, merely exhausted. Nothing food and sleep won't remedy.' Poppy's words were a little too hearty and Sam knew that, though Edge might not be ill, Poppy was worried.

'Did you know he was in Egypt?'

'No. We received a letter from him only a couple of months ago from Brazil, but it must have been sent long before.'

'Good morning.'

Janet wavered. Clearly she wanted to rush to Edge, but perhaps it was the sight of a very different but far more familiar Edge that stopped her. Daoud had done more than shave him, he'd trimmed his hair and found a set of clothes left by Lucas or Chase.

In the flowing gown and the long cotton strip worn like the natives to protect the head and face from the sand and sun Sam had hardly recognised him. Now she was thrown back eight years to the last time she'd seen Edge—in this very room, she realised. He'd stood just as straight and withdrawn and watchful. And yet this was a different man. He'd lived a whole lifetime in those eight years, as had she.

'Good morning, Edge. Would you care for tea?' she asked. His gaze moved to her and then settled on the tea pot by her hand.

'Yes, thank you, Lady Carruthers.'

Oh, for heaven's sake, Edge.

The words almost spurted out of her, but she held them back and held out the cup.

'Your tea, Lord Edward.'

'You are very kind, Lady Carruthers.' Something almost like amusement flickered in his eyes, but then Poppy's patience ran out.

'Now, boy, tell us when you arrived, why you didn't inform us of your arrival, and what on earth—'

'Let him eat first, Poppy,' Janet interrupted and Edge sat by her.

'It is all right, Aunt. I cannot stay long so you may as well hear everything now. Rafe has disappeared.'

'Rafe? What is that fellow up to now? I'd expected he would be settling in as the new Duke of Greybourne.'

'Unfortunately not. I received a communication from the embassy in Istanbul that Rafe was killed alongside the Khedive's son Ismail in Nubia. The Greybourne lawyers instigated an inquiry, but that could take months so I came myself.'

'He...he is dead?' Janet faltered and Edge smiled, reaching out to take her hand. The transformation was so extreme Sam felt herself tense as if she'd just noticed a crocodile moving in the reeds.

'No, I don't believe so, Aunt. In fact, I have reason to believe that letter was sent by Rafe himself. I need to find out why.'

'But you cannot go there,' Janet said, horrified. 'That whole area is in upheaval. You could be killed!'

'I am glad I didn't stop here on the way, then, Aunt Janet. I wouldn't wish for you to worry.'

'You already went?'

'Yes. There are still skirmishes, but Defterdar Bey has the area well under his brutal thumb.

I don't know quite what Rafe is about, but I do know he did not take part in those battles.'

'How do you know? He is a mercenary, is he not?'

'He is, but for several years now he has chosen to involve himself in financial rather than political concerns. More to the point, Ismail was killed in November of last year and I spoke with a…an acquaintance of Rafe's who met him and his valet Birdie in Alexandria only last month before he headed south. I followed his trail and there were enough people who recognised my description. They call him Nadab.'

'Scar,' Poppy translated, frowning.

'Yes. I never imagined I would be grateful for Rafe's accident. In Syene he was joined by a young man and they hired a guide and camels to take them north through the western deserts. I was several days behind so I decided to try to cut around them by way of the river.'

Sam watched Edge as he spoke. She'd forgotten how blank his face could be. People showed more emotion speaking of the weather. But she knew better—she could see tiny signs, in the dip of his long eyelashes that shielded deep grey-green eyes, the flicker of tension in the lines cut on either side of his mouth.

Janet sighed. 'I know he swore not to take a penny of Greybourne money as long as your father lived, but why must he continue in this stubbornness now he is Duke?'

'I don't know,' Edge admitted. 'Six months ago he told me he intended to return to England and tried to convince me to go with him.'

'*Were* you planning to return?' Poppy asked and Edge's smile turned wry.

'No. But that is beside the point. What matters now is that I hope I have gained some ground on them by coming by way of the river, perhaps even enough to outflank them if I come through the oases. Which made me think of al-Walid. No one could cross his territory without him knowing, correct? If you could give me some testimonial, I will proceed there and if I find nothing I will continue to Cairo. I paid dragomen there and in Alexandria to keep an eye out for him so hopefully at some point my luck will turn.'

'You appear to have had more than your share of luck already, my boy. Walking from Zarqa! What next?'

'It seemed the most reasonable option.'

'Reasonable! One more day and you wouldn't even have found us here. We were to leave for Cairo tomorrow and then back to England.'

'Then I am glad you are here, but I am certain Daoud or Youssef could have helped me. All I need is a camel or a good sturdy horse and some form of message for—'

'We will come with you, Edge,' Janet interrupted softly. 'We can continue as well from Bahariya as from here and in truth it has been far too long since we visited al-Walid.' She held up her hand as Edge tried to protest. 'You might be younger and stronger, Edge, but Poppy and I are more practised at desert travel. Good, now that is settled I shall have a word with Ayisha and Daoud about provisions, and of course we must bring gifts. I know just the thing. Come along, Poppy dear.'

She wandered out as she spoke, patting Edge on the head as she passed, as if he was still the young boy they took in almost thirty years ago rather than a man of thirty-four who was taller than she even when seated.

'Uncle...'

'Admit defeat, my boy. You know our Janet.'

The room fell very silent as Poppy closed the door. Sam poured more mint tea into her cup and after a moment's hesitation refilled his cup as well. He watched, his mouth tense. She knew that expression, having been so often the recipient of it. He was annoyed.

'Can't you convince her this is unnecessary, Lady Carruthers?' he said. 'You used to wrap her around your little finger. Tell her you prefer to travel by *dahabiya*.'

Sam's little finger tingled, but so did her temper. It was a peculiar feeling; she hadn't been angry in quite a while.

'*Tell* her,' she repeated and his eyes narrowed.

'It was a suggestion, not a command. For your own benefit and comfort.'

'No, for *your* benefit and comfort. As usual.'

'As usual?' There was a dangerous lowering of his tone and the peculiar feeling quickened— anger tasted warm, thick. She'd forgotten that.

'Yes. Ten years ago you convinced Poppy not to allow me to join the expedition to Bahariya.' She felt rather foolish raising this old grievance now and rather surprised by how sharp it still was.

'Precisely, ten years ago. I was perfectly justi- fied in objecting to taking a child into the mid- dle of the desert. Your brothers and I very nearly didn't make it back.'

'From what I heard Poppy tell Janet you and Lucas and Chase would not have been in danger either if you had not strayed from the town on your own. Since I would have remained, sensi- bly, with Poppy and Huxley and al-Walid, I would have been safe. Besides, I was sixteen. Hardly a child.'

He bent his glare on his teacup.

'Would you care for some more tea?' she asked and had the satisfaction of making him snap,

'No. Thank you.'

'You are welcome.' She braced herself as they moved from annoyed to angry. Good.

'Perhaps you weren't a child, but you acted like one. Within a week of our return you had me thrown in gaol and then Poppy and Huxley were almost chased out of Qetara when you kidnapped Sheikh Khalidi's cats.'

'Oh! That is unfair! You were thrown into gaol because Khalidi's daughter was fool enough to fancy herself in love with you and came to Bab el-Nur to beg you to stay in Egypt. I certainly didn't ask you to try to break Abu-Abas's nose when Khalidi sent him to return Fatima home.'

'What the devil was I to do when you threw yourself between him and Fatima like a demented Don Quixote?'

He had a point so she moved swiftly to more defensible ground.

'Besides, if I hadn't tried, and failed, to kidnap Khalidi's adored cats you probably would have remained in that horrid gaol far longer.'

'He planned to release me anyway—he was merely making the point that not even foreigners could assault his men with impunity. Simply because your actions did not end in disaster does not mean they were justified. It was reckless and foolish and you could have been seriously hurt. You always had more luck than sense.'

She'd forgotten fury. She'd forgotten wanting to launch herself at someone as she had at Abu-Abas when he ordered the soldiers to take Edge away. But she was no longer a child and she would not gratify his insults by confirming them.

'And you always had more sense than heart,

Edge. I promise you, next time you are tossed in gaol I shan't lift a finger. I shall reserve my loyalty for people who appreciate it.'

He turned away, but she saw the flush that showed darker under his sun-browned skin.

'I don't know why I am arguing with you,' he grumbled. 'I don't argue with anyone but you and as usual it's a waste of time. Come to Bahariya if you wish.'

'How magnanimous.'

'Don't be snide. You've won, Lady Carruthers.'

It didn't feel like a victory. She felt as weary as he looked.

'It is not a contest, Edge. And please stop calling me Lady Carruthers like that. If you object so much to my presence, I will travel with Ayisha and the luggage on the *dahabiya* while you go with Poppy and Janet.'

He didn't answer. All she could see was his profile, an outline that was etched in her mind with the familiarity of a childhood landscape—the kind you woke up to every day and hardly noticed until you went away. Without thinking she leaned across the table, hand extended.

'They probably want you to themselves anyway, Edge. They've missed you terribly.'

His hands curled around his cup and his long eyelashes lowered further. She started to rise, but he reached out and caught her hand on the table.

'Wait. You might as well come. They won't be

calm thinking of you on the *dahabiya* without them. I apologise. It is only that… I am worried about Rafe.'

She tried to concentrate on his words, not on her hand which felt like a large and dangerous animal had rolled over in its sleep and pinned it to the table.

'You said he is a mercenary. Surely he is able to care for himself?'

'He is, but I don't understand why he came here in the first place. He always told me he would never come to Egypt.'

'Oh. Why?' She sat down again, careful not to dislodge his hand.

'Why?'

'Why not Egypt? One would think he would be curious, knowing how much you loved it.'

His eyes finally fixed fully on hers—with the sun filtering in through the shutters behind him they now looked a deep forest-green. She could almost see shadows moving between the trees.

'Rafe and I assumed most of our childhoods that we were each the one being punished—me by being sent away, he by remaining. Life is rarely what one thinks. In any case he came to hate the idea of Egypt so whatever brought him here must be serious. If he is in trouble, I must find him.'

His hand was still on hers, warm and large and rough against her skin. The gesture and the admission were both so unlike Edge she did not

know what to do. She thought of her brothers—
she would cross deserts for them and not think
twice.

'I'm glad you care for him so much, Edge.'

He took his hand away and went to the door.

'I owe him a great deal. More than I can repay.
I must speak with Poppy now.'

Chapter Two

~~~~~~~~~~~~~~~~~~~~~~~~~~~~~~

Jephteh pointed to the darkness below the cliff, his fingers biting into Gabriel's shoulder. 'Mortals are prodigiously foolish, boy. You will die the moment you strike those rocks, yet you waste your precious last moments wondering what lies in those shadows.'
—*Captives of the Hidden City,*
Desert Boy Book Four

Bahariya wasn't quite what Sam had expected. Once they'd passed the rippling tan and gold sand dunes, what met her gaze was not an encampment of tents, but a sprawling town of mudbrick structures tucked between date groves.

At least they were finally there, she thought with relief, because every last inch of her ached and she had to consciously stop herself from licking her lips because they dried so quickly in the desert breeze it felt like they might crack open like overripe fruit.

Her body felt like it had taken a beating but her pride was faring the worst.

Edge must be almost as out of practice at riding a camel as she, but he sat as gracefully on the dusty cloth saddle as Daoud and Youssef while she felt her joints might need re-attaching.

She tried to rub her leg without being obvious and Edge glanced at her briefly, but as usual she could not tell what he was thinking, or if he was thinking at all. It was like riding beside a living statue. She wished she could draw him just as he was—with the protective cotton scarf and his skin darkened by the sun he looked like he belonged here.

At least until he looked at you with those deep-water eyes. They'd always reminded her of moonlight reflecting off a lake, leaving you wondering if it was merely inches deep and full of nothing more than muck and algae or a crevasse stretching miles into the earth and filled with fantastical creatures like the Lake of Sorrow in the third *Desert Boy* book.

She wondered if Edge had ever come across the *Desert Boy* books, or if Poppy and Janet ever told him she was the illustrator of the novels that had become one the most successful novels in England. It was part of this silly descent into childish impulses since his arrival that she wanted him to know. He would probably not be impressed and he definitely wouldn't understand how important the *Desert Boy* books were for her. She hardly dared admit it to herself. Other than Lucas and Chase, who were already fading away from her into their marriages, the books were the one firm anchor in her life. Which was ludicrous considering she didn't even know who wrote them.

A trickle of perspiration ran down her cheek and she brushed at it, grateful for the faint coolness it brought with it. Out here in the emptiness of the desert everything felt insubstantial. Perhaps she could just keep on riding, aching joints and all, and never have to make a decision about her future.

'Almost there.' Edge guided his camel closer to hers and she scowled at his commiserating smile.

'That sounds suspiciously like "I told you so, Sam".'

'I never strike an opponent when they're down. You look like one nudge would topple you from that poor camel.'

'Trust you to pity the camel, Edge.'

His smile widened, but his attention was drawn away by the crowd gathering as they entered the town. They were mostly women and children in plain cotton robes, eyes wide with curiosity. They stopped near a well between the buildings and Sam gathered her resolution to dismount, but before she could move Edge was beside her, holding out his hand.

'It's been years since you've ridden a camel let alone for so many hours, Sam. You'll need help.'

He'd unwound his headscarf and his face and hair were dust-streaked, his temples and cheeks marked by dark rivulets of perspiration. She could only imagine what she looked like, she thought with a rush of embarrassment. But even unkempt and dusty he looked unfairly handsome. No, even more handsome than usual. He looked raw and unvarnished, like a statue before it was sanded into perfection.

'Well? You can't stay up there all day. If there is trouble awaiting us, we will need you to scare them off.'

It was an olive branch and she felt foolish at the magnitude of her relief.

'How do you do that?' she asked.

'Do what?'

'Laugh without laughing.'

The lines at the corners of his eyes deepened.

'Years of training. It wouldn't do to encourage you.'

He unhooked her leg from the saddle and swung her down to the ground before she'd even adjusted her balance. She grabbed hold of his arms, steadying herself and thoroughly resenting that he was right—her legs were as stiff as logs and bursts of sparkling pain danced up from the soles of her feet. She managed to snap off her groan by gritting her teeth.

'That bad?' he murmured, his arm supporting her, his other hand splayed on her waist as she half-leaned her elbows against him.

'Someone has put needles in my boots while I wasn't watching,' she replied, trying not to think of the hard surface of his chest, the dark, warm smell of his body so close to hers.

'I knew I shouldn't have allowed you to come.'

'You did not *allow* me, Edge. I'm not a child.'

'No. You're not.' He let her go, turning to follow the others towards a series of large tents pitched beside the date groves. She bit back a curse and steadied herself against the camel instead. He was the only man who could ensure she acted like a child, blast him.

She'd promised herself she wouldn't fall into her old behaviour around him. *Any* of her old be-haviours. And yet here she was, either prickling like the hedgehog she used to call him or being aware of every nuance of his expressions.

She wasn't a child any longer and her foolish infatuation was a thing of the past. She was now an experienced widow and could appreciate what a fine specimen of manhood he presented without making a fool of herself. And that was *that*, she assured herself as she hobbled after him to join Poppy and Janet.

They were escorted to a large tent set in the shade of palm trees and greeted with effusive warmth by the white-haired Sheikh and his wife

Aziza. Sam's Arabic had improved since she'd returned, but there were still times when her weary
mind stopped making the effort to understand
and this was just such a time. She surreptitiously
worked away at the needles still tingling along her
legs until she noticed everyone had turned to her.

'So. You are the youngest Sinclair, yes?' al-
Walid said, slapping his knees. 'You are very like
your brothers.'

'You remember them?' Sam asked, not certain
if this was a compliment.

'Of course. There was trouble when they came
here last. Remember?' He turned to Edge.

'Of course. A Bedawi tribe took offence at our
exploring Senusret's ruin. We had a worrisome
moment until you and Poppy came to our rescue.

Al-Walid laughed.

'A worrisome moment! You three were nearly
skewered on a spit like lambs over a fire! I forgot
you speak like a rock after sitting out in the cold-
est night. I named you well, Geb.'

'Geb?' Sam asked and al-Walid's laughing eyes
turned to her.

'Geb. God of earth. You do not know the story?'

Sam shook her head, her curiosity sparked as
much by Edge's annoyed frown as by al-Walid's
enthusiasm.

'Good. Now I have something to share by the
fire tonight. But first—Aziza's honey cakes!' he

announced as women entered the tent bearing trays.

'You like?' Aziza's smile was confident which was hardly as surprising as Sam reached for her third helping of the date-filled cakes. Sam laughed and nodded, licking the sticky residue on her lips.

'These are dangerous; it is impossible to eat only one!'

'Truly these are the only reason al-Walid married me.' Aziza sighed, but her smile belied her words and al-Walid gave a snort of dismissal.

'It is lucky I had not tasted your cakes before I bargained with your father or I would have dispensed with your dowry completely. Whenever the neighbouring tribes stir the dust, I remind them that to insult me is to forfeit these delights. Our disputes rarely pass the rising of a new moon.'

'A very interesting negotiation tactic. We never thought to employ anything so sensible during the war.' Edge smiled at Aziza.

'That is because you are English,' al-Walid dismissed. 'The French would win every battle. You are lucky your stubbornness compensates for your lack of taste. Now tell me why you are here, Geb.'

'Why do you presume we are here on my business and not Poppy's?'

'Because you are simmering like a pot on a campfire and your brow is as dark as a sandstorm on the horizon. Or would you prefer to discuss this in four eyes?'

Edge shook his head.

'No, I would be grateful for Sayidti Aziza's thoughts as well. You are right, it is my problems that bring us here. Or rather my brother's.'

When Edge finished recounting his quest al-Walid beckoned to one of the men beside him and after a few swift words the man departed and with him al-Walid's solemn mood.

'By darkness tomorrow we shall know if your brother has come through our desert. Now go rest and tonight we shall hold a feast to celebrate old friends and new.'

'Good Lord, I shall need a camel to move me,' Poppy groaned as he rose and helped Janet to her feet from the low cushioned stools beside the campfire outside al-Walid's tent.

'You are retiring for the night so soon?' al-Walid asked.

'You must excuse our old bones, my friend.'

'Of course, but the young must at least remain until I fulfil my promise to tell them about Geb and Nuut, yes?'

'That excuses me, I dare say,' Edge said, beginning to rise.

'Sit down, Geb.' al-Walid waved him back. 'You are still but halfway on your journey through life.'

Edge grimaced.

'That is a depressing thought.'

Janet touched his arm as she passed.

'The second half shall be better, Edge.'

Sam waited for Edge's expression to reflect his disdain of such a very Janet-like comment, but though he shook his head he smiled at her.

'From your mouth to Allah's ear, Aunt.'

Al-Walid leaned back, staring at the darkened sky. Sam eyed the cushions next to her with longing, wishing she was brave enough to stretch out like al-Walid. In her previous life she would not have thought twice about doing just that. Behind them the fabric of the tent flapped as the evening winds pummelled it like a beast trying to escape, but beyond the vain flapping the only sound was the shushing of the wind in the palms.

'This is a good wind,' al-Walid said. 'It will be cool tonight and some dew tomorrow. Shu is hard at work.'

'Shu?' Sam asked.

'The god of air and wind, *aanisah*.'

'Do you believe in the old gods, then?'

'We believe first in Allah and in Mohammed his prophet, but the old gods are part of this land my ancestors came to before our memory began. It is smart to heed them because they gathered much wisdom about the desert. Shu was the father of Nuut, goddess of the sky. Have you heard of her?'

Sam had, but she wanted to hear al-Walid's tale so she shook her head. Out of the corner of her eye she caught a flash of Edge's smile, but ignored him. She didn't care if she was behaving like a child. She felt like one again and it was wonderful.

'Nuut and Geb were inseparable and one day the greatest god of all, Ra, grew jealous of their closeness so he set Shu to keep the lovers apart— that is why the air stands between the earth and the sky, do you see?'

'Yes, but how sad!'

'Awful,' Edge interposed, his voice as dry as the desert. 'He was such a successful guardian they only succeeded in siring five children.'

'It is still sad. Five stolen encounters hardly amount to a happy relationship.'

'Five children would naturally imply a great many more than five encounters,' Edge replied. 'Given the limited likelihood of conception at each encounter that would mean—' He broke off and Sam couldn't help laughing.

'Must you ruin the story with both pedantry *and* prudishness, Edge? Where is your sense of romance and excitement? Besides, these were gods—perhaps part of their divine properties was to time their *encounters* perfectly and each encounter was so magical as to…'

'Yes, very well. Why don't you allow Sheikh al-Walid to continue?'

Sam smiled at his discomfort and turned back to al-Walid.

'Did Ra punish them?'

'No, their children prospered and ruled the

earth, but also caused much strife. In the temple of Senusret beyond the valley you can see the images of Geb and Nuut—Geb is composed of earth and trees and Nuut is arced above him, made of the night sky and stars with hair both dark and touched with sunset. Very like you, Najimat al-Layl.'

Sam gasped in surprise. 'That is what Ayisha our housekeeper calls me; how did you know?'

'Poppy *effendim* has spoken much of his household over the years. Your name was well chosen, Night Star—your eyes are like stars and your hair shades of darkness.'

'It was not meant as a compliment, Sheikh al-Walid,' Edge interposed. 'Ayisha named her thus because Sam… Lady Carruthers often wandered at night and set the whole household searching for her.'

'Thank you for clarifying that, Edge,' Sam said with a bite and Edge bowed.

'You are welcome, Sam.'

She turned her shoulder to him.

'But why do you call Edge Geb, Sheikh al-Walid?'

'Ah, yes. The name was given him by the tribe that tried to capture him and your brothers at Senusret's temple. It is told that at the peak of the battle the god Geb appeared on the temple roof in the form of a statue with emeralds for eyes and brought with him a great sandstorm, whipping the very earth from under them. We came across them riding away from this apparition and they warned us not to risk our souls by proceeding and angering Geb.'

'But that could not possibly have been Edge,' Sam said primly. 'He does not approve of climbing on the antiquities. Do you, Lord Edward?'

'Under normal circumstances I do not. I was merely trying to assess how many men we were facing and whether they were trying to outflank us. I believe self-preservation justifies my actions rather more than your habit of using antiquities as a painting perch.' His voice was pure Edge, but his mouth was relaxed and indulgent.

'Of course it does, oh, mighty Geb,' she replied. 'I'm certain you always have a reasonable excuse for breaking your own rules.'

'Not always, Sam.' His eyes narrowed into the jewelled slits that had helped send the Bedawi warriors into flight. She felt it, too, the quivering of the earth beneath her, as if a herd of horses burst suddenly from their pen. He might not have been referring to that moment eight years ago when he kissed her back, if such a brief response could have been called a kiss, but the memory rose as clear as yesterday, erasing the chasm of time between them.

The wind picked up, her hair snaking about her face and neck. She brushed it back, but her hands felt clumsy, twice their size and filled with sand.

'Shu is hard at work,' said al-Walid. 'Perhaps he feels he must intercede more forcefully than usual. *Insha'alla* tomorrow brings good news, Geb. Rest well, Najimat al-Layl.'

He wandered off and Sam was immediately aware of the silence. It wasn't soundless, but filled with the threshing of the palms and the huffs of animals further away. But it was still a silence that wrapped around them like the emptiness of a great ocean. Edge was staring into the darkness, his sharp-cut profile gilded by the last glimmers of the campfire. Above them the stars were growing, multiplying, gathering into a lacy ribbon arced across the sky. Even in Qetara she had never seen so many or so clearly.

'We are lucky there is no moon. It is rare to see such an abundance of stars,' Edge said in reflection of her thoughts and she shivered. 'Are you cold?'

'No, not at all. It's the…weight of them. I could never paint this in a million years.'

He nodded and stood and she felt a burst of pain, like a surprise blow to her chest. She didn't want to retire yet.

'Come. There is still too much light and noise here,' he said, holding out his hand.

Come?

Without asking he helped her to her feet and led her past the well.

'Edge. The house is over there.'

'In a moment. You should see this. Even in the desert a night like this is rare.'

Within moments the remnants of sound and light from the encampment fell away. The ground was hard and pebbled and at first Sam stumbled a little on the uneven earth, but Edge held her arm firmly but without pressure. He seemed to know precisely where he was going though there was nothing to see but the faint milky surface of the ground.

The further they walked, the less her eyes strained to see. The ground became luminescent, a cream swathe of silk pockmarked by the indigo shadows cast by each pebble and rock. Above them the sky was everything, a massive dome hung with a myriad of silvery eyes, blinking or staring but strangely still. Sam didn't even notice they'd stopped. She was reduced to nothing but an awareness of being both insignificant and part of everything. The fabric of space was breathing with her, in and out, shimmering and dancing through her.

'I'm breathing stars…' she whispered. 'I'm swimming in them.'

'Don't swim away. I'll never find you in this infinity.' His voice was low and rough as the ground beneath them. 'If you walk twenty yards in the wrong direction, you will be lost and might never find your way back.'

Sam turned. Very faint in the distance behind

them was the pale glow of what could be the village, but other than that there was no sign of life, of anything. She looked up at the darkness that was Edge. Even this close he was nothing but a monolithic form with faint outlines of the same silky cream as the ground, as if he'd been transformed into a statue of obsidian and alabaster—hard and soft. Pared down to his truth.

She tried to push the thought away—it was nervousness brought on by the vastness of the desert, the memories of this old life of hers when she'd still felt so real, so alive, so absolutely unthinkingly herself.

It was deceptive, just like the sense of distance in the darkness was deceptive. Edge was right—if you allowed yourself to go too far into this strange dream, you might never find your way back.

'That is why I depend on you, Edge,' she said lightly. 'I know you will never allow yourself to lose track of the real world. I dare say you know precisely how far we have come and when to stop so we do not lose our way.'

'You think me a very unexciting fellow, don't you, Sam?'

She flushed.

'I think you do not allow yourself to be carried away. But there is nothing wrong with being sensible. There have been many, many times I'd wished I was more so.'

'You've changed.'

'Of course. Eight years is a long time. It would have been surprising had I not changed.'

'It isn't the years, Sam. What happened to you?'

'What happened to me? Good God, Edge, you do nothing in half-measures, do you?'

She tried to laugh but a whole sky's worth of pain was filling her, expanding like the inundation of the Nile—swift and unstoppable. 'Let's return.'

'Not yet. Are you crying?'

'Not yet, but I shall if you keep prodding. I'm tired, my legs ache and I'm terrified of returning to England and it is all too much. You may be made of stone, Mr God of the Earth, but I'm not. If you wish to stay here, I shall find my own way back.'

'Perhaps it would do you good to cry out here where no one can hear you. I need to make amends for interrupting you on the Howling Cliffs.'

She didn't know whether to laugh or kick him for his dispassionate practicality.

The truth was she didn't want to return yet. She wanted to stay cocooned in the night, wrapped in the strange thoughts bubbling inside her, but somehow separated from them by his presence. In the dark she made out the shape of a large flat boulder and sat with a sigh.

'I never really understood you, Edge.'

'There isn't much to understand about a lump of rock.'

His voice was flat, but suddenly she could hear

the currents beneath, as if not seeing his face she could hear things his expression would never give away. There was bitterness and resentment and darker things.

She held out her hand without thinking.

'Come sit with me.'

'I had better not.'

'Don't play the prude, Edge. Just sit.'

He sat and she closed her eyes, soaking up the warmth of his body so close to hers. Above the silvery scents of the desert night air and the ochre of the earth there was his scent—it was out of character—warm and encompassing, like the sensations sparked by the deepest, darkest of wines. She wanted to lean into it and then sink.

She touched her palm to her chest. The pain inside her was gone. Strange—it had been so harsh and enormous just moments ago and it was gone. All she felt now was…heat, as if the desert still held the warmth of the noon sun and was sending it upwards through her, through him…

'You are the least lump-like person I know,' she said and he laughed, bending forward to lean his arms on his thighs as he picked something up from the desert floor. But he didn't speak so she continued, working her way through her thoughts.

'You are like watching the sea from a ship's deck on a moonless night—you never know quite what is beneath the surface, but you are quite certain a great deal is going on there and that one is safer on solid ground.'

Where on earth had that come from?

'I am not certain if being the dark abode of sea monsters is any better than a rock.'

'No,' she agreed, a little scared of the image she'd conjured. 'Perhaps not. I meant it as a compliment, though. Clearly I am not very adept at them.'

'You were always more honest than was comfortable, Sam.'

'In other words I always spoke before I thought. Madcap Sam.'

'Don't make it into an insult. Your honesty was never cruel or cavalier. Sometimes you put too much thought into it, in fact. What will you do when you return to England?'

Sam wanted to stay on the topic of her honesty. Or rather on his strangely complimentary interpretation of her. But she accepted his change of subject.

'I do not know. Now my brothers are married I shall have to find a solution.'

'They don't want you living with them?'

'It is not that. They do, but soon they shall have children and—' She broke off, realisation hitting her, her hand closing over his. 'Oh, God, I'm so sorry, Edge.'

He placed his free hand over hers, hard.

'Don't tiptoe around me, Sam. I can't abide it.

Especially not from you. The worst is no one will talk about Jacob or they do what you just did—apologise and run away. Jacob was the best thing that happened in my life. I would not have traded a moment of my time with him for anything else.'

Her hand was buzzing under his and it was a struggle to stay still.

'I'm glad you had him.'

The image of Maria flashed in her mind, starker than usual in the darkness. The three-year-old's dark curls woven into the sky, her smile shimmering with stars. She'd had only a year with Ricki's natural daughter, but she'd loved her and when she'd drowned it had cracked Sam's heart all over again. It could not compare to Edge's loss, but she understood what he meant. She wanted so much to share the story with Edge, but guilt held her silent. Ricki bore the brunt of responsibility for Maria's death, but none of it would have happened if Sam hadn't been fool enough to think she could escape her pain and loneliness by marrying the charming and gregarious Lord Carruthers.

The silence stretched until he spoke again.

'I heard Janet telling Poppy she plans to introduce you to some of the younger antiquarians when they reach London.'

'It is rude to eavesdrop.'

He tossed the stone he held and picked up another.

'They thought I was asleep.'

'Still rude.' She could feel him watching her, her whole left side felt branded and fuzzy. 'Janet is probably right and it would be best. I am tired of not having a corner of my own.'

It sounded so weak, so utterly out of proportion with her fears and half-formed hopes. Watching her brothers find such contentment had brought back this thirst inside her—to create a home of her own. A family. But after the mistakes she had made with Ricki she was too afraid to trust her judgement about men. The thought of finding herself in that hell…again. By choice…again. She didn't think she could do that.

'You miss your husband.' Edge's words cut through her fog and they were so far from the truth her throat closed with shame and guilt. A memory returned, vivid and bitter—Ricki rising from the last time he shared her bed, his body slick with sweat as he loomed over her, flinging insults and threats, but all she could hear was the scream inside her head and the prayer that he would hold true to his threat never to touch her again until she begged him to. A shiver of remembered disgust at both of them rippled through her and Edge stood abruptly.

'It is late. We should return.'

She rose as well, feeling utterly defeated and not even sure why.

'You *have* changed,' he said after walking a while. 'In the past you never would have agreed to return without at least a token argument. I don't know if that's a good thing, Sam.'

'Make up your mind, Edge. You spent years lecturing me for being wild and now you're bemoaning how tame I've become. Be damned to you,' she snarled and marched off.

'Sam…' He caught up with her, but she walked faster.

'I don't want more of your twisted brand of wisdom, Edge. Go away.'

'You're heading the wrong way.'

She stopped. Her jaw ached with a kind of fury she could not remember ever feeling, not even at Ricki. It felt like it might raise the whole of the desert around her into biblical eruption. Maybe this was what desert sandstorms were—somewhere a woman unleashed them when the ferocity she held inside could be contained no longer. Sandstorms, volcanos, typhoons… She felt she could unleash them all right now.

I am Sam. I am Sam. I am…

'No one will hear you if you want to howl at the world again.'

'Don't be nice to me, Edge,' she snapped.

'I'm merely stating a fact.'

'*You* will hear me and probably say something obnoxious. Again.'

'Here. If I say anything, you have my permission to throw this at me.'

He held out a fist-sized stone. Without thinking she took it and threw it. Hard. It hit a boulder with a sharp clack and a small burst of dust visible even in the darkness.

'You've a good arm,' he observed without heat. 'Were you aiming for that, or was it mere chance?'

'You are lucky you waited to speak until after I threw it. Don't you *ever* lose your temper?'

'Not often. Not for a while at least.'

'When was the last time?'

'When?' He looked up at the sky, frowning. 'I can't remember.'

'You used to lose it often enough at me.'

He smiled, still at the stars.

'That was different. *I* was different back then.'

'Why don't *you* take a dose of your own medicine and howl at the sky? It might do you more good than me.'

He let out a long breath and began walking again.

'I used to. That was one benefit of living on a lonely stretch of shore with only fishermen around me. Whenever there was a storm that is precisely what I did the first year I was there. Then I didn't feel like it any more.'

'Do you feel like anything any more?' She retorted, still angry and determined not to let the image of Edge raging at the storm soften her. She *wanted* to be angry at him. But he just shrugged again, as if shaking her off.

'No, not really. It is quite pleasant this way. It suits me. But it doesn't suit you.'

'Go fall down a well, Edge.'

'I dare say I will if I spend enough time with you. Or into the Nile like the time you took the felucca without Daoud's permission.'

'I would have been fine if you hadn't insisted on coming aboard when I was pulling away from the jetty.'

'Probably. I always did make bad worse, didn't I? I deserved every one of your nicknames. It would have been far better if I'd listened to you instead of you to me. Then I might have…'

She heard the clean note of pain at the memory of his son and she took his hand again without thinking. It was warmer than hers and a little rough, his callouses rubbing against her palm as his hand wrapped around hers in turn. The sky felt like it was pulsing above them, a deep, steady throb. She watched the outline of his chest as he breathed, a slow rise and fall like the thick rolling waves of the Mediterranean. With strange panic she felt her own breathing fall into the rhythm, like a musician entering the orchestra late. Her heartbeat was completely on its own, though— hard and slapping at her insides as if trying to wake her from sinking into a dangerous sleep.

Into a dangerous dream.

She'd fallen into it once, but she wouldn't again. It was the result of being back in Egypt with memories of everything that had happened... Edge standing below the ram's statue, looking exasperated, but with that glimmer of rueful amusement she'd often missed or misunderstood. She'd seen only what he chose to show the world and not the conflicting currents that clashed beneath his wary surface.

Again she thought of al-Walid's story.

'I keep thinking of what they saw,' she said and he turned to her.

'Who?'

'Those men who saw you on the temple with the sandstorm rising behind you. It must have been terrifying.'

'*I* was certainly terrified. We thought that might be our final misdemeanour.'

'That wasn't what I meant and you know it. They must have thought you conjured the storm yourself.'

'Which makes as much sense as believing you conjured the stars in the sky behind you... On second thoughts, I could well believe that right now, Najimat al-Layl. In fact, I'm surprised the wind has fallen. Shu is failing in his role.'

Edge truly had the most amazing voice, Sam thought as her heartbeat whipped up again, her mind groping to remember what al-Walid had said about Shu and Geb and Nuut.

And intercourse.

The desert turned cold at night, but Sam didn't feel it in the least.

'Come, we should return.' He reached out his hand.

'I'm not ready.'

'Don't be foolish, Sam. It is late. Come.'

'But I want to do something foolish. It has been far too long.'

'Too long? Today you refused to rest even though you were ready to fall off that camel and the day before that you were railing at the skies from the Howling Cliffs. I'm afraid to ask what you did the day before that.'

'Well, at least I didn't insist on walking alone from Zarqa.'

His laugh was a rusty rumble.

'*Touché.* I think you are owed at least one more foolish act to measure up to mine. Go ahead, climb something. There's another boulder over there.'

'Very well.' She walked past the boulder he indicated, heading for the darker shape beyond it.

'Sam…that's a hill!'

'Wait for me here if you're scared. You never did know how to enjoy yourself.'

She wasn't surprised to hear the scrape of pebbles and muffled muttering behind her as she climbed. Like the honourable man he was, Edge was so easy to manipulate. He could no more leave her alone in the desert than he could take a hammer to a statue.

'This is beyond foolish, Sam. You can't even see where you are going. If you fall into another bat-infested tomb I'm going to leave you to it this time!'

'That only happened once! You'll remember that on your deathbed, I dare say.'

'I probably will, if I live long enough to die on a bed which is distinctly less probable with you around. And I know all about enjoying myself.'

'Yes, spending hours cleaning a broken piece of pottery. Scintillating.'

'No, not that.'

They'd reached the top of the hill and she barely stopped in time to prevent herself from stepping into darkness. There was something in his tone that told her he'd reached the end of his temper's leash as well. Strangely it made her want to smile. He'd scared her a little these last couple of days—he'd been so...empty. Not like the Edge she'd remembered.

In the darkness she could only make out the tense lines of his jaw and the deepened grooves by his mouth. Suddenly standing at the tip of the little cliff with the substantial bulk of this dark, angry giant looming over her felt distinctly unwise.

This is Edge, she reassured herself. He won't hurt you. Not like that at least.

But then what did she know? Eight years and

losing one's family changed a person. She knew that. What she didn't know was who he had become.

'Edge...'

'You think I'm as useless and dull as those broken pieces of pottery you used to make fun of, don't you?'

'No... Edge, I didn't mean...'

'Yes, you did. Lord Hedgehog, Stay-Away-from-the-Ledge-Edge. I lost track of how many ways you mangled my name. It is rather ironic that you were the one who saddled me with the name Edge only to then contort it into all manner of insults about how boring I am.'

'Edge, *no*. I only said such things because I was upset you never wanted me to be part of what you were doing.'

That was a little too much truth. She could see it in the narrowing of his eyes, the tight line of his mouth. Embarrassed heat flared through her. She'd learned nothing in eight years. All her hard-earned poise was as flimsy as a paper boat on the Nile. Without thinking she tried to move around him and stepped into nothingness.

She didn't end up in a heap at the bottom of the hill as she deserved. Instead it was worse. He hauled her against him, bracing his legs apart. For a moment they both teetered but then he steadied, his arms so tight around her she could feel the hard pressure of his hipbone against her stomach, his knee parting her legs.

'Now you'll say I told you so,' she gasped.

'No, I'll say you owe me. Again.'

'It wouldn't have been so bad this time. We can't have climbed that high.'

His hands softened, sliding down her back, and she sank back from her tiptoes, his knee scraping her skirts against the inside of her thighs.

'Shall I let you go and see?' His voice was lower, taunting. She swallowed. She was shaking and not with fear.

'No.'

Don't let me go.

'Then say thank you for saving me again, Edge.'

'Thank you for saving me again, Edge.' She rose again on tiptoes and touched her mouth to his.

Eight years melted. She melted.

Oh, no.

She could hear those two words again and again, like a bell tolling. *Oh, no...oh, no...oh, no...*

I still want this.

Any second now he would push her away as he had eight years ago, probably off the cliff, but she didn't care. She was caught by the firm warmth of his lips, softening where they were slightly parted, his breath just a whisper of indrawn air on hers, as if he'd stopped breathing altogether.

She knew what was coming—the lecture, the dismissal…

Her hands curved about his nape, slipping into his hair, so much silkier than she'd remembered, nothing like Ricki's shaggy curls. And his scent… It wrapped around her, warm and unique. Unforgettable.

He hadn't saved her, he'd damned her.

Again.

Damn *him*.

She untangled her hands, detached her mouth, bracing herself against his shoulders for when he put her aside. She wasn't brave enough to meet his eyes so she stared at the pulsing beat at the side of his throat, at the shadowed line of his jaw, every inch of her telling her to kiss him again, touch…take.

But neither of them moved. Perhaps they'd turned to pillars of salt like Lot's wife as she looked back in yearning.

Then his hands moved, one pulling her closer, the other cupping her cheek, his thumb rough against her lower lip, as if erasing the memory of her embrace. Then it softened, brushing with the same gentle touch he used to give his precious antiquities.

'Shall I show you how I enjoy myself, Sam?'

It wasn't at all like eight years ago. That had been her very first kiss and she'd been all confusion and it had taken her a while to realise it was even a kiss and only then to realise it was over.

But she'd never stopped wondering why those brief, girlish embraces had meant so much. They'd marked her so potently she'd consciously set out to erase them with every man she'd kissed that foolish year in Venice before she'd finally accepted Ricki's courtship. She'd tried to replicate the way Edge's kiss connected with every parcel of skin and ran through every bone and made everything tingle and ache. She kept searching for that same flash of truth, that sense of *Yes. This!* And found not a whisper of it.

Until now.

Though even as his lips moved against hers, he wasn't even truly kissing her, just exploring her mouth with his, almost curious. His hand was doing the same to the lines of her cheek and throat, learning her as a blind man would something he feared was fragile. Or dangerous.

It was gentle, but it wasn't at all. Each sweep of his lips on hers, every stroke of his fingers, was fire trailing over abraded skin. He applied no pressure, but it both hurt and made her strain towards him, trying to feed or relieve the strange inner cry. She planted her hand on his chest and discovered the lie—there was nothing gentle or soft about his pulse—it was harsh and faster even than hers. Whatever he showed on the surface he was on fire inside and in a second her whole body went up in answering flames and her lips parted with a whimper under his, her tongue touching the smooth warmth of his upper lip.

For a moment she thought they were falling again, the way his arms gathered her to him, crushing her against his body. He could have pushed her off the cliff and had less of an impact. He wasn't gentle any longer, his mouth hard and demanding on hers as his hand sank into her hair, his other drawing one long line down her back to close on her behind, pressing her against him and making her shudder and rise towards him as if trying to reach something or escape it. She moaned as his tongue withdrew to trace her lips, burning and defining them. Her body was alight, on fire, every inch of her wanting its turn. Her hands were fisted in his shirt and she dragged it up and slid her arms up his back and moaned at the sheer pleasure of feeling him. She'd never touched him like this, but it felt like coming home.

This was so very, very wrong.

He must have thought the same because he suddenly froze with something between a curse and an expelled breath. Slowly she sank back on to her heels and he disentangled himself and stepped back. Lord Edward Edgerton was back.

'We should return. It's been a long day and we are both tired.'

Chapter Three

The Jackal sniggered, pawing at Gabriel's torn shirt. 'Only a fool would ask the River God the same question twice and expect the same answer. Leila would know better.'

'Leila is gone,' Gabriel snarled, and turned towards the water once again.

—Temple of the River God,
Desert Boy Book Two

'They went where?'

Janet looked up from pitting dates alongside Aziza in the shade of the small courtyard.

'To the temple of Senusret, my dear. Poppy has been itching to see it again after all these years. Since we cannot expect any news until later in the day it is best the men occupy themselves. They haven't our patience, you know.'

'The *men*,' Sam huffed and Janet smiled.

'Yes, my dear, I know you haven't the patience either. But I noticed you did not sleep much last night and so I chose not to wake you. Come help us with the dates. I want to watch so I can show Ayisha when we return to Qetara in autumn.'

Aziza looked up from her significantly larger stack of pitted dates.

'I have six older brothers, Najimat al-Layl, and I know what it is like to wish to follow where they lead. Even to lead where they might follow. Sometimes I think it is best not to have daughters, the world is never fair to them.'

Sam moved closer, picking up a cured date and splitting it with her fingers. The sticky, fibrous meat gave way and she resisted the urge to sink her teeth into its warm sweetness.

'I want a daughter and I want her to do more than I dared to do.'

'That is a good dream. One day you shall have just such a daughter.' Aziza nodded, pitting five to her one.

Sam's stomach closed like a fist around the stab of pain at the memory of Maria, her hair a tumble of dark curls about the plump face, her eyes wide as she listened to the story Sam was reading. Perhaps in time Ricki might have stopped trying to punish her for not loving him and perhaps in time she'd have learned to care for the sulky boy that hid under the boisterous exterior, at least enough to open herself to his advances again, perhaps even welcome them. But that possibility died when Maria drowned because of Ricki's drunken callousness. And then again, definitively, three years later when Ricki drowned as well.

Sam knew she had no real right to mourn Maria's loss so long after her death. She wasn't her child, not like Jacob had been Edge's son. Perhaps it was no longer Maria she was mourning, but the absence of a dream of her own daughter. A family. A home.

She'd been pushing that wish away for a long time, but it kept growing. Perhaps it was the realisation they were returning to England. Or the unsettling encounter with Edge. Whatever the case she couldn't ignore it any longer.

She wanted a home of her own. A family. Already the images were forming as if she was drawing them herself—a girl and a boy, dark haired, green eyed…

She blinked them away as quickly as she could, but they lingered like the halo of a bright light on the inside of her eyelids.

The idea, once broached, would not be tucked away. She would not have thought of it if Edge had not walked out of the desert and into her world, but he had. She was twenty-six, widowed and wealthy enough to buy herself a house and hire a proper companion to give her countenance, but she wanted more than that. She wanted a home, a partner, someone who loved Egypt and travel and freedom.

Someone whose touch made her wonder if

she'd been wrong to believe Ricki when he'd said that there was something wrong with her woman-hood. That she was incapable of feeling what others did. Because in the fire of that kiss Edge had ignited on the hilltop she'd sensed a whole land-scape awaiting her, accessible if she only reached for it.

Someone she could trust. Someone she could be herself with and however much Edge pushed back at her, she realised she had been more her-self in the past three days than in…years.

Herself… In all her twenty-six years she'd been herself with fewer people than she could count on two hands…

But even if she considered it, why would Edge? He had nothing at all to gain.

It was madness.

She tried to put the idea away, but as she watched the women work, splitting, pitting, stack-ing dates, her mind was putting up brick upon brick of an idea, far faster than she could disman-tle it with logic and objections and reality. She needed to obliterate it—or have Edge do that for her. Once she saw him in the light of day again it would become all too evident just how mad the idea was.

'Aziza, is there someone who could take me there? To the temple?'

'My boy Abdul, if you must go.' There was sympathy in Aziza's eyes and pity, too.

* * *

Edge left al-Walid and Poppy crouched by the tumble of rocks at the far end of Senusret's temple and walked along the vividly painted walls. Amazingly nothing much had changed in a decade. It was still a beautiful escape from the starkness of the desert—the colours were remarkably fresh, better preserved than many temples he'd seen along the Nile.

He inspected an oval-encircled cartouche—a club and a jackal positioned above several abstract shapes. Poppy had showed him a copy of Champollion's revolutionary new philological theories regarding the hieroglyphs and Edge was inclined to agree he was on the right path. It would be interesting to see how this field developed—to reach the point where he could understand the meaning of the hieroglyphs with the same ease as reading English.

Perhaps once he tracked down Rafe and returned to London he would visit the Society of Antiquaries and refresh his mind on the latest state of scholarship. He'd been away so long his mind had atrophied but there was still so much to learn. To do.

He reached out to touch the cartouche and stopped himself, smiling wryly. He'd admonished Sam often enough and here he was doing the same. She always had to touch everything, experience it with all her senses before capturing it

in the quick and intuitively brilliant sketches that
made her illustrations for his books so captivating.

His conscience snapped at him again. His one
firm stipulation from Mr Durham, his publisher,
was that his authorship of the *Desert Boy* books
remain a secret from everyone, even the illustrator. He'd wanted no direct communication with
Sam and he had no intention of changing that
aspect of their relationship now. But he still had
enough of a conscience to feel guilty about encouraging Poppy and al-Walid to leave early without waiting for her and denying her the chance to
see what he knew she would love to draw.

She should be here.

His excuse that she needed to rest had been just
that—an excuse, and a petty and insincere and
cowardly one. Qualities he despised.

Especially cowardly.

Sam wasn't to blame for the fact that he was
sorely regretting indulging his lingering curiosity by kissing her last night. There must be something very wrong with him that a half-innocent
kiss snatched years ago could have etched itself
into his body as definitely as the ancient Egyptians carved their world on to this temple wall.
He'd thought it was half-guilt, half-surprise that
had made him react so strongly and so uncharac-
teristically to her innocent kiss eight years ago.
The discovery of Sam not as Lucas and Chase's
younger sister and the bane of his existence but

as a young woman with a lush body and the most extraordinary eyes... He'd never even noticed that ocean grey-blue until she'd knocked him to the ground, literally forcing herself on him... Or her mouth... Or the long legs tangled with his and the surprisingly large breasts so evident under the cotton *kamisa*. He'd barely even noticed she had breasts until those last weeks. Perhaps he *had* hit his head when he fell that day—he couldn't understand why else he had been so stunned he'd reacted like a boy of sixteen rather than a man of twenty-six.

But when she touched her mouth to his... again...

Hell.

It was absurd that he'd remembered the feel of her mouth after eight years when he could barely remember Dora's or most of the women who shared his bed since. Succumbing to curiosity and kissing Sam again had been a mistake.

He clenched his jaw as the same fire surged through him as had possessed him on the hill last night. He hated this. Had hated it then. Hated it last night, hated it now.

Once he found Rafe he fully intended to return to the life he'd built after Jacob's death—it was comfortable there on his emotional plateau, confining all his flights of fancy to his writing. It might be as drab and boring as Sam accused him of being, but he'd been content.

Damn Rafe.

Blast Sam.

No, it was wrong to blame her for his misstep yesterday, just as it was wrong to resent her for sowing the first seeds of doubt about his marriage. He could not blame his and Dora's failures on that encounter with Sam eight years ago. It had been a catalyst, not a cause. It wasn't Sam's fault he realised there was little he found of interest beyond Dora's vivid beauty and charm and it certainly wasn't Sam's fault Dora discovered she had nothing in common with what lay behind the façade of the wealthy war hero Captain Lord Edward Edgerton.

He'd still hoped that once they had children they would find a common ground and grow together. What a young, naïve fool he'd been. Jacob's birth and illness had only weakened Dora, encouraged by her overprotective mother with her love of ailments real and imagined, and he'd done very little to help. He'd found it hard to watch her apathy to their beautiful son and his joy in the babe only seemed to make her more fretful. So he hadn't truly objected when her mother whisked Dora away to recover in Bath after her difficult birth. He'd wished her well and settled in to enjoy his son.

When Jacob fell ill he'd waited for her to return, but once again Dora had given way to her mother's decree that she wasn't strong enough to expose herself to the fever. When the fever passed, leaving Jacob damaged for life and the doctors shaking their heads over the chances of Jacob's surviving into adulthood, Edge had hoped that Dora and her mother, both so very fascinated by their own ailments, would be empathetic to Jacob's, but he'd been as wrong as wrong could be.

He'd finally insisted she return to Chesham, but that brief visit had been a disaster. Dora had been devastated by her one encounter with Jacob and Mrs Wadham had taken her away that very week. The final straw came swiftly in the form of a letter from his father saying Mrs Wadham and Lady Edward had called at Greybourne on their way to Bath and that it was felt it best to send Jacob to be cared for elsewhere if Lady Edward was to return to Chesham and try to produce a healthy heir.

Rafe had been staying at Chesham during these challenging months and Edge had handed him that letter, then tossed it in the fire and never spoke another word with Dora or his parents. It was Rafe who sent word to them when Jacob finally died and Rafe who first received word that Dora had died of influenza two years later in Bath.

Edge walked out of the temple into the blazing sun, tilting his head back, hoping it would eclipse the heat and confusion inside him.

His eyes flew open as something came between him and the sun and stared in shock as a figure moved up the dune on the side of the temple. For a moment he thought it was a desert *sarab* conjured by his libido and conscience. But the rivulets of sand slipping down from the roof as she came to stand on its rim were not typical of desert illusions. His memory chimed in happily with the memory of her standing on another temple long ago, him reaching up…and finding himself flat on his back with an armful of warm…

Hell.

'Sam! What the devil are you doing here? Come down at once!' he demanded.

'You can see the whole desert from here,' she replied with a happy sigh and that only made it worse. 'My goodness! What *are* those? They look like giant mushrooms.'

'They are rocks. Now get down before you break something.'

She touched the tip of her boot to the long stone lintel that covered the entranceway.

'It feels solid to me. Clearly Senusret was worthy of his reputation as a master builder.'

'I meant your bones, not the blasted temple.'

'Edge!' Her eyes widened, her mouth curving into a smile that was far more old Sam than new. Or more young Sam than old. Or just more annoying Sam than the proper one whose emergence he'd so foolishly worried about. She must have loved her husband deeply to empty herself so brutally of life and laughter and to be filled with the grief she'd shown at the Howling Cliffs. He'd heard about the dashing Lord Ricardo Carruthers—it wasn't surprising Sam still hadn't recovered from her loss. It was wrong, though. Sam should be as she was now—with that glimmer of mischief lighting her inner flame, laughing at him. He'd always felt both comforted and uncomfortable when her impish humour targeted him. Right now it felt like a benediction; proof there was hope yet for this world.

She moved back a step, sending another cascade of sand like a veil over the entrance.

'Is this better?'

'No, it is not. What are you doing now?' he demanded as she rooted around in her cloth bag.

'I want to sketch those mushrooms.'

'Rocks.'

'They cannot possibly be natural rocks. Only look at them. That one looks like a parasol run amuck.'

Despite himself he turned. 'Which one?'

'You cannot see it from down there.'

Edge surrendered before he even began the fight this time. Clearly she had no intention of coming down and he would likely have an apoplexy waiting for her to fall. At least if he was close he could grab her before she did something foolish…again…

Oh, Sam. What the devil am I going to do with you?

'There. See how beautiful it is from up here?' she whispered when he stopped beside her. They stood so close the wind was wrapping her skirts about his legs like a morning mist.

'We are barely ten feet off the ground standing on a pile of stones. Hardly an Alpine peak.'

'It is not a "pile of stones". It is a magical temple that can be moved by the power of one's thoughts. Where would you command it to take you, Edge?'

'There is nowhere I would rather be.'

The words were out before he could think and he very much hoped she interpreted them as apathy. It wasn't that he wished to be here beside her, precisely. It was merely true that there was nowhere he would rather be.

After a moment's silence, she returned to the view.

'That formation looks like a tipsy mushroom, doesn't it? And that one like a rabbit with one floppy ear and a bad squint.'

'It looks like a rock.'

'So do you, at the moment. Surely they are not natural, are they?'

'They are. The stone around here is soft and the wind has sculpted it over millennia in an Aeolian…'

'Oily Inn?' Sam asked, sitting down and unwrapping a cloth parcel. The scent of honey and dates snaked around him and his stomach tightened with another form of hunger. Blast Sam.

'Aeolian. Named after the Greek god of wind, it means quick-moving wind and sand scour away the softer rock to reveal harder stone beneath. According to Hutton's *Theory of the Earth…*'

'Do take a seat.' Sam patted the sand next to her and Edge surrendered again. He sat, brushing his hands on his dusty trousers, and took the slice of cake Sam offered. She smiled and licked her fingers and a little earthquake roared through him. The memory of his mouth on hers in the dark—her taste…

'So. What is Hutton's theory of the earth?' she coaxed and he wished it was polite to snarl.

'That the earth is balanced on the back of a camel stumbling about inebriated with *raki* which is why there are earthquakes.'

She laughed, handed him the cloth-wrapped cake and began sketching.

'That is a marvellous image, but I thought you were constitutionally incapable of mouthing an untruth.'

He held the warm parcel in his hands, wishing his conscience was less developed. For a moment he considered telling her the truth about the scope of his powers of confabulation.

'I know how to lie when I must, Sam.'

'About what?'

Her smile faded, her pencil poised above her

drawing. Already in a few strokes she'd outlined the horizon, the twisted rock formations rising like billows of smoke from the ground. He could already see the finished illustration—that mysterious foreign landscape, beckoning the reader, drawing them in to a world promising adventure...and eventually salvation. What would she do if he told her that he was the author of the *Desert Boy* books? That all these years...

He gathered air for the admission, but the foolish image he'd created faltered, the camel stumbling, the earth rolling off its unsteady back and down a crack to...nothingness.

No, that was one Pandora's box best kept sealed. It simply was not worth the risk.

When he didn't answer she returned to her sketch and for a while there was no sound but the muted voices of al-Walid and Poppy from inside the temple and the scrape of Sam's pencil on paper. It had always been a puzzle to him how mercurial Sam could be as still and precise as any watchmaker when she was sketching. He knew he'd disappeared for her, he felt he himself was disappearing a little into the world she was weaving for him without even knowing it was for him.

Ever since he'd asked Durham to commission her as illustrator of his books he'd seen again and again how precisely she captured what he wasn't even certain he'd conveyed in words. There was a terrifying gap between what he saw in his mind and what he was able to write. By some strange magic Sam closed that gap as if she could crawl into his mind and harvest the first vivid images that stood at the heart of each chapter, the sensations that gave it the beating heart and drew the readers in. That sense of encroachment had even made him suggest finding another illustrator, but Durham would have none of it.

'Heaven forfend!' Durham had objected. 'It is true there are more talented illustrators in matters technical, but I do not know of another who could capture the emotions that quiver between the characters of your tales. One always feels that any moment that world will come to life and we shall all be swept into the adventure. I fear readers already attached to her images might feel cheated by any change midstream, so to speak, and that might affect our sales, Lord Edward.'

I don't give a rat's ass about sales, Edge had wanted to respond, but it was not true. The first book was published when Jacob was barely a year old, just before he fell ill. Edge had loved reading to Jacob—his son's cinnamon eyes would light with pleasure at the cadence of his reading and his laugh made Edge's heart expand to encompass the universe. Edge had no idea if his stories reached Jacob, but he knew without a doubt the illustrations did—whenever a page contained an illustration, Jacob's plump, stubborn fingers would stop

Edge from turning the page until Jacob looked his fill.

Unlike the Egyptians Edge did not believe in life after death, neither in heaven or hell or anything in between. But he wanted desperately to believe in it so he could imagine Jacob still existed somewhere other than in his dried husk of a heart. And if that was so, every book he wrote, and every illustration Sam drew, was for Jacob.

'What is wrong, Edge?'

He hadn't noticed she'd stopped drawing or that she was watching him. He turned away.

'It's boiling out here. At least come inside the temple. There's even a statue of Senusret in there for you to climb on. You just might fit on his lap.'

Well, that was a mistake. The sharp knife of grief did lose its sting, but it was replaced by the image of her lush posterior on the statue's granite lap, wriggling as she settled, the stone warming…

'Help me up, then.' She extended a hand and he took and helped her to her feet, her hand warm and dry in his. She gave a little moan as she balanced herself on the shifting sand. 'My legs are still stiff after that ride yesterday. I wish women could go to a *hamam* and have someone—'

'Blast it, Sam,' he interrupted before that image also took root in his already disordered mind— his hands moving over her legs, kneading the taut muscles, skimming up her thighs, warm… 'You cannot speak of such things in public. I thought you'd finally grown up.'

He saw anger flash in her eyes and was almost grateful for it. He'd be grateful if she pushed him off the temple roof if it countered his deteriorating impulses.

'Well, I thought the same of you. You were hardly such a prude last night.' She moved past him towards the bank of sand and this time he did not try to help her down.

Sam knew the moment they entered Bahariya that news of Rafe had arrived. There was a welcoming committee, led by Aziza with Janet by her side standing almost on tiptoe in her excitement. Edge reached them first.

'They've found him?'

'News of him, my dear.' Janet grasped his hand, her other extended towards Poppy. 'They stopped in Farafra several days ago and so are likely in Cairo by now.'

Edge turned to al-Walid.

'Please convey my gratitude to your people. This means I must leave tomorrow at dawn.'

Sam followed Janet and the women, her thoughts stumbling over each other. Following Edge to the temple had only jumbled her thoughts further. She felt both more uncomfortable and comfortable with Edge than anyone she knew and that wasn't helping in the least. There would be no time to explore her half-formed thoughts and plans. They'd only muddied the waters further. Tomorrow Edge would be gone and she would soon be returning to London and to whatever future she could build for herself.

Nothing had changed.

A small, sharp voice spoke at her very core.

You are right. Nothing will change unless you change it. So do something, Sam Sinclair. You are tired of being swept along, rudderless. So do something...

Chapter Four

Leila knelt by the silvered rim of the lake, placed her hand on the cool water, and called up her fate.

—*Lost in the Valley of the Moon,*
Desert Boy Book Three

'Edge? Are you awake?'

For a moment he thought he'd mistaken the whisper of the wind for her voice. But then the cloth entrance shifted and a figure slipped into his tent. He surged to his feet, his whisper grating in his ears.

'What the devil are you doing here, Sam?'

'I need to speak with you.'

'We can speak tomorrow before I leave. Now go away before you are seen.'

'By whom? I hardly think any of al-Walid's people will denounce me to the patronesses of Almack's.'

A pale blur showed as her mouth curved into a

smile and his hands twitched. That smile was attached directly to an inner core of heat and here in the darkness, after a very unfruitful attempt not to sink into equally unfruitful fantasies, his defences were especially weak.

He could see her more clearly now, the oval of her face and the deeper shadows of her eyes. He was as tense as if a wild animal searching for shelter had just prowled into his tent. No, Sam bent on testing him to his limits was more dangerous than any desert predator.

'That is hardly the point. Surely this can wait until morning?'

'No it cannot. It requires a degree of privacy. For heaven's sake, Edge. I shan't pounce on you, you know.'

Oh, hell. I wish you would.

'Very well. Just be quick about it. I would rather not be discovered entertaining you here.'

'You aren't entertaining in the least at the moment, Edge. Though you might be entertained yourself once I tell you why I'm here.'

He frowned. Her voice was high and raspy. She was nervous; *very* nervous. She kept shifting her weight, too, as if preparing for a bout of pugilism.

'I have a proposition, Edge.'

A proposition.

His body felt fractured—heat pulsed from his stomach muscles while a cold weight pressed at his lungs and shoulders like a mantle of snow.

He didn't like the feeling. He was tired, worried, confused. He wanted to recapture that pleasant numbness he'd worked hard to attain since Jacob's death.

But... A proposition. From Sam.

The words echoed through his mind, intermingling with the thoughts that had been keeping him from sleep—memories of her taste, the feel of her in the darkness. Her scent—even arm's length from her it engulfed him. It was like standing in a garden in mid-bloom. Spring. She smelt of spring and he was as hard as the rock formations she'd admired.

And why not? They were both widowed and had no ties. The physical attraction was undeniable and Sam was clearly no stranger to such encounters. He'd been isolated from gossip after Jacob's death, but he'd heard enough about Sam's many flirtations before her marriage in Venice. The Sinclairs were always newsworthy and Dora and her mother delighted in gossip even when it was being played out in foreign climes. The fact that it involved an Austrian prince, a Russian count, and the very dashing Lord Ricardo Carruthers all vying for the attentions of the scandalous Sinclair sister had pushed it to the forefront of London gossip that summer.

So why not assent to a proposition? Perhaps it would finally put to rest the foolish fantasy she'd planted in his mind all those years ago and the hunger she'd fanned since he'd seen her on the Howling Cliffs. There was nothing wrong with acting like the animals they were. These sensations might be the only things that were right in his life at the moment.

'*You think too much, Lord Glower-from-the-Hoity-Toity-Ledge,*' she'd told him often enough. Well, she was right. For the moment he should stop thinking. It was hell on his libido.

'Edge?'

He dragged himself out of his thoughts.

'What?'

'All I ask is that you listen to me before you say no or call me mad. Because it is a little mad, well, more than a little. But I think, perhaps, it could benefit us both. Well, benefit me more than you, but perhaps it might offer some…oh, the devil, I'm blathering. No, don't say anything yet, please. Just listen. *Please.*'

Her hands rose, two pale smudges, fingers spread wide, as if warning him to keep his distance. He took a deep breath, his body tingling with far greater disappointment than he wanted to credit. This did not sound like the proposition he'd begun to imagine.

'Very well. I am listening.'

'I know you have more important matters on your mind, but all I ask is that you consider it. And I mean *truly* consider it, not just be your proper self and say you will consider it while you tell yourself inside that this is only Sam being foolish Sam…'

'Sam, tell me what it is you want. If it is something I can do, within reason, then I shall.'

She laughed and dropped her hands.

'Within reason. That is a matter of opinion…'

'Sam!'

She breathed in sharply and almost exhaled the words.

'I want you to marry me.'

She might have struck him right in the sternum with a cannonball and had less of an impact. He even pressed his hand to his chest as ice-cold shock burst through him. The closest he'd felt to this was when the unseen French *voltigeur*'s shot caught him in the shoulder that day at the foothill of the Pyrenees. Disbelief and denial had been as powerful as the pain. As if by a force of will he could unmake those fateful moments.

But now disbelief wasn't laced with denial, but with heat. The ravenous panther that had burst into being since he'd been foolish enough to touch her again was clawing at his back, trying to push past him and devour her whole.

'Say something.' Her voice was still shaky so he tried to steady himself. He shoved the panther back into the shadows, trying to see her expression in the gloom of the tent.

'I'm a rather dull fellow, as you pointed out,

Lady Carruthers. If this is a jest, you will need to explain it to me.'

'This is no jest. I am sincere…oh, never mind, you idiotish clod. I might as well try to talk to a lump of clay as evoke a human response out of you.' She sounded on the verge of tears and Edge moved between her and the entrance.

'Wait.'

'I don't wish to speak to you any more.' She grabbed his shirt and tried to haul him aside.

'Well, too bad.' He caught her hands, but did not try to detach them from his shirt, just wrapped his own around them. 'You cannot say something like that without…explaining.'

'I can say what I wish. I'm tired of thinking about everything I say. I had an idea and you said it was a bad one. No surprise there. After all, I'm only Sam the impulsive madcap…'

'Sam, stop.'

'Let me go, Edge. I didn't mean it.' She squirmed and gave a little tug to her hands, but not enough to pull them free. Her knuckles were pressed against his chest and he could feel the beat of his own pulse hammer against them, each strike followed by a shower of sparks coursing through his veins, spreading heat.

'You never say anything you don't mean, Sam. That is part of your problem.'

She closed her eyes and breathed in and he saw again the shift between Sams—this one was a strange mix of measured Sam and a Sam he wasn't familiar with.

'Yes, you are right,' she replied. 'I did mean it. These past months, since I returned to Egypt… this is the first time I've felt alive in years. I don't want to return to England and sink back into that half-life I lived. Yes, I'm wealthy and could find a companion and travel the world, but I want more. I want to travel and return often to Egypt, but I also want a family and a home and I want to have that with someone I can trust and talk to and who knows me, good and bad. Then I realised these are all things that I have…with you. And then there is…this.'

'This?'

She rubbed her knuckles against his chest and *this* flooded him with liquid fire.

'This. I'm not a child, Edge. I couldn't imagine marrying someone I did not wish to share… intimacy with. It would be…unbearable. None of the men poor Janet introduced me to in Cairo had *this*. I haven't felt *this* in…in years. I might have been a child eight years ago, but even then I felt *this*. For me, at least, it is rare.' She looked up. He could feel her trying to read his expression in the dark. 'It isn't just me, is it? You do feel a…an attraction?'

She'd slipped back into hesitation and even though he knew he was on dangerous ground he needed to chase away her doubt.

'Yes, Sam. I thought that was obvious. I've never been a good actor.'

She sighed with relief, her fingers curling into the fabric of his shirt and even if he'd lied, his body couldn't. It was aching, pleading with him. He moved closer, aware he was stepping out on to the same plank as she.

'That's true.' She laughed a little, her breath cool against the perspiration at the base of his throat. 'When you did allow anything past your stony façade one could be certain it was purely you. And that is why... Edge—if there was time I would try to be patient and plot your downfall in a civilised manner, but there isn't time. Tomorrow you will be off again and I might not see you ever again or at least until we are old and grey and I cannot bear living with the regret of not asking if you would consider marrying me. I *feel* this is the right thing to do, the *best* thing to do. You say I'm impetuous and I dare say this proves everything you've ever said about me, but I couldn't not try, do you see?'

'Sam, you do realise what you are offering...it means the rest of your life.'

'Of course I realise that, Edge. I think...you are lonely as well, aren't you? I know there is part of you that prefers to remain that way, but doesn't part of you want something more than to return to your exile in Brazil? I'm tired of mine. I want *more*.'

Brazil. His lungs constricted just at the thought. That bridge had burned behind him and he'd not even realised it. Sam had opened a Pandora's box and he didn't think he was strong enough to close it.

Another chance. At being a husband, a father. With Sam.

He'd set down that path with Dora in good faith eight years ago and ruined both their lives. He shouldn't even consider it with Sam of all people. To be responsible for *her* future happiness. He *shouldn't* consider it, but merely by asking she was changing the course of his life.

'No,' he answered. 'There is nothing to return to.'

'Then what shall you do when you find Rafe?'

'I don't know.'

'Where do you wish to go?'

Here. I want to stay here and let the world care for itself. I want to see if this ease I feel with you is real because it is unlike anything I've felt with anyone else. Even with Rafe—and I've trusted him with my life.

The words didn't come anywhere near his lips.

'I don't know, Sam.'

'Do you ever want to have a family again?'

'Yes. Yes, I do.' The words left him before he could stop them. Jacob's face rose before him, clearer than it had been in a long while—smiling as he smeared a jam-covered hand down the page of Edge's first copy of the *Desert Boy* book. It wasn't the words that had caught his son's attention, but Sam's illustration of Gabriel being jostled between a camel, a donkey and a one-eyed jackal.

'So will you at least consider what I proposed, Edge?'

'Yes.'

Her laugh was shaky as she finally untangled her hands and stepped back.

'Good. Thank you. Goodnight, Edge.'

She grasped the cloth door of the tent and the panther reached through him and sank its teeth into its prey.

'I accept.'

'You…what?'

'Accept. Your proposal.'

'But… I did not mean you had to give me an answer immediately…'

'Shall I withdraw my acceptance?'

'No! No, but…'

'We will tell Poppy and Janet in the morning and discuss the particulars.'

'Edge, I…thank…'

He stifled the words before she could speak them. He didn't want her thanks. He wanted… *this*—his hands in her hair, his mind already unravelling it over her shoulders, her mouth softening under his… Like the night before shivering heat swamped him as every parcel of his body fought to embrace or escape *this*.

She was right, whatever else existed or didn't exist in this world, he couldn't deny *this*. In mere days it had become a certainty and that scared the hell out of him. He softened the kiss, pulling away.

'It's late. Time to go, Sam.'

'But…'

'Now. Before I change my mind.'

About saying yes and about letting you leave this tent before I ask you to stay.

For once she obeyed him without a word, whisking into the dark like the last tendril of smoke from a campfire. He followed until she was safe inside and then stood for a long time in the darkness, wondering whether all those years of exile and isolation had finally pushed him over some precipice of insanity.

Chapter Five

Gabriel gaped into the pit. 'There is nothing there but darkness, Leila.'

'I am there. I told you the day will come when you must choose to trust me, Gabriel. That is today.'

— *Treasures of Siwa,*
Desert Boy Book Five

'**W**ith this ring I thee wed, with my body I thee worship...'

Edge's deep voice had been as flat as a millpond, but the words kept playing in her mind, just as her fingers kept playing with the simple gold ring on her finger.

She had no idea where he found it or when. The three days since her proposal were a confusing blur. Both Poppy and Janet had surprised her by being delighted at Edge's laconically delivered news of their betrothal, utterly unconcerned that their nephew was about to marry a woman he had not seen in eight years.

Once in Cairo, Edge disappeared, returning with the news that a man matching Rafe's distinctive description had booked passage to England on a ship which had sailed from Alexandria that very day.

He didn't look at Sam as he spoke and when he added he'd requested the consul general help him find passage on the first fast ship to England she steeled herself for the inevitable. Here was a perfect excuse for Edge to withdraw from her proposal, or at least postpone it long enough to come to his senses. Perhaps so would she.

But then he'd thoroughly stunned her. Apparently he'd done more at the consul general's than arrange passage. She'd listened in shock as he'd informed her that the same vicar who performed Chase and Ellie's wedding was still in Cairo and more than willing to perform the ceremony should they choose to marry before leaving Egypt.

If she chose.

If.

She'd searched his face for some indication of his wishes, but this was Edge. He'd put the pieces on the board—the move was hers.

Sam touched her ring again. It was surprisingly delicate, very different from Ricki's elaborate gold and ruby family heirloom that chafed her fingers and which she'd lost in the canal the day Maria drowned. The moment Edge slipped the ring on her finger at the vicar's command the world shrank and hushed, like the moment birds chirping raucously in a tree at dusk settled suddenly into the calm of night. She'd still wobbled when they'd kneeled and his hand had caught hers and just for a moment he'd shown an emotion, even if it was worry.

Married.

Again.

Edge was now her husband.

'My dear, dear Sam. I'm so very, very happy.' Janet clasped Sam's hand almost convulsively, her other hand pressing a now-mangled handkerchief to her eyes. She'd cried quietly throughout the brief ceremony in the drawing room of the British consul general's house, nestling under Poppy's arm. 'You both deserve happiness after all you have been through. I know you were forever at daggers drawn when you were young, but sometimes that is the best way. You know the worst of each other which is so much more than most couples do when entering matrimony, you know.'

That much was true, Sam thought as she patted Janet's hand. She was still too shocked to do more than smile at the people who had joined the impromptu congratulatory toast that followed the brief ceremony. Behind her smile her mind kept echoing with the same thoughts.

Married. Again. What have I done?

This was either a most brilliant move on her part or an impulsive recipe for disaster. This time she had climbed something from which she could easily fall and break her neck.

She squirmed with the same mix of excitement and terror that hadn't let her go since she'd entered Edge's tent. She'd expected him to throw her out on her ear with a good lecture at worst or with a stolid 'I am flattered by your proposal but you are clearly suffering from desert fever, now go to sleep like a good girl'.

She should be content, happy. Edge might be a trifle...difficult, but he was good, conscientious, intelligent. Even kind when he let his shell fall away. Not to mention as handsome as sin and could kiss as if he had traded something very valuable to the devil for that skill.

There was no reason to be shaking with fear.

Yet she was.

'Lady Edward, my warmest congratulations!' The consul general joined them, beaming. 'Are there any more Sinclairs for us to wed here in Cairo? We are most willing to continue in this pleasant vein.'

Spoken aloud the words sounded even more foreign than in her mind.

Lady Edward.

In the past that name had plagued her—it sparked twists of pain and the image of a golden-haired beauty waltzing in Edge's arms under the light of a thousand candles. When her girlish hopes for her own marriage to Ricki turned to ashes she realised that image had goaded her into seeking a male version of the perfect and charming Theodora Wadham. She'd latched on to Ricki's golden curls and infectious laughter, his pleasure in dancing the night away, his adoration of her... She'd been too young to see how much of that pleasure had been fuelled by wine and how much of his adoration fuelled by a need to possess the prize others sought.

Ricki's perfect image faded fast, but not Lady Edward's. At night as she lay under Ricki's heavy body waiting for it to be over, her mind tortured her with images of the golden sylph in Edge's arms, being loved in a manner utterly different from Ricki's heedless, drunken pawing... Eventually even those images faded and she just lay there.

Until the day Ricki taunted her once too often with her insipidity and coldness and the truth came roaring out of her—that she never had or ever would love him, that she'd married him only because she wanted a home and family and could never have that with the man she loved. Even now that memory was a taste of purgatory—her venom spilling out and then the realisation that despite his drunken clumsiness and childish posturing her husband actually cared. But it had been too late. There had been no taking back the truth.

'More champagne, Lady Edward?'

Sam accepted the glass from Sir Henry, watching her husband over its rim.

Her husband.

That tall, handsome, serious-looking man listening to Poppy and the vicar with a slight smile softening the sharp-hewn lines of his face. Despite his outward calm, he exuded a raw but leashed power. She could see the other guests watching him as they might watch a wild animal only half-tamed by years of captivity, fascinated but wary that any moment he might forget his civilised veneer and succumb to an atavistic urge to devour. Not that he seemed to notice. Even as a young man he'd been just as unaware. She'd overheard her brothers ribbing him that this was why his mistresses were usually older than he—it took a mature and determined woman to make it absolutely clear they were interested.

Just as she had.

The thought and its implications made her shiver.

Edge looked over suddenly, his eyes shaded despite the glare of candles. He detached himself and moved towards her and she tried to gauge his mood but could see nothing in his darkened eyes but polite interest as they skimmed over her. He turned to nod to Sir Henry.

'Thank you for arranging passage so swiftly, Sir Henry.'

'Think nothing of it, Lord Edward. HMS *Lark* is one of the navy's swiftest vessels and could have you in Portsmouth in under three weeks if weather allows. Pity you cannot stay to see the marvellous new finds. Truly exquisite. But perhaps you will be returning next winter?'

'Perhaps.'

'Depending on your lovely wife, I am certain.'

'Mr and Mrs Carmichael will remain a little longer, but my wife and I had best leave as we must now prepare for an early departure tomorrow morning.'

'Of course, of course. Everyone will understand.' Sir Henry laughed, his cheeks redder than Sam's.

Once in the carriage the sounds and smells of Cairo took over. Sam watched the darkened streets and wished again that Edge could have found Rafe innocently lodged in one of the hotels. Then there would have been time to adjust, to become reacquainted, explore Egypt together...

She threw him another glance, but he was looking out the other window, his mouth a straight line.

She had no idea what to say to him.

Are you regretting this marriage? Resenting me? Thinking only of reaching England and finding your brother? Or of something else entirely?

'You look very lovely.'

She started at his words—though he hardly sounded as if he meant them.

'So do you,' she said anyway and the corner of his mouth curved a little.

'I've never been called lovely before.'

'Well, perhaps that is not the best adjective.'

'What is, then?' He finally turned to her, but still she could see nothing in his eyes but faint amusement. It scared her—that this man was her husband and she could not read him at all. She had the strangest sensation that though he looked like the Edge she'd once known he was someone else entirely.

She'd married a stranger.

'What is wrong?' His eyes narrowed as they moved over her face. She forced a smile.

'I don't know. I think I'm tired. No, nervous. No, I'm scared I've forced your hand and you will come to resent me.'

That was more honest than she'd intended, but at least it sparked something in his gaze.

'Sam of old wouldn't be so plagued by doubts.'

'I don't know if that is true. But in any case Sam of old is long gone, Edge.'

He reached out to trace a line from her cheekbone to the corner of her mouth, paused, and then continued, settling on the curve of her lower lip. He applied no pressure, but her lips parted and she had to consciously draw air into her lungs. She wanted desperately to moisten her lips, but her nerve utterly deserted her. Sam of old's bravado, sparked by the raw beauty of the desert, had lasted long enough to shift her life on to an entirely new course, but now the fear was back.

'Is she? Gone?'

'I don't know.'

His hand dropped and he looked away.

'I hope she's not completely gone, Sam. You'll need her strength to tolerate me.'

'I think it's rather the other way around. I dare say you are regretting this already.'

He laughed, utterly surprising her as he pulled her on to his lap, his breath warm against her temple as he spoke.

'At the moment I'm only regretting we will only have one night to explore the attractions of our alliance, Najimat al-Layl.'

His lips brushed softly over her ear, resting for a moment on her earlobe, and she shivered as his tongue traced its curve.

'I like when you call me that,' she whispered. 'Even though it is merely another reminder of what a nuisance I was.'

His hands moved over her back, loosening the laces of her dress under the cover of her light cloak, sliding under the fabric, warm and firm, making her skin dance with skittish pleasure. She arched against them, trying to meet or escape the pleasure unravelling through her.

'You were impossible, Night Star. I kept waiting breathlessly for the next disaster.' He murmured the words against her cheek, brushing his lips lightly over hers. His mouth was cool, but he was a blaze of dark heat wrapping around her, singeing her from the outside in.

This was what he wanted from her, probably all he wanted from her.

The attractions of our alliance...

It should worry her, but right now the only thing that worried her was as he said—that they would have only one night before they set out on the long journey back to England which meant for three weeks or so the best accommodation they would have would be the narrow bed of a naval frigate.

She turned to him, her hands on his shoulders. In the darkness of the carriage his eyes glinted at her, challenging, his lips parted.

'Yes, Sam?'

His hair was thick and silky warm against her fingers, her lips tingling with the need to feel it, to feel him. She could taste the memory of their kiss in the dark, feel the texture of his mouth on hers.

Her husband's mouth...

'Edge... Kiss me...'

His hands sank deep into her hair as she whispered against his lips, holding her there, pressing her closer.

'Don't stop.' The words rumbled between them and then were lost as the kiss deepened.

When he finally drew away, setting her back on the seat with a muffled curse, it took her a stunned moment to realise they'd reached the Carmichaels' house in Cairo.

At the top of the staircase she turned towards her room, but Edge caught her hand.

'This way. My room tonight, Madame Wife.'

Heat flared through her—a mix of fear and anticipation. Her palm was hot and damp against his and the coward in her wished she could somehow jump ahead ten years to a time when everything had smoothed out, *she* had smoothed out into a calmer, more sensible person who was content to be content. Who wasn't scared.

He closed the door behind him and she stared at the bed.

Years ago she'd stood just so in her husband's room. Beyond the windows she'd seen the roofs of Venice and a sky tinged with the setting sun and known she'd made a horrible mistake for all the worst reasons.

Right now she didn't know anything but that the bed was enormous and that Edge was standing right behind her as if ready to push her off a cliff. Surely there was a chasm between them and the bed that would be impossible to cross. It was not at all possible they would in a matter of moments be in it. Together.

All those kisses, that heat, that hope, would end in...*that*.

'What is it?'

She tried to answer him, but couldn't.

'Are you worried?'

She swallowed and nodded.

'Are you tired? Would you rather sleep?'

Sleep? She would never sleep again in a million years. She swallowed again and shook her head.

He took her hand and drew her towards a door at the side of the room. It led to a small parlour with a desk and a cushioned *mastaba* bench under the window overlooking the inner garden. Jasmine vines poked in through the carved shutters, the scent powerful and soothing.

'Sit.' He eased her on to the bench and moved away and she almost grabbed for his hand again. God, she was behaving like a terrified virgin. He must think her ridiculous.

He returned with a glass of brandy and she sipped it, grateful to have something to hold in her hands. The cushions shifted as he sat beside her.

'What will you do when we reach London?' she asked hurriedly.

'Search for Rafe. Hopefully he will have presented himself at Greybourne or at least alerted the lawyers of his return. Once I ascertain he is well I will beat him to a pulp for dragging me halfway around the world. If he isn't there, I shall have to find him. You know that, don't you?'

'Of course. I would do the same.'

'Yes, you undoubtedly would. What will *you* do when we reach London? Will your brothers be there? It would be preferable if you stayed with them rather than a hotel until I can make arrangements.'

'Of course we shall stay at Sinclair House. But…should we not go see your family?'

'We just have. They stood behind us at the ceremony and are hopefully enjoying the consul general's champagne as we speak.'

'I didn't mean Janet and Poppy. When was the last time you saw your mother or sisters?'

He swirled his brandy and a trickle skimmed over the rim on to his finger. He switched hands and licked off the liquid and Sam caught herself leaning forward. Then his words snapped her back to reality.

'Four years ago.'

'Four?'

'You sound shocked. I left England not long after Jacob died. Or rather after Rafe removed me to Cumbria.'

'You make it sound like you were a piece of furniture.'

'Close enough. I don't even remember being removed.'

Sam let that sink in, her heart aching, and grateful he was telling her this. There was nothing in his voice, neither heat nor coolness. He might just as well have been telling her about geological formations, but she knew there was a whole kingdom under that bland layer.

'I'm so glad he was there when you needed him.'

He smiled at the floor, shifting his shoulders. He'd taken off his coat and cravat and she could see his muscles move under the linen, the taut tendons of his throat, the warm colour of his skin. He smelled of the forest, not the desert—deep and cool and inviting.

'Yes, I dare say. Poor Rafe. Playing nursemaid was new to him.'

'Where did he take you?'

'He has a house up in the hills above Grasmere. It is tiny and in the middle of absolutely nowhere, but he goes there when he needs to…when he needs to be alone. We stayed there for several months and then sailed to Jamaica.'

'I see why he is so important to you. I will do everything I can to help.'

'Yes, I know. That is what worries me.' He finally looked at her, his grey-green eyes warm with laughter. She knew he was doing his best to put her at ease and it worked. She poked her elbow in his ribs.

'Most amusing. I *can* be useful at times, but I shall try not to interfere unless you ask me. So while you are canvassing the lawyers I shall work on my drawings. Chase was right—it was important to return to Egypt and see everything afresh. Now I only hope Mr Bunny writes more books so I can use my new inspiration.'

'Mr *what*?'

'Mr Bunny. That is what I call the author of the *Desert Boy* books.'

'But why Mr *Bunny* of all things?' He sounded so disgusted she laughed.

'Bunny as in hare, or a hare's tail. Every time I try to imagine what he looks like the image slips away like the hare in our garden used to disappear into its warren when I tried to catch it.'

'I'm surprised you didn't stake a tent beside the hole and wait for it to reappear.'

'I did linger until I saw the one I'd been chasing pop out of another hole on the other side of the lawn. You think me stubborn, but I am too impatient to waste time on lost causes.'

'Are you? And I would say you are more tenacious than stubborn. You don't stick to your guns unless it involves what you consider a higher principle.'

'My God, Edge. Was that a compliment?'

The dips at the corners of his mouth deepened.

'It was close. Would you care for a compliment? You have the most beautiful eyes I've ever seen. They are never the same colour each time I look at them.'

'Oh.' Sam swallowed.

He touched the crest of her cheek. His mouth

was still faintly smiling, but his eyes were darker, storm clouds streaked with jade.

'You're blushing. You're usually only that colour when you're furious at me. Surely you've received more fulsome compliments?'

'I...yes.'

'Do you always blush like that?'

She shook her head. She felt as though she was being backed off a cliff by a stalking wolf. *It is only Edge, stop acting like a green girl who's never seen a man before in her life.* Not that Edge was any man. He was by far the most attractive man she'd ever known, even more so now than when he'd been younger.

And she was married to him.

'Am I making you uncomfortable?' It was the hesitant note that reached her.

'Not *uncomfortable* uncomfortable. I'm merely not accustomed to you...you always treated me like a grubby, aggravating girl.'

'Not so much recently.' The fugitive smile was gone and her heat escalated, like the desert approaching midday. He hesitated and added, 'And not the last time I saw you eight years ago either.'

'No...but that was my fault. You were kinder than I deserved.'

'Kind. I don't remember being or feeling kind.'

'No. You were angry with me and you had every right to be.'

His hands fisted and his mouth closed tight.

She wished she'd kept her own mouth shut. She hadn't wanted to chase away his smile and the ever-so-faint hint of flirtatiousness.

A coil of hair fell over her ear and she tucked it back, his gaze following her motion.

'How do those pins manage to hold up all that hair?' His fingers touched her hair briefly and she tried to smile.

'Badly. And sometimes painfully. I prefer it dressed simply, but Janet insisted this occasion deserved rather more pomp.' She touched the arrangement, but he moved her hand away.

'Let me.'

Edge proceeded with meticulous care, as if there was a written treatise on how to undress hair in the least painful but most unsettling manner. Weight by weight her hair slid down, settling on her shoulders and then rushing down her back.

'You smell like spring. Beautiful...' He breathed in the word, his fingers fanning through her hair and letting it fall over her shoulder. The scent of the bath oils with which she'd washed away the desert joined the jasmine, the brandy and the deeper, darker scent of Edge that was as foreign and familiar as the desert. They were all mixing together, stirred by his hands as they moved gently in her hair.

'It doesn't have to be tonight, Sam, but soon I will see all this glory spread on my pillow. On me.'

The words, half-absent, undid her. It *had* to be

tonight, or the tension would likely send her into a nervous decline. She sank her hands into his shirt.

'Not soon. Now, Edge.'

He'd taken his time undressing her hair, but her dress was off before she even realised. It slithered to the ground and the flower-scented air snaked up her stockinged legs and under her thin chemise. Then his fingers brushed lightly over her shoulders, curling over the straps of her chemise and sending spears of lightning that made her breasts ache. She wanted to lean into him and disappear into his warmth. But she also wanted to tear away his hands and run.

This wouldn't stop with Edge's bone-melting, world-shifting kisses. She *knew* where this was heading—into that bed, into that...

She *couldn't*...

She'd hated it with Ricki. Perhaps not at first, she'd been too anxious for everything to work that she'd ignored the discomfort. But soon she'd come to hate it—the heavy, thumping, pushing and prodding and Ricki's wine-scented breath and his tongue making her gag... What if Ricki was right? That despite the fire that rampaged through her at Edge's touch there was something utterly wrong with her? That this, too, would end with her lying resentful and tense under Edge as she had under Ricki felt obscene, like defiling a temple. Edge did not deserve that from her.

'I'm awful at this. *Awful.*'

His hands stilled. She closed her eyes. Hard.

'Awful,' she repeated for good measure and wished the world would suddenly and unequivocally end.

His hands moved lower, closing very gently on her arms, but she didn't open her eyes.

'Sam… I don't understand.'

'I don't wish to speak of it. I can't. I'm so sorry, Edge. Perhaps if we go back there now and tell them this was a mistake you could yet demand an annulment. I never should have done this to you. You deserve better and I'm the most horrid person in the world to have foisted myself on you…'

She continued talking as he led her into the bedroom, but at the sight of that monstrous bed she took two steps backwards.

'Don't worry, Sam, we aren't going to do anything, I promise. Only lie down and rest.'

He brought her to the bed, peeled back the cover and then pressed her down very gently, moving her to one side so he could move her hair out from under her, like a child.

'There. Now close your eyes.'

'I can't possibly sleep.'

'I know. But close your eyes for a moment.'

She stiffened as he lay down behind her, but he merely placed a hand gently on her arm, his fingers resting in the crook of her elbow, and she felt her heartbeat against them, as fast and sharp as rockfall.

'Do you remember the time we were invited to the marriage celebration of Khalidi's younger daughter in Qetara? What was her name?'

She wished he hadn't brought up memories of that year. That had been the week before the fateful day she'd fallen off the statue and realised she'd cared far too much for Edge. Why on earth must he bring that up now?

'Her name was Suleima. That was the first time I tasted raki. It was horrid.'

His laugh was low and warm against her nape and she shivered a little.

'Yes. But it did wonders for your dancing skills. I remember we were searching for you to return home and I found you in the garden, dancing with Fatima and Suleima.'

'They couldn't be where the men were and we wanted to dance so we came to the garden where we could hear the music better. I remember you were shocked.'

'I…yes, I dare say I was. I had a very set view of the world then. When we arrived at Khalidi's you were dressed as properly as any young English girl, but the girl dancing barefoot in the garden with her hair down her back…' His fingers smoothed out a length of her hair.

'You called me a noisome child.'

'I shouldn't have called you that. I *was* shocked.

Not by you, Sam. A little exasperated we had to go searching again, yes, but not shocked. It was hardly the first time you'd behaved true to Sam form. What…upset me was that I wanted to sink my hands into your hair and feel it run through them. That was not the reaction I expected from myself so I became angry at you.'

'Again.'

'Again. You were right about me. I tried to force the world into a certain mould. It felt safer that way. You didn't fit that mould and at that moment neither did my…reactions. I had very little patience for human fallibility.'

'That's not true. You were endlessly patient with people even if you hated being so. Just not with your own fallibility, perhaps.'

'And you are being far too forgiving. You must have wished me at the devil at least once a day when I was at Bab el-Nur.'

'At least. Almost as often as you wished me there.'

'Definitely more than once a day.' He laughed as he leaned over to blow out the lamp, the only light now a faint glow from outside, like a distant torch.

Edge's hand was brushing softly over the curve of her shoulder and she no longer had to force her eyes shut. It felt good, like the warm desert wind or the music weaving through the wooden shutters. She hummed the memory of that music, deep and haunting.

'Yes, that was it…as if the night sky was singing,' he murmured and eased her over on her stomach, his hand stroking gently down her back. 'Don't stop.'

It felt so good, just the sweep of his hand, like waves flowing and receding. She wanted to feel it directly on her skin. She wanted to feel his warmth closer to her. She wanted…

He took his hand away and she squirmed.

'Don't stop.'

'I'm not. It will be more comfortable like this.' He raised her and with complete casualness he slipped off her chemise and lay her down again, pulling the cotton sheet over them. She should have felt embarrassed or scared, but the fear didn't come. She was even a little disappointed when he didn't pull her to him, but only stretched beside her and continued stroking her back in long, languid motions.

He was right. It was so much better like this, though *'comfortable'* was not the right word. It was soothing, blissful, warm and warming. She'd never thought of her back as anything more than…her back. Now, like an ignored feline suddenly getting all the stroking attention after years of living in the wild, she was luxuriating under his hands, arcing and stretching and seeking more. And all the other parts of her were becoming envious.

She turned to try to capture the trail of his sweeping fingers, her behind tingling each time his hand swept within reach and then away. Her shoulders curved, her arm rising in hope his fingers would slide under and over towards where her breasts felt suddenly full, the spears of lightning no longer painful but urgent. She was a constellation of new stars revolving around a growing sun of heat and darkness at her core—a new centre of tension, very different from what held her back, but just as frightening. It was a pulsing beating of drums, just like the music still humming through her.

'Are you sleepy?' His lips feathered over her shoulder-blade and a flame licked up the right half of her body.

Sleepy? *Sleepy?*

'No. Don't stop.'

'I won't.' His hand was freer now, not stopping at the limits of her back, venturing to slide into the dip of her waist, over her hip, just brushing the line between her and the bed and sending darts of heat and need along her abdomen. It was utterly foreign and yet utterly right.

Then it retreating to the slopes of her back again before venturing lower again, curving over her backside and stopping. His hand was large and warm and she felt it shake a little and could feel his breathing, too, had changed. He wasn't as calm as he wished her to believe and she smiled against her pillow. She no longer wanted him calm. She shifted, arching her backside a little into his palm, and heard him breath in and out. Then his hand continued.

It was a sweet, building agony and she didn't want it to end. She was lit up inside and out, soothed and excited and desperate to move and wanting to stay just as she was, revered like this for ever and ever. She wasn't humming any longer, or she was, but a different hum—a mixture of murmurs and moans that she didn't try to stem because she felt their impact on him. His breathing was deeper, audible, his hand losing its finesse, tightening on her hip. His leg came to be pressed against hers as well, as exciting as the pressure of his hands. Then he buried his face against her nape and took a deep breath before moving away completely.

'Goodnight, Sam.' His voice was raw and her eyes flew open.

'Goodnight?'

'That's the limit of my self-control. I think we should stop now and… Sam…' her name sank into a groan as she turned over, her leg sliding against his '…there is no need to rush…'

'Hush…' She kissed his throat, from the silk beneath his ear to the roughness of stubble along his jaw. He tasted so good, so very good. And his mouth… Her body was still humming, hungry for the contact he'd withdrawn. She moved closer, sighing against his lips as her breasts pressed against his arm and chest.

'It's like lying on sun-warmed granite…' Without thinking she rubbed herself against him a little, luxuriating in the slide of skin on skin. She'd never realised how good that could feel— their bodies sparking against each other like living flints. A sharper, hotter spark drew her even closer, her leg rising over his.

'That doesn't sound very comfortable.' His voice was choked and she felt his erection pulse against her thigh and she gave it a testing brush with her leg and was rewarded by another groan, his arms coming around her, his hand closing on her behind as he raised her more fully on top of him.

'It isn't comfortable, it is… I don't want to sleep. I want everything, Edge.'

The next moment she was under him, being kissed into oblivion, his hands doing to her front what they'd wreaked on her back, trailing destruction and moving lower.

She'd watched his hands countless times when he worked alongside Poppy and Huxley at the tomb, or later in the room at Bab el-Nur where they recorded their findings. But she'd never realised quite how magical they were, that sure, gentle touch was so much part of his nature. On her skin it felt as though he was discovering her, too, unearthing her from a wasteland, every brush of his skin on hers, ever kiss and taste unveiling a hidden essence that marked who and what she really was. She felt like she was discovering her body with him.

But even as her body came into focus, alive and vivid, her mind was fading. He spoke to her, soft endearments and encouragements as she whimpered or as her own hands clasped around him as if he was holding her above an abyss and any moment now he would let go and she would either fall away into bliss or oblivion.

Though she'd stopped thinking, reality snapped back when his fingers brushed over the hair at the apex of her thighs and skimmed over the sensitive skin of her womanhood. The starburst of sensations only shocked her further, her legs clamping shut.

'What are you doing?' she hissed and he raised his head. His cheekbones were marked with colour, his lids heavy. He looked half-lost to passion and that only made her blood heat further, but not enough to chase away her fear.

'Sam…' He appeared at a loss for a moment, then he pressed his lips to the corner of her mouth. 'If you aren't ready, there is no hurry.'

Ready. She knew what ready meant. All this heaven was merely prelude to the fumbling, the pushing, and the shoving. At least that meant it would soon be over. She wished he could have just…kept doing whatever he had done before this part had to happen. She sighed.

'I am ready.'

He raised himself a little further, ran his tongue over his lower lip and her gaze fixed on that surface. She wanted to taste it…

'I am not planning to do anything else this evening but pleasure you. And if you prefer to rest now, I understand. This is hardly a…conventional situation. I don't wish to hurry you.'

She felt ashamed, a failure before she'd even begun. He might be more mature than Ricki, less clumsy, but soon the recriminations would begin and this time she would truly shrivel because this time she *wanted* to feel. And to give.

'I don't want to sleep. I want to make you happy.'

'Don't look so agonised, Sam. This requires trust and we are neither of us very adept at that. Here, close your eyes again. The fate of the world does not hinge on anything that happens or doesn't happen tonight.'

She placed her hand on his where it lay on the bed beside her.

'I *want* to trust you.'

'Then close your eyes and trust me enough to know I will stop the moment you tell me to. I've never lied…to you, Sam.'

Her eyes flickered at the strange hesitation in

his voice, but whatever was beneath it, she knew
it was true. She trusted Edge. As much as she
trusted Lucas and Chase. How strange. Then she
let her eyelids sink and settle, her hand just resting against his hip as he settled beside her again.

'Good,' he murmured. 'Now breathe.'

She breathed.

'In *and* out.'

She breathed in and out. His lips were brushing her hair, his hand resting lightly on her lower
abdomen, brushing idly at the valley next to her
hip bone, sending sprinkles of sensation down her
leg and up to her breasts. Her body happily took
back the clamouring rhythm of need and when
his hand moved back over her thigh she trusted
him. When he parted her legs again with his leg
she rubbed against him, recapturing that sensation of strength and heat.

When his fingers slipped between the curls and
glided along the silky centre she still wasn't prepared for the shiver of pleasure that swept through
her as they found the sensitised nub waiting for
him, but she pushed back at the fear that this, too,
was a trap.

This was Edge and, whatever else, she trusted
him.

She concentrated on the sensation of his lips
moving very lightly against her cheek and neck,
trying not to think about what he was doing down
there, but her body was splitting from her mind,

focusing on his fingers and the tension they were building. Then he lowered his head, his lips brushing the swell of her breast. Her shoulders hunched in a mix of yearning and resistance and a shivering moan rolled through her. He echoed it and that sound, between delight and abandonment, melted another layer of fear. She didn't care any more what happened next. All she cared about was being closer, moving against his marvellous, beautiful hands.

Her own hands were moving, too, mapping his body as he'd mapped hers, shaping him into her memory, swimming between amazement at what his fingers and mouth were doing to her and how brilliant a creation his body was. She couldn't even remember what it felt like to touch Ricki, but she would remember each angle and dip of Edge's body until she died. Which felt like it would happen very soon because what he was doing to her was unbearable...unbearably unbearable, but beautiful.

He was right—it was beautiful. *She* was beautiful. And coming apart. This could not be safe. At the peak of the wave she tried to fight her way back to safety, her legs trying to close, her nails sinking into his back. But it was too late, she heard his voice against her ear, his breath warm like the desert wind.

'I know, Sam. Let go, sweetheart, let it happen. Trust me.'

So she let it happen, let go of the cliff face, but she didn't fall—she floated, a great wave was raising her and all she had to do was... She cried out and lost her hold and fell apart into sweet, honeyed pleasure.

'Edge...oh, no...'

She felt his laugh against her throat as she floated down from bliss, but also the muscles of his back quiver under her hands. She didn't want him to be tense when she felt so very, very blissful so she stroked his back to the rhythm of her body's slowing pulse, soaking up his tension— the bunching of muscles as he held himself above her, the sharp angles of his shoulder blades that shifted as she traced them, the ridging of his spine and then the rise of his buttocks.

She wanted to see him, but she hadn't the energy to open her eyes.

She wanted to feel him inside her, at the centre of this slowly pulsing heat with its memory of pleasure.

That thought woke her a little. She'd never liked it when Ricki pushed inside her, but now she wanted all the tension knotting Edge's back and legs connected to her, she wanted to feel his release against her just as he'd felt hers.

Why wasn't he *doing* anything?

She woke further, opened her eyes and met his. They weren't blank now. The ocean was in full storm and populated by sea dragons. The grooves beside his mouth were dark slashes beneath the carved granite of his cheekbones.

'Why did you stop?' Her voice was fuzzy and his head dipped a little.

'I don't want…to hurry you.' His voice wasn't fuzzy, it was choked. 'You're tired. It has been a long…week. There is no reason to hurry.'

Hurry?

Her mind was thoroughly awake now. Didn't he want to…no, his arousal was hard and pulsing against her thigh—there was no doubt he wanted to consummate the union. As for being considerate, well, that was carrying chivalry several leagues too far. Surely he could not mistake she had enjoyed…more than enjoyed herself. She had never comprehended that such pleasure was within her reach merely by the wave of a hand. What a horrid waste of time. Now the very last thing she wanted was to deny him what he'd given her.

'I'm not tired. Don't you wish…?' She searched for the words and suddenly he groaned, resting his forehead against hers. It was as damp and hot as his body.

'Yes, I wish. Blast it, Sam.'

'Then stop cursing me and do something about it, you stubborn lug.'

His laugh was choked as he shifted, sinking between her legs, sliding one hand under her thigh to raise it. His hard heat pressed into her and she angled her hips to take him in as she had learned to do to make Ricki's entry less painful. But unlike Ricki's swift grunting thrusts, Edge entered her with excruciating slowness, as if savouring every inch of the voyage. She had never experienced this before—the slow coming together, the way her body gathered him in, the sensation of his thighs against hers, her body adjusting, shifting to take him in deeper and deeper. Then he stopped and for a moment they stayed just like that. And then with a sigh she raised her behind and rocked against him lightly. Just testing.

His head was leaning against hers, his breath on her ear, and he caught her lobe between his teeth, his words a hiss against the sensitive hollows of her ear.

'Don't, one move and I'm finished. I don't want to finish. Ever.'

'One move? Like this?'

'Sam…'

He gave up restraints as if the cords holding him were torn. She held on as he moved inside and against her, his mouth against her, the words muffled, just her name rising as he climaxed as well. When he sank down on top of her she wrapped her arms around his back and let herself drift.

My husband.

It wasn't terrifying any longer. Perhaps tomorrow it would be again, she thought half-absently as the world faded away, but right now it made perfect sense.

Chapter Six

*The hawk swung low and settled on Leila's
shoulder. 'That Gabriel being is still behind
us. Stubborn.'*

*'He thinks he is protecting me,' Leila
scoffed. 'Why are humans so very foolish?'*
—*The Sprite Queen,
Desert Boy Book One*

Sam inspected her cabin aboard HMS *Lark*. The
linen closet at Sinclair House would fit three of
these. Once she stepped inside there would be
room perhaps for a cat and two mice. The cot itself looked like a window ledge—long and just
about wide enough for a few flowering pots, but
for sleep? Sam could understand why Edge had
chosen a hammock below decks rather than accept
the Post Captain's offer of the only other cabin
on the ship.

'Well, at least if I fall I won't roll far,' Sam said
and Edge nudged her inside, placing her sketching

bag on a narrow shelf that served as a table. Even with half his body still in the passage the cabin shrank from tiny to stifling. He sighed, brushing back hair disordered by ducking under so many low lintels and missing a few.

'I knew this was a bad idea. You should return with Poppy and Janet and wait until they sail on a more reasonable vessel built for actual passengers. There is still time; they won't return to Cairo until tomorrow.'

That stung. As had their discussion that morning when they reached Alexandria and Edge realised that *HMS Lark* was a sixth-rate frigate—as fast as any ship sailing the Mediterranean, but hardly built for comfort. The Post Captain, a mere couple of years older than Sam, had been shocked to learn he was expected to transport 'A woman'. His shock had fizzled a little beneath Edge's glacial stare, but the realities of the arrangements on the frigate had made his point just as well. Edge had tried to convince her to wait with Poppy and Janet until they sailed on the next available merchant ship, but Sam had done her calculations. Waiting for a slower ship meant they would arrive weeks after Edge. He might be hurt trying to find Rafe or he might even follow his brother's trail to the Antipodes and the next time she would see him would be in another eight years. The fact that Edge could make this suggestion as if it was nothing more than her taking the carriage while he rode a hack on the way back from Richmond Park only made her blood boil.

So they'd had their first argument as a married couple.

Well, she'd argued while Edge stood like one of the Colossi of Memnon, staring past her and perhaps hoping she'd wear herself out like a tantrum-throwing toddler. She hadn't and she wouldn't but in the end she'd adopted the same approach—stony coldness and staying put. At least he hadn't physically removed her from the ship when Poppy and Janet returned to the carriage, but he had told them to wait on the quay until he 'resolved the matter'.

Perhaps he'd expected her to change her mind when she saw the living arrangements.

Well, he'd sorely underestimated her.

She plopped herself resolutely on the cot. Not a smart move since it was hard and the rim of wood holding in the thin mattress was a great deal more painful than it looked. She would remember that if she had fantasies about rolling over to relieve a crick in her back in the middle of the night. She sucked in a breath and let it out.

'No.'

'Sam…'

'No! I know you, Edge. When you reach London you will insist on searching for Rafe on your own even when I tell you that my uncle can probably find him for you like that…' She snapped her fingers. 'And you will probably make a hash of things.'

'Thank you for that vote of confidence, Sam, but I told you I have no intention of involving the law in this search.'

'My uncle is not the law. He is a law unto himself.'

'We are not having this conversation. Sam…'

'Go find your hammock. I'm staying.'

He didn't slam the door, but neither did he close it, which was almost as much of a protest.

Two weeks was a long time to sustain a silent sulk, but then Edge was a master of the art.

It didn't show on the surface. He remained impeccably polite, just like an automaton of a boy she'd seen in Venice that could bow, tip its hat and extend its hand to an invisible handshake. In an automaton these achievements were awe-inspiring; in a man this mechanical performance of politeness and propriety was intimidating to the lesser men aboard the *Lark* and infuriating to Sam, who knew full well he was giving her one long cold shoulder.

It added to the aches in her own shoulders from sleeping on the miniscule cot and wasn't doing wonders for her temper. It was particularly awful in comparison to their amazing night in Cairo. The memory of bliss and pleasure faded with each passing day, cold look and aching muscle.

She couldn't even relieve her tension by moving about the ship. There wasn't much of a ship to move about in and most of it was populated by hammocks, crates and cannons below decks and sailors above decks who swung between admiring awe and superstitious disgust at her presence. After a young ensign almost toppled overboard when she ventured above deck Captain Meacham begged her to remain in her cabin for her own safety, as he put it, but his gaze conveyed something else entirely. He looked so young and harassed she agreed.

Edge, wisely, said nothing, meeting her glare as she returned to her cabin with a look as blank and empty as a grazing cow. But she knew that behind that Pharaonic façade was one big 'I told you so'.

She'd kicked her cot when she was back in her room, which didn't help at all except to knock her narrow pillow to the floor, but at least that gave her the good idea of placing the mattress there as well which made her night marginally more comfortable since she didn't have to worry about falling, just rolling when the ship pitched.

The only relief was during mealtimes when she and Edge joined the officers. She dug deep to resurrect the social skills she'd discovered that fateful year of her debut in Venice and realised she had not completely lost her ability to charm and by the time they passed Gibraltar the young officers were sharing their hopes for their naval careers with her.

But the more they thawed, the more Edge ossified. He was unfailingly polite, but he concentrated all his conversation on the ship's surgeon who shared his interest in Greco-Roman culture. Every time she tried to join their conversation he became so deferential she barely restrained the urge to kick him under the table.

She wondered what these men thought of their marriage. She wondered most of all what Edge thought of their marriage. With a kind of superstitious fear she clung to the hope that once they reached London they would somehow mend matters between them. All she had to do was survive that long without Edge's ominous calm breaking and having him toss her overboard.

It broke three days before they reached England, set off by the most inconsequential thing. That particular evening the waves made dinner a challenging exercise and Sam excused herself early, followed by Edge, maintaining the façade of an attentive spouse. Just as she reached her door the ship pitched and Sam almost went with it, but Edge caught her, bracing himself against the wall. For a moment as the ship righted itself they stood there in a parody of an embrace. Sam closed her eyes, breathing him in, her skin warming and softening even as her mind warned her any moment now he would put her away.

He did precisely that. Very carefully untangling himself and reaching past her to open the door. In a fit of desperation Sam grabbed his coat and pulled him inside. Only his quick reaction saved him from smashing his head against the lintel and before he could recover she shut the door behind him and pressed her back to it.

The tiny space shrank by several sizes, emptying of air. She rushed into speech before he put her aside again and marched out.

'I'm sorry, Edge. I know you're furious and I'm a horrid person, but please…can't we stop this stalemate? It is exhausting. I feel like I am under siege.'

'*You* feel like you are under siege!' Edge wiped a hand over his mouth and jaw as if physically strangling the words. His eyes were dark with anger and she pressed back against the door. Perhaps forcing this particular panther into a cage with her was not the most intelligent move at the moment.

She raised her hands. She would have waved a white handkerchief, but he did not look in the mood for whimsical gestures.

'I know you are regretting marrying me—'

'What I am regretting,' he interrupted, 'is not throwing you over my shoulder and taking you back to Poppy and Janet so you could travel to

England in a more…proper manner. I should have listened to Captain Meacham instead of you.'

'He doesn't appear to mind my presence on board any longer…'

'Of course he doesn't mind your presence! The young fool is infatuated with you. I'm only grateful you've preserved enough sense to stay below decks or we'd find ourselves run aground on the first shoal if he mooned after you on deck the way you encourage him to do across the dinner table.'

'I do not encourage him! And he does not moon.'

'Fine. Drool.'

'Captain Meacham's manners are impeccable. As opposed to yours, Lord Friday-Faced-Fussock.'

'If you are going to resort to childish name calling, try for accuracy rather than alliteration. Fussock means a lazy woman.'

'It does? That wasn't at all the image I had in my mind.'

'I won't ask what was. My point stands.'

'What is your point?'

'That you're a menace! If I have to sit through one more…' He swiped his face again.

'I'll stay in my cabin,' she offered, a little shocked at the degree of his anger and with his belief she really meant to encourage poor Captain Meacham. 'I am tired of trying to be charming anyway. I was never good at it and it is almost as exhausting as weathering your disapproval. You may tell them I always become ill once we pass Gibraltar.'

As if to make her point, the ship tipped and sank beneath them again. She reached out to steady herself and her palms met his chest. The ship rolled back, but she stayed there. The urge to move closer and sink into his warmth was so powerful she stepped back and immediately regretted it. She was behaving ridiculously. She was a widow, not a newly deflowered virgin.

If anything he'd re-flowered her that night in Cairo. That was what it had felt like with the scent of the gardens weaving into the warm air around them as he'd coaxed her into heaven. He'd made her body bloom. She hesitated and then placed her palm once more against his chest. His pulse wasn't as fast as hers, but it still felt swift and harsh.

'I apologise for forcing myself on board, but it is done, Edge. Can we not start over?'

She searched his face for some sign of softening. His eyes fell from hers and suddenly he looked more sulky than furious and her heart eased a little. Before she could press her advantage his gaze flickered to the cot, away, and then back.

'Where is your mattress?'

'My mattress? Over there—I roll it up after I use it, it takes up too much space if I leave it on the floor.'

'On the…you are sleeping on the floor?'

'That way if I fall off there isn't far to go.'

'Why didn't you tell me you were having trouble sleeping?' he demanded and she smiled at his outrage. This was the Edge she could cope with.

'Because I hate when people say I told you so. I have heard that enough times from you to last me several lifetimes. Besides, it is not so very uncomfortable.'

'Yes, but what if there are…?'

'What?'

'Nothing. If you cannot sleep on the cot, I will bring a hammock. It attaches to these.' He indicated the steel hooks embedded in the walls, but her mind fixated on his avoidance, her eyes skittering around the room. They were on a ship, for God's sake. Why had it never occurred to she might be sharing the floor with the ubiquitous naval rat? She brushed at her dress, her hair, but the image rose as sharply as if she'd actually awoken to it—the scuffling, snuffling, scratching… the sudden pressure as the small forms skittered over her legs… Her arms crossed over her chest, her hands at her throat in an instinctive defence.

'Sam, you are perfectly fine, this room is well sealed, I'm sorry I said anything.'

He placed his hands on hers, his fingers moving soothingly on them, against the soft skin beneath her jaw, stroking the tense sinew along the side of her neck.

'I am *not* afraid of rats,' she denied, but her

voice wasn't as firm as she wanted. 'It is only…
I imagined…'

'Yes, your imagination was always too fertile
for your own good. And a sensible person *should*
be afraid of rats—they carry disea—' He stopped
again at her glare and his face shifted into an all-
out grin. Out of nowhere she remembered something Khalidi's daughter Fatima had said about
Edge more than a dozen years ago.

*'He has the smile of a god. He does not bestow
it often, but when he does it is as if the sun and the
moon and all the stars all join hands to bless you.'*

At the time Sam remembered being thoroughly
disgusted with Fatima's infatuated adoration of
Edge. She'd had no patience for such nonsense at
fourteen and even less when Fatima's foolishness
landed Edge in gaol. To be fair it was as much
Sam's fault, since Edge had only been protecting
her when she tried to stop Khalidi's deputy from
taking Fatima out of Bab el-Nur. Another of her
well-meaning crusades gone wrong, as Edge had
pointed out. He'd been even less impressed with
her failed attempt to rescue him from gaol and
had studiously ignored her for weeks afterwards.

His beautiful smile dimmed as she remained
silent.

'Sam, there really is nothing to worry about.
Don't look like that.'

'I'm not.'

His hands traced the juncture between her neck

and shoulder and it wasn't soothing any longer. Her body heated, the hair at her nape rising as nerves tingled down her spine. His eyes rested on her lips and his jaw flexed, deepening the lines beside his mouth. She was desperate to lick her lips, her tongue was pressing against her teeth, begging. She couldn't stop herself from sucking her lower lip in a little, testing it. Yes, she was ready, so ready for…

'A hammock. I will fetch you a hammock,' Edge said and left the cabin.

She was still staring at the door when he returned with a cloth hammock.

'You expect me to sleep on that?' she demanded. He smiled over his shoulder and heat fuzzed through her, her body tensing even as her mind relaxed at this sign that they were at least halfway to a truce. When he was done she came to inspect his work.

'Edge, I shall fall out!'

'You won't. It is harder to fall than it looks. Try it.'

She eyed the dun-coloured fabric and he touched the tip of her nose.

'You look like I've soaked it in bilge water. Come now, don't be a coward.'

It was a blatant provocation, but it hit its mark. She placed her hands on the hammock.

'Glaring at it won't help, Sam. You need to turn around and…well, sit on it.'

She indulged in another futile glare, but did as she was told. For a moment when it took her weight she flailed back, her feet shooting upwards. She squeaked and grabbed at the cloth, sure the next thing she would see would be the ceiling as she hit the floor, but Edge steadied it.

'Very gracefully done,' he said, his face suspiciously blank. 'Now swing your feet up, but this time try to get them inside.'

She was tempted to tell him to rip the blasted thing down, but she also wanted to conquer this absurd contraption. After all every fool on board knew how to sleep in one; she refused to admit defeat.

She swung one leg up and then the other, absurdly aware of her skirts riding up. This time instead of rocking side to side, it wobbled back and forth like a horse trying to buck.

'You can't sit upright in it once your legs are up. Lie back,' Edge said. He sounded underwater.

'If you laugh at me, Edge…'

'Not much you can do to me from there, Princess. Just lie back.'

She lay back, her dress bunched under her bottom and her arms pinned to her sides by the fabric. She wriggled them free and clasped the sides.

'I feel like a mummy,' she grumbled.

'You look marginally better than most mummies. Less comfortable, though.'

'This is punishment for forcing myself on to the *Lark*, correct?'

He gave up trying not to smile.

'If you could only try to relax for a moment, Sam, you will see it is not so bad. Close your eyes.'

'I'd rather eat nails dipped in boot blacking.'

He took her shawl from a peg on the wall and tossed it over her face.

'Now be quiet and stop fidgeting.'

She swiped the shawl from her face and folded it between her arms, but closed her eyes. Edge was so stubborn he probably wouldn't allow her out of this blasted cocoon until she did as she was bid. Then she would return the mattress to the cot and resign herself to sleeping motionless.

His finger traced a line down the middle of her forehead.

'You always had that line—a natural-born glowerer.'

'That is not a word. And you are a fine one to talk about glowering.'

'Keep your eyes closed, I said.' He was nudging the hammock very gently, and she thought of the apple tree in Burford where they'd lived just before her father died. Lucas and Chase built a swing and she would curl her body into a ball and watch the sky. She had very few memories from that time, but she remembered the gentle creak and swish of the rope and the clouds tangling in the branches over her head as the world's breath carried her back and forth, back and forth.

She had the oddest sensation that the hammock was suspended over nothingness. She was just a darkness floating in another shade of darkness. The pressure on her eyes changed and she opened them and realised he'd extinguished the lamp, its acrid scent fading around her as she swung gently. She could not see him, but she felt his warmth, like a chimney after the fire fades. She wanted to reach out and anchor herself to him, but she was too pleasantly sleepy. She yawned, her head falling to rest against the fabric.

'I'm floating... Did you put something in my wine?' she murmured, her voice swallowed by the darkness.

'I will if you don't keep quiet; you are the least restful female I know, Princess.'

She smiled. Princess. He'd called her Princess. Twice. It wasn't an endearment, but there was affection there, reluctant thought it was and for the first time she accepted that, however difficult matters were between them, Edge liked her. She knew she wasn't a princess and he was certainly no prince. But he did like her when he wasn't as annoyed as the devil with her. It was a beginning. And he had made this lovely swing for her.

'This is quite nice. A pity you can't join me.'

The rhythm stuttered a bit, but then fell back into a soothing ebb and flow. She was dozing when he stopped and she mumbled an objection, but it was lost to the brush of his mouth on hers. He'd probably only meant to give her a quick salute, but one shouldn't give a sip of wine to a sot and expect them to tamely hand back the bottle. She threaded her hands into his hair, parted her lips beneath his and kissed him.

Never kiss a siren in the dark—that should be inscribed on his tombstone.

Every time he kissed her in the dark he stepped further down the plank—under the desert sky, in the tent, in this floating torture chamber...

Whatever defences he'd constructed to cope with this hellish voyage went overboard like a drunken sailor the moment her fingers slipped against his nape, her lips parting against his with a small sigh of pleasure, that plump lower lip she'd been sucking on warm and damp between his.

He hadn't meant to kiss her. He'd meant to show her how to use the blasted hammock and then go find his for another tortured, sleepless night. For two weeks he'd lain in his hammock surrounded by snoring sailors and tried not to think of Sam curled up in that little cubby-like cot, her hair in a dark plait over her shoulder and her cotton nightshift covering her like a dusting of fine snow over hills and valleys waiting to be melted. Just at that point when sleep overcame discomfort and frustration he'd finally allow himself to imagine precisely that—the fabric fading like a film of dew on the desert planes, shimmering away and leaving just... Sam.

That night in Cairo had been a mistake. He would have been wiser to wait until they reached England to consummate their marriage. Because one night of volcanic lovemaking after a year of abstinence, only to be followed by weeks of a hammock while his wife flirted with two rosy-cheeked naval innocents while ignoring him...

It didn't help that she looked as lovely every day as if she'd slept ten hours in a cloud. It didn't help that that body-searing night kept playing through his mind like a popular tune that refused to be chased away. Playing through his body and with his body until he ached.

He'd forgotten about aching. It had nothing to do with abstinence, apparently. Trying to sleep in a hammock with a persistent erection and a bubbling temper was not a combination he was accustomed to and he didn't wish to become accustomed to it.

But there was nothing he could do to stop fantasising about their marriage night. About the feather-soft skin of her inner thighs under his fingers or how she rubbed herself against him... those soft, half-embarrassed moans as she began giving away to pleasure. And her scent…orange blossom and…and butter biscuits.

Hell and damnation. He was frustrated and tired, and still a little in shock that they were married.

And now she'd spiked every one of his guns with her admission she'd been sleeping on the floor this whole time and said nothing… God, he wanted to climb into the hammock with her and do something about this ache.

'Sam…' He tried to pull back, but her hands tightened in his hair, sending fire down his back.

'Your hair is so silky and warm. I love touching it,' she murmured against his mouth. It should have meant nothing, but a groan exploded in his head like cymbals. He managed to keep hold of the hammock and not fall on top of her, but his arms shook with the effort as her teeth grazed his lip before licking it.

'And you taste of Aziza's honey cake,' she whispered and another cymbal crash rang through his body. That didn't even make sense, he wanted to say and gave up. He dug his arm under her and hauled her out of the hammock and into his arms. Her breath left her in a surprised whoosh and then she laughed, pushing back at the deflated hammock that was swinging wildly and batting them in the dark.

'All your good work undone. I'll never manage to get in again.'

He moved forward until he bumped into the table and set her down there, securing his hands in her hair and finally, finally kissed her the way he had in all those aggravating dreams that had plagued him the past two weeks.

In the dark her muffled whimpers and moans were a thousand times more intoxicating and he couldn't stop touching, tasting, his fingertips singing with awareness of the shifting textures of her skin, this silk, that satin, the roughness of her elbow—he lingered over that, remembering her bent over her drawings, her sleeves hitched up, that line between her brows as sharp as a spear. And then the mother-of-pearl sweep of the inside of her elbow…he turned it over and breathed it in, open-mouthed, brushing it with his lips to the rhythm of her pulse and heard the soft *thunk* as her head fell back against the wooden wall, the rasp of her breath, the way her legs clamped about his hips. He hadn't even realised he'd come to stand between her legs.

His hands slipped gently over her body, just softly on the outer swell of her breasts, he would make his way there later, he promised her silently as his hands slipped over her thighs. They twitched under his touch and she grabbed his shirt, pulling him closer.

'I'll help you back in when we're done,' he murmured against her throat as he undid her gown, shifting her so that it slid to the ground, grateful having no maid meant she'd dispensed with stays.

'When we're done,' she confirmed, tugging his shirt from his trousers. 'I just don't quite know how we *will* be done. I can barely fit in that cot on my own...'

'How limber are you, little mountain goat?' He nuzzled Sam's scent just below and behind her ear—silky soft and warm and it flowed through him like melting honey. Yes, orange blossom and biscuits. God, he was hungry for her.

'Limber...?' He felt the word through the skin of her throat. Her hands were pushing into his hair, sifting it like she would the soft sand of the delta as he tasted her, licking her earlobe and catching it with his teeth as a silvery shudder quivered through her. He smiled and kissed the soft skin there, aware that it was absurd to be pleased he was already beginning to find her weak spots, like the one right there, just beside her hip bone where the skin stretched towards her navel. He let his fingers linger and tease that indentation through the soft lawn chemise, loving the answering shivers that tightened her long legs around him.

'Yes, limber. That bed presents a problem. We shall have to be creative.'

'Oh. Tell me what to do and I shall try.'

He brushed his mouth over hers, a little surprised to feel his own mouth curved in a smile.

She sounded both dreamy and determined. Typical Sam.

'All you must do for the moment is close your eyes and relax, Night Star. I shall do the rest.'

Chapter Seven

The camel's hoof pressed Gabriel deeper into the sand, its grizzled chin and twisted teeth less than an inch from Gabriel's face.

'If you had asked for help, boy, we wouldn't be here. And they call my kind stubborn!'

—*Captives of the Hidden City,*
Desert Boy Book Four

Sam knew she had to move, but she didn't want to. Edge yawned, his body stretching against hers, his arms pulling her more securely on to his lap as he leaned back against the wall of the narrow cot. It felt so good to be held. To surface from a fuzzy cloud of pleasure into comfort.

To think that just a few hours ago she'd been miserably convinced Edge was regretting his completely uncharacteristic impulsiveness in marrying her. He certainly hadn't been complaining a few moments ago. He'd been...

She shivered in appreciation and growing anticipation and gave herself a silent reprimand. The man was exhausted, the setting was as uncomfortable as could be imagined, besides—twice in one night? It was probably not done. She rather suspected most of what she'd just done with Edge was not *done*. She very much doubted Dora had ever agreed to be seduced on a narrow wooden table and certainly would never have whimpered so loudly he'd had to muffle her cries with his mouth.

He yawned again, burrowing his face into her hair, his arms slackening for a moment before gripping again as if he was fighting sleep.

'Go to sleep, Edge. You looked utterly exhausted at dinner. You are not a good advertisement for the restful qualities of hammocks, you know.'

'It wasn't the hammock that kept me awake, Sam,' he mumbled against her hair and then untangled himself from her, groping around for his clothes. He made it out the door without bumping into anything or strangling himself in the hammock. The man must have eyes like a cat.

When he was gone she snuggled deep under the blanket, tucking it under her bare feet and wishing she was tucked around his warm body. She stared at the vague shifting in the dark that marked the still-swinging hammock.

Tomorrow she would brave that contraption again.

* * *

Where was he?

It wasn't that she'd expected Edge to be beating down her door at dawn, but it was already midday and she was sorely tempted to hunt him down and tell him it was foolish to return to sulking after last night.

Well, she refused to beg. Instead she began a new drawing and finally became so engrossed she didn't hear the tapping. It was the dull thud against the door that caught her attention and she hurried to open it.

'Edge!'

He winced at her cry, but didn't move. He was leaning on the doorjamb with both hands and he looked horrible.

She took his hand and pulled him inside. He flinched, turning away from the lamp.

'The light...' Edge's voice was always deep, but now it was subterranean, a clenched rumble. He moved without any of his usual grace, as if his body was solidifying into stone as he walked. She forced him on to the cot, shuttered the oil lamp so it left only a glowing rim of gold.

'Are you about to be sick?'

'No. Head.'

Head. A flash of memory returned, of her mother retreating into the darkness of her room. The doctor, a venerable man from Padua, proclaimed hemicrania in the name of science and grief in the name of the soul. He'd prescribed a list of tonics, but admitted that silence, darkness and rest were the only cures he'd found to be universally effective. Sometimes her mother would be violently ill and only then settle into the agonised pain of darkness, but the worst usually passed in a day or so. As in many things Sam and her brothers learned to provide whatever alleviated the symptoms of their mother's grief, knowing they could never chase it away completely.

Sam inspected the rigid statue seated on her cot as if in the docks awaiting judgement and sighed.

He winced.

She was about to debate taking off his boots when she realised he wasn't wearing any.

'When did this start?' she whispered.

'S'morning.'

'It's noon. Why didn't you come sooner?'

He didn't bother answering. She put her arm around his shoulders and guided him down on to the pillow. He was about as helpful as one of the statues he resembled, but she persevered. When his head settled on the pillow he groaned as if she was disembowelling him and she prepared to grab the basin, but he merely grimaced.

'Too much noise. People.'

Meaning he would not have come even now unless he'd been desperate. She stifled another frustrated sigh; keeping quiet wasn't her forte but she'd try.

She took the linen strip she used to clean her brushes, dipped it in water and very gently placed it on his forehead. A rivulet ran over his temple and into his hair. His whole body stiffened, but after a moment he seemed to abandon all hope of salvation and gave himself over to agony. She sat beside him, measuring every movement and sound. Even in the dark she could see the flickering of the muscles along his jaw, the tense straining of the tendons of his neck.

She had no idea how much time passed until his body began relaxing. She saw it in the lines about his eyes first, and then his jaw, softening the deep grooves by his mouth. His lips parted a little as if about to speak, but closed again, not quite as tense.

He had a beautiful mouth, drawn with confidence and skill, a mouth a Michelangelo would have paid good money to draw. She reached for her pad, but realised even the sound of pencil on paper might feel like a cannonade to him.

He finally slept, his hands uncurling from their death grips. One arm slipped off the narrow bed and he mumbled, but didn't wake as she gently draped it back over him. After a while she braved covering him and still later she turned her chair back to the table and began sketching as quietly as she could in the shifting gold glow of the lamp.

* * *

'Sam…'

She put down her pencil very gently and turned. He was watching her and the fact that his eyes were open without squinting was a very good sign. She smiled.

'A little better?'

'Leagues better. I'm sorry.'

'You're an idiot. Don't rise. You need to sleep still.'

'I should return…'

'You should sleep. Everyone else is.'

'What? What time is it?'

'Some time near dawn, I think they just rang two bells.'

'I've slept…a whole day?' He sounded appalled. He levered himself very warily into a sitting position and rubbed at his left temple. Hastily she placed a clean sheet of paper over her drawing. She preferred he not know she sketched him while he was unconscious.

'Still bad?'

'No, just echoes.'

'Have you always had megrims?'

He scowled and winced.

'I do not have megrims. Megrims are what women have when they wish to keep their husband at bay. It was merely a headache.'

'That is not only very unfair to bedevilled wives but also inaccurate. Megrims are a documented ailment. Doctor Carlucci was an authority on them and he said hemicranias were written about by Galen himself. My mother had them. Did you have these during the war?'

'Of course not.'

'Why of course not? Lucas and Chase told me the war did bad things to many soldiers.'

'True, but it started long after that. About a year after Jacob died. It does not happen often. You need not fear you have wed an invalid.'

'I fear I have wed the stubbornest man this side of the equator.'

His mouth relaxed and he leaned against the wall, flexing his legs carefully before him. He was so big, he had to angle his stockinged feet away so they wouldn't slide under her chair. Her own toes curled in against the urge to extend her feet to meet his.

'We're a fair pot and kettle then, aren't we?' he said. 'You could give a mule lessons in holding its ground.'

'A cross between a mountain goat and a mule— two very sturdy animals. You should be grateful you acquired me so cheaply; in Egypt you would have to part with many camels for the privilege of marrying such a sturdy wife.'

He rubbed his jaw, an audible rasp in the quiet of the cabin. Her body tingled and she called it to order. The man was in no state for any of that.

'Sturdy Sam.' There was still that smile in his

voice and she wondered if it was kind to wish he suffer from megrims more often.

'That sounds like a poorly named village fair exhibit: *Sturdy Sam and her Spectacular Stalactites.*'

'Thank you, Sam.' His voice was quiet, cutting through her nonsense and flooding her with embarrassment.

'That is an even worse name. Though it rhymes with Thank you, ma'am. You could have the makings of a limerick there.'

'You never could take gratitude or compliments very well. I seem to remember the first time I heard you use a profanity was when I told you that you had drawn a fine copy of a wall carving at Karnak. Something about my being related to a dung beetle. I forgot that.'

'Well, now that you've remembered, keep it in mind.'

'I shall try.'

His smile widened and so did the pit under her feet, but then he frowned.

'You said you slept. Don't tell me you slept on the floor, without even a mattress or a pillow!'

'Of course not. I slept in the hammock.'

He looked in disbelief at the limp hammock hanging from one hook and she laughed.

'It is true. I mastered the fine art of hanging it and getting in without cracking my skull. I am very glad you were lost to the world, though, because my entry and exit still lack grace, but you are quite right, I slept better than on that rack of a cot.'

He didn't answer and absurdly she felt a wave of long-forgotten shyness join her embarrassment. She fiddled with her pencil.

'Are you hungry?'

He stretched again and shook his head.

'No. My appetite takes a while to recover after having nails slammed into my eye with a sledge-hammer.'

'Is that what it feels like?'

'Close enough. On a good episode. When I'm not being stubborn and trying to push through it like a good soldier. But I do need to go take care of other more pressing issues. And find my boots. At the moment I can't remember how or where I took them off.'

He stood very carefully and gave a small sigh of relief. At the door he turned.

'Thank you, Sam.'

And left.

Chapter Eight

'He is no warrior,' Sekhmet scoffed, looking down at Gabriel's sleeping form, her claws gleaming silver in the moonlight.

Leila cast her shadow between him and the goddess. 'Yet he did not run with the others. He is here.'

—The Sprite Queen,
Desert Boy Book One

Egypt had been moving swiftly towards summer, but England still wasn't convinced it was spring. The moment they sighted the grey and green coastline the world lost its sunny briskness and sank into a sulking drizzle that lasted all the way to London.

The same grey veil fell on Edge as well. It was his first time back in England in years and he was dreading it. He was even beginning to think fondly of HMS *Lark*, which was surely a sign of severe desperation. Sam tried to make conversation during the coach ride, but his mind refused to provide anything beyond monosyllables and she finally let him be. He hoped she would attribute it to what she insisted on calling a megrim. He could see the benefits such ailments served. Not that he wanted to keep Sam at bay, he merely...

He didn't want to be here.

England was not a good place for him. All the light he'd ever really experienced in England was centred on that brief period with Jacob at Chesham House when he'd been shocked to discover he not only loved being a father, but was a good one.

Not a bad brother either—Rafe had surprised both of them by staying at Chesham for almost a year before he had to return to his affairs. Jacob had made the grey Greybournes bloom. And then wither.

Now he was back.

And married again.

It would be a miracle if he didn't ruin this.

The carriage clacked to a stop and Edge stepped on to the pavement in front of an imposing Palladian-styled house. Sinclair House presented a perfect façade and probably hid a multitude of sins. He helped Sam descend from the carriage and her hand jerked a little in his, pulling him out of his self-absorption.

'Sam? What is it?'

She shook her head, the ribbons of her bonnet dancing in the wind.

'I haven't been back here since I was a child. My last memory was of fleeing outside into the snow with Lucas and Chase because my father and uncle were trying to run each other through. This was not a happy house. Perhaps after we find Rafe we could return to Qetara?'

She gave a little laugh, as if trying to make light of her words, but he nodded.

'But by *dahabiya* up the Nile this time, I'm still aching from that camel ride...'

The door opened and a wiry white-haired man in livery stared at them in disbelief.

'Miss Sam!' Aside from being inaccurate, for a servant this greeting was utterly inappropriate, but Sam detached her hand from Edge's and hurried up the steps.

'Tubbs!'

Edge's mother would probably have swooned at such breaches of etiquette. At least the man waited until Sam hurried into the hallway before pressing her hand warmly between his. Sam turned to Edge, her nose red and eyes damp.

'Edge, this is Tubbs. He always took care of us. Tubbs, this is Edge... Lord Edward Edgerton, my husband.' She laughed at the butler's expression. 'Impossible. I've finally succeeded in surprising the imperturbable Tubbs.'

The butler transformed himself into a specimen well suited to Greybourne, his gaze settling somewhere past Edge's left shoulder.

'My congratulations, Lord Edward, Lady Edward. Do Lord Sinclair or Mr Sinclair know of this? It was not mentioned.'

'No, not yet, Tubbs. It was rather a…surprise. Are they here?'

'Lord and Lady Sinclair are expected back this evening. Master Chase and Mrs Sinclair are in Paris, I believe, or perhaps Switzerland by now.' His stiffness melted into an affectionate smile. 'Married. Goodness. Mrs Tubbs will be beside herself. I must see to the rooms. There have been quite a few changes here this past year as you can see, Miss Sa—Lady Edward.'

'This is only until I make arrangements for accommodation elsewhere,' Edge interjected, feeling resentful though he did not know why.

Tubbs bowed, resuming his dignity.

'Of course, my lord.'

Edge set his jaw, but before he could turn to Sam an almighty yowl sounded above them and a black cloud streaked down the stairs. Edge moved between Sam and the projectile, but this was clearly a case of unnecessary chivalry because instead of shredding him, the feline, as the streaking object turned out to be, merely wove with impressive agility between his boots and climbed Sam like a ferret, leaving visible rents in her cloak.

'Inky!'

Sam laughed and cradled the monster, stroking the purring mass as best she could. The cat tolerated this for a few rumbling beats and then leapt to the ground, directed its snow-capped tail heavenwards and stalked off without a backwards glance.

'Well, Lady Sinclair will be pleased to see Inky can recover her spirits. She has been sulking since her return from Egypt and there have been no more offerings of mice in inappropriate places for quite some time. Clearly she has missed you, Miss Sam.'

Edge again locked his jaw against a completely incomprehensible urge to correct the butler. It was not like him to care one way or the other about titles and Miss Sam sounded far better than Lady Edward. She sounded like she belonged here.

He, on the other hand...

'Is my uncle in London, Tubbs?' Sam asked and Tubbs's face underwent another transformation, blanking of all expression.

'I do not know. Shall I make enquiries, Lady Edward?'

'Yes, please.'

Edge held his peace until Tubbs led them to a drawing room and departed. Sam sat on a pale blue *chaise longue* with a sigh and cast her bonnet on to a low table. It rolled on to the floor and Edge picked it up, smoothing out the ribbons as tension flicked along his nerves.

'Sam, we discussed the issue of your uncle…'

'I don't think we could call your blank refusal to accept help a discussion.'

'And we certainly cannot call your refusal to listen to my objections a discussion.'

'True. Therefore, it is safe to say we did not discuss this, but it is none the less the right course of action.'

'I am certain your uncle has better things to do than…'

'Don't be stuffy, Edge. There is no one better equipped to help you than Oswald. Please stop pacing and sit down.'

He stopped pacing, but kept the length of the room between them.

'How many times must I make it clear that my brother might well be involved in something which does not bear scrutiny? The last thing I want is to have a representative of the government investigating him.'

'Oswald would never reveal a confidence and he would never hurt me.'

'Very touching. You cannot guarantee that and, besides, it is not you he would be hurting but Rafe.'

'And through Rafe you and through you me. He would not do that. You don't know him, Edge.'

She held out her hand and his mind ran ahead to whatever rooms this Tubbs was organising for them, but he reined his worst instincts back—he had no time for this. His primary concern at the moment was to find Rafe. Then he would consider his future options, calmly.

'There is still time for me to see the lawyers today. With any luck Rafe has contacted them and this discussion will prove pointless. Promise me you will not speak to your uncle about Rafe behind my back.'

'Edge...'

'Promise me.'

'I promise I will not mention Rafe until you return.'

'That is not what I asked.'

'It is all I will promise at the moment.'

He knew that look—brows lowered, her lips pulling into a pucker that had nothing to do with an invitation to be kissed. She was mounting the battlements again. Somewhere from behind the front ranks of his annoyance he felt a smile forming.

'Edge.' The fight melted from her expression and she looked smaller suddenly. He wavered. He *really* did not wish to go to see the lawyers. He would have given a great deal to go with Sam now and slip into a nice hot bath and into...

There was a sharp hiss and the black cat emerged from beneath the *chaise longue*, wrapping itself about Sam's feet and glaring at him. He glared back. What was it called? Inky. He felt he was sinking into some inky substance and it was time to extract himself.

'Goodbye, Sam. I will return…later. In fact, I ought to go out to Greybourne as soon as possible and speak with the steward there. I might have to stay the night. I shall send word if that is the case.'

'Of course. Do inform me if you find your brother.' Her own voice was now as stiff and blank as his.

'Sam…'

'You should be off, Edge. It is already afternoon and you have a great deal to do.'

Oh, for heaven's sake, just leave, man.

He left. He had no patience for himself or stubborn wives or glaring felines at the moment. He wanted peace and quiet.

Not very likely for the foreseeable future.

Chapter Nine

Jephteh's staff glinted gold in the light of the torches, its tip hovering an inch from Leila's heart. 'You may be Queen of Sprites but you too will bow to Jephteh, Priest above all Priests.'

Leila swatted the staff away. 'I am more likely to bow to a mule's behind, you rotted carcass.'

—Captives of the Hidden City,
Desert Boy Book Four

The heavy rumble of carriage wheels slowed and Sam looked up from her drawing. It was a bad habit she'd developed since Edge walked out of Sinclair House two weeks ago and disappeared.

'That's old Freely's carriage. He lives across the road,' Lucas said and Sam detached her eyes from the window and turned to her brother.

He was standing beside Olivia, his hand absently toying with one of her red-brown curls as she bent in concentration over a stack of correspondence arranged with military precision on a large desk.

'How do you know?' Sam asked, trying to smile.

Olivia signed and put aside one document and glanced up at Lucas, her hazel eyes warming into honey.

'He just does. All those years looking over his shoulder. He is like one of those old biddies who always seem to know what is happening on their street. I dare say you know where poor old Mr Freely has been.'

He tweaked her curl and bent to brush a kiss on her forehead.

'Since it is Wednesday I presume he has been to visit his mistress in Kensington.'

Olivia's eyes widened and he laughed.

'Too gullible, love. I have no idea where he has been, nor do I care. All that concerns me is in this house and wherever Chase is off gallivanting with Ellie.' He looked across at Sam again, his smile fading. 'And Edge, of course. That concerns me.'

'Lucas…' Olivia placed her hand on his, but Sam shrugged and retreated to her drawing. No doubt Lucas would have dealt better with the shock of her sudden marriage if Edge had been there to take the brunt of his first reaction instead of disappearing for two weeks. In that respect she thoroughly agreed with Lucas.

Two weeks, punctuated by two notes. One to inform her he was going directly from the lawyers to Greybourne House in Hampshire. Another to inform her he was travelling north to Rafe's house in Cumbria. Both signed *'E'*. Not even *'Edge'*. Not even *'Yours'*. Heaven forbid.

And now nothing for a week.

'He will return. Edge is nothing if not conscientious.' Oh, God, she was beginning to sound like Edge. She heard nothing in her voice of her loneliness or of the fear that this would be her future. That her marriage to Edge, despite the passion he'd shown and the care he'd taken of her, would end in cold distance. Instead of a home she might have trapped herself into worse loneliness than the one she'd been trying to escape.

'I know,' Lucas replied. 'I am not concerned he will disappear back to Brazil. I am concerned he will become embroiled in Greybourne's dubious affairs. I know you promised Edge not to summon Oswald, but if this new husband of yours sees nothing wrong with leaving you in London and wandering off...'

'Lucas, enough. She gave her word,' Olivia intervened and Lucas turned his glare on her and threw up his hands.

Sam rubbed a smudge on the paper. She hated causing friction between Lucas and Olivia and she knew he was right, but so was Olivia. It was a small thing, a promise, but as foolish as it might be she felt not honouring it could risk unravelling the frail tapestry of their union.

Patience is a virtue.

Patience was an agonising twisting of her innards. She hated being patient. She wanted Edge to walk in the door right now, tell her Rafe was alive and well and dedicating himself to leek farming and now they could finally...

There she drew a blank. She tried and tried to imagine what her life with Edge would look like. What their *home* would be like. Somehow in Egypt it had all made perfect, wonderful sense, then faltered on the *Lark*, recovered thanks to a hammock and a headache, and now it was fading again.

Perhaps she'd been suffering from some desert malady and invented the whole thing. Perhaps Edge *had* disappeared and would never return. Perhaps he was somewhere suffering from another horrible megrim with no one to help him...

'Sam... Sam, I'm an idiot. I'm sorry.' Lucas bent over her, his hand on her shoulder. The door snicked shut and she realised Olivia had left them. She bent and stroked Inky.

'And I'm sorry you and Olivia are arguing because of me.'

He grinned.

'No, we aren't. Livvy knows full well I fume when I'm worried and has learned to ignore me, thank God. But she is also concerned. She wants me to stay here instead of going with her to York-shire for her brother's wedding.'

'No! Lucas...'

'Calm down, there is no way in hell I will leave her to face the people who humiliated her alone. In fact, I am looking forward to terrorising a few of them and one in particular. But I give you two choices. If Edge, blast his dour soul, has not re-turned by the time we leave, you either come with us or I set Oswald on to him. Now I'll go soothe my worried wife and you finish your drawing.' He glanced at it. 'Is that Senusret's temple? Edge must have changed a great deal to agree to climb a temple and act as model.'

Sam squinted at the figure.

'It isn't Edge. It is Gabriel, from the *Desert Boy* books.'

'Looks like Edge to me. I wonder if he will be flattered to feature in a romantic novel?'

'I doubt he will even look at it. He didn't show any interest in the books.' That stung. After their reconciliation aboard the *Lark* she'd shown him her copies of the first two books, but he'd changed the subject very effectively, making her forget until quite a bit later he hadn't even looked at her illustrations.

'Then he *has* changed,' Lucas said. 'He used to read aloud to Janet and Mama every night. I think he enjoyed it as much as we all did. Remem-ber? You would lie on the *mastaba* staring at the ceiling and making shapes with your hands as he read and when he dared stop you would bark out commands that he continue as if you were the Khedive himself.'

Sam laughed.

'What a nuisance I was.'

'Yes, you were. Managed us all like a little field marshal. Now that I think of it, Livvy should be grateful to you—I think it was all that practice being manoeuvred by a pint-sized dictator that made it so easy for her to order me about.'

'Edge said the same, but I did *not* order you about.'

'Ordered. Us. About. And before you begin worrying about that as well, allow me to point out that Edge derived quite a bit of enjoyment out of riling you. Your husband is not as straightforward as he appears, Sam. Which is precisely why I want a word with him.'

On that parting shot he left the room and Sam allowed her shoulders to droop. She wanted a word with Edge as well. More than a word. With every passing day of silence the chasm grew. She knew he was probably in no danger and yet...

She wanted to see him. She *needed* to see him.

Devil take him.

Sam was lying on the upper deck of the *dahabiya*, staring at the stars, the scent of jasmine drifting above the murkier smell of the river. But then the crescent moon became a gaping jaw and the fabric of the night twisted into a beast with searing comets for eyes streaking towards her. Any moment she would be devoured but her body would not move. Then the river splashed and seethed and two dark columns rose from the depths, wrapping about the beast which writhed as it was dragged down. Then she was falling, too, waiting for the cold to strike her...

The floor struck her instead. Luckily she woke mid-tumble, landing on her knees with a dull thud, her hands still twisted in the sheets.

Only a dream.

If it was a dream, why did she hear water? And why was there light under the dressing-room door?

She shook off the sheets and very quietly opened the door.

Definitely not a dream.

She'd dreamed of Edge naked these past weeks, but not in the bath. This image was likely to join the rest of those tormenting her since that night in Cairo.

One of the wonderful changes Lucas had made to Sinclair House was three very large baths in the separate suite of rooms meant for each sibling. They were connected via an ingenious apparatus of pipes to cisterns of water heated by a great fireplace in the attics that also served to heat the servants' quarters. It was decadent and utterly marvellous, though a trifle large. Right now it did not appear so big—Edge took up quite a bit of the generous structure.

He was wreathed in steam, leaning back against the raised rim with his eyes closed, his damp arms draped along the sides. His face was flushed and damp, opal water droplets shimmering along his shoulders, pooling in the hollows above his collarbone and speared in the straight dark hair that fanned across his torso and disappeared into the water. It was too dark to see beneath the surface, but her imagination was recruiting the all-too-brief memories of their encounters and her mind happily imagined following that arrow of hair down into the steaming water.

She forced her gaze to his face. He looked tired, the lines beside his mouth even deeper than she remembered, but otherwise he looked unharmed, chasing away the lingering fear of the portent of her dream. The fist of worry relaxed, but anger tightened its hold instead. Not even the sight of his beautiful body and the answering heat that shot through her could counter it. No, it made it worse. A hundred times worse.

There was an ewer of water on a side table and she tested it. Cold. Good.

She barely managed to pour half its contents on to her nemesis when he was on his feet and out of the bath. Prudently she stepped back, holding the ewer out like a weapon as water poured off his body on to the carpet. He looked enormous, not that different from the beast rising out of the Nile in her dream. She took another step back.

'What the devil… *Sam!*'

'I could say the same… *Edge.*'

'This is one hell of a welcome.'

'It isn't a welcome, you poltroon. This is one hundredth of what I would like to do to you. How dare you disappear like that and then sneak in here like a thief without a word to me that you have returned. How *dare* you!'

Her voice was shaking and she clamped her mouth shut. She hadn't meant to show her fear, but it was already too late. The fury on his face gave way to concern and then to consternation. He took a towel to wrap about his waist, but it did not help in the least. Her mind clung to the image of gold and bronze firelight shimmering along every muscle, sinew, hollow and length, heating her with the need to touch, to bring him close to her. She knew that image would sink deep into her mind, filter into her dreams. She wanted with equal fervour to touch him and sketch him.

'Sam, I'm sorry…' he said as he secured the linen, reminding her she was angry. No—furious.

'Don't bother apologising because I shan't forgive you. You *abandoned* me, Edge. As if I was nothing. I learned not to expect anything from my father and mother and certainly not from Ricki, but apparently I am still a fool since I expected some basic respect from you.'

'Sam, listen…'

'No! Why should I? You couldn't even be bothered to send me more than two useless notes. *Off to Cumbria. E.* Do the postal services charge by the letter now? You should be grateful this was only cold water because believe me, for the first time I can understand the meaning of the phrase heaping hot coals on someone's head.'

'Sam…'

She set down the ewer with dignity and stalked back into her bedroom.

'Yinaal abuk wa abu abuk!' The curse rose into a squeak as Edge hauled her off her feet and deposited her in the water.

'You can curse me and my sire just as well from here. Stop splashing about; you are wasting all this wonderfully hot water. This is almost as good as a *hamam*. Move over, I require more room than you.'

'Don't you dare!'

'I'm losing counts of all the dares you are tossing at me, Sam. God, that is good…' He sank into the water, closing his eyes again and she scooted on to her knees to avoid his legs, considering her options.

'Why don't you take off your shift and enjoy this luxury, Sam? Or you could keep it on; I like the way it…' His voice faded, his hand settling on her thigh under the water. 'Come here, Sam.'

She melted. At least her body turned into warm, melting pudding, but her will held her where she was. He shifted forward and the water lapped at the swells of her breasts, mixing warm water and cool air. His gaze was fixed on them, his lips parted.

'Come, Sam.' There was a hot desert wind in those words that had nothing to do with the steam around them. It was so strong inside her she dug her heels in. This mountain goat would not be so easily dislodged.

'No.'

'Why not?'

'Why not? Do you think you can just appear after two weeks, toss me in a bath and move on? I doubt you ever dared disappear like this on your darling Dora.'

He leaned back.

'You are quite right, she disappeared on me.'

'Well, I…what? What do you mean she disappeared on you?'

'That is not quite accurate. Her mother bundled her off to Bath soon after she gave birth.'

As a distraction, his twist in the confrontation was masterly. Curiosity was the Sinclair Achilles heel.

'She was ill?'

'Her mother said she was, but then her mother

turned being an imagined invalid into an art form. To be fair Dora suffered while she was carrying and everyone agreed she needed to recover her strength.'

'But…what of Jacob?'

'Jacob did well with his nursemaid and me.'

'And you were…you had no objection?'

His mouth curved and the mockery was all self-targeted.

'After my anger cooled I discovered having Jacob and Chesham to myself suited me perfectly. You know I am not a sociable fellow, Sam. I've just proven that again, haven't I?'

'But you were barely married a year when Jacob was born.'

'True. That says it all, doesn't it? I warned you, Sam—I win no prizes as a husband. I might have blamed Dora at the time and been only too happy to regain my solitude when she went to Bath, but it was my fault. I married her for all the wrong reasons and then blamed her for my disappointment. She did not deserve that. If I had been a decent man, I would have gone after her and tried to find a middle ground between us. She might have left Chesham, but I didn't try to fetch her back.'

He was breathing hard, the water rippling with his tension.

'My only consolation was that she was happier playing the invalid in Bath, just like her mother, and I was happier playing the hermit at Chesham, just like my father. You already know I am not sociable, now you know I am an abysmal husband. You've made an ill bargain, Sam.'

Sam stilled. There was agony in his voice, well hidden, but agony. And self-contempt. Even through her anger she felt something shift, like the gears on a clock. The image that had tortured her for years began to crumble—his perfect wife, his perfect life only shattered by the death of their son... The thought that he'd been as disappointed and betrayed as she had been... That he'd been alone with his beloved son, caring for him and watching him die. Alone.

Her arms were aching to reach for him, to wrap themselves around that pain like a blanket and chase away his bitterness at himself. But her own heart was too bruised.

'I hate that you had to suffer alone, Edge. I wish... But that cannot be an excuse. This has nothing to do with being sociable—it has to do with respect. If you wish to play hermit, you have my leave to do so, within reason, but you will keep me informed so I do not sit every day wondering if you are ill, or suffering, or something terrible has happened. You are not alone any longer...'

He reached forward, his hands closing on her arms, and she fell silent. His eyes were a sharp jade green flickering with firelight.

'I'm sorry.'

His eyes moved lower, following his fingers as

they trailed down her arms, into the water, brushing against her ribs. She covered her abdomen with her arms and he withdrew, his gaze capturing hers.

'Sam. Are you…are you with child?'

She snapped her arms away so swiftly they hit the sides of the bath.

'No. No, I'm not.'

'Are you certain?'

'Of course I am. I do understand the rudimentary mechanisms of my body, my lord.'

'Don't call me that.' He leaned back, the heat in his eyes completely gone and the sulky curve to his mouth making him look younger.

Her anger faded, beaten back by the memory of her confusion when her monthly course arrived—she'd been relieved because it was too soon to bring a child into their unsettled union and yet…

They sat for a moment facing each other. Then he rubbed his face, shoving his hands into his damp hair.

'I'm too tired for this at the moment, Sam. Please, can't we…just for now cry peace?'

She sighed. She was tired as well. Exhausted.

He leaned forward, tracing a line down her arm. Goosebumps chased his caress and her legs, already quaking from being held so tight, slipped between his. It was both better and worse. His eyes drifted lower again, two jade and silver slits, like a wolf's through the brush, and she realised her breasts had firmed, her nipples darker and visible through her soaked nightshift. She instinctively covered them with her arms and he let out a long breath and closed his eyes again. He looked so beaten she had to dig her fingers into her arms to stop herself from reaching out.

'Edge. Is there news of Rafe?'

'No. He was briefly at his house in Cumbria, but returned south again. He hasn't been to Greybourne. I went there first.'

'Did you see your mother?'

'It was unfortunately unavoidable.'

'Was she…was she not happy to see you?'

'I have no idea. My mother is not a demonstrative woman. She said she'd expected me in England sooner given Rafe's disappearance. There were some estate matters she was not authorised to address.'

'Oh. Did you tell her…about us?'

His mouth quirked at the corners. It did not look like a smile.

'I did.'

'Was she shocked?'

'My mother is not easily shocked.'

'That is not an answer.'

'It was to the question you asked.'

'You are being purposely difficult.'

He leaned his head back and sighed, sending the steam into a billowing dance.

'She was polite. I have no idea what she was thinking. I never know what she is thinking.'

'Now you know how I feel.'

He sat up abruptly, the water sloshing around them. 'That is not true. I'm not like her.'

'I didn't say you were; I have no idea what she is like. I do know you are very, *very* hard to read. Even now I don't know whether you are glad to be here or merely waiting to be off again.'

He brushed his hand over the rippling surface of the water. His lower lip was gilded by firelight, accentuating the slightly sulky look of a chastened schoolboy.

'She has this room. The Rose Room. It hasn't changed since I was a boy. It is one of the few things I remember about Greybourne other than snow. I was sitting with her there and I remembered…' He rubbed his arm and Sam held still until he continued. 'We were reading a children's book. She has a good voice. Very deep…'

'Do you remember the story?'

'No…something about animals living by a river. She has pale hair, not like my father. I don't know why I am telling you this. It is foolish.'

'No, it isn't. Whatever she did, you have so few memories of her, you should cherish them.'

'I'd rather not waste mental powers remembering the people who discarded me.'

'They didn't precisely discard you, they sent you to Poppy and Janet who loved you unconditionally. Do you know I was jealous of you as a child? I used to wish they were my parents.'

He shook his head, but he was smiling.

'What a discontented lot we humans are. Your mother might have had her weaknesses but she fought like a tiger to keep you, no matter how far into the dark she sank.'

'Yes, that is true,' she admitted, suddenly uncomfortable with how revealing her words were. 'Do you remember your father?'

His smile faded, his gaze falling to the cooling water.

'My only memories of him were from morning prayers. Every morning we all kneeled in the great hall for eternity and a day while he bellowed sermons at us.'

'That sounds horrible.'

'It was boring and hard on the knees, not horrible. Unless one of us coughed or nodded off. Then… I'd forgotten, too, what a temper my father had. He would roar like a wounded bear and loom over you. The more I remember the more I realise Rafe was right, I was lucky to be sent away.'

'That doesn't make it any easier to understand as a child.'

He finally looked up, his fingers stilling on the water's surface.

'No. Poppy and Janet were so different I had no idea what to expect at first. On the way to Egypt we docked in Malta and for a few moments I was separated from them. Then Poppy was looming over me and I waited for my punishment…but they hugged me and bought me a notebook so I would have a captain's log and always write where I was going. I remember what it smelled like—saddles and cinnamon. Strange.'

The knot inside her untangled as he spoke. She had no idea what tomorrow would bring, but for now the aching loneliness was gone.

'Are you cold? Your hair is wet because of me.' He touched the goosebumps on her folded arms and she shivered and shook her head, the tip of her plait shifting in the water.

Not only my hair.

The answer, shockingly improper, hovered on her lips. She was quite certain she did not speak the words but his eyes caught hers and stayed there.

'Come here, Sam. Please,' he added very quietly and this time she came.

Chapter Ten

*'Why should I accept succour from the likes
of you? There is not a glimmer of magic in
you,' scoffed the Sprite Queen.*

*Gabriel drew himself to his full height.
'Because I am the only one who offered,
Queen-Who-Misplaced-Her-Realm.'*

—*The Sprite Queen,
Desert Boy Book One*

The bed was beautifully soft and warm, like
being tucked into a cloud and gently roasted by
the sun, but Edge knew without opening his eyes
Sam wasn't there.

He smiled at the memory of the pitcher of
freezing water she'd upended on him. He'd deserved it. He'd known the day he left he was being
a stubborn fool.

He would make it up to her. Once he found
Rafe he would let her decide on the next step. But

first he needed to find the fool and that meant admitting she was right—he needed help.

He yawned and stretched and lurched into a sitting position as his hand touched something soft and rumbling. A pair of round grey eyes that were most definitely not Sam's glared back at him.

'Inky. Keeping an eye on me?'

Inky bared pretty white fangs and Edge inspected the bed, but no dead mice were evident. The grey stare was becoming unnerving so Edge put back the blanket and hesitated. It would be carrying Sam's accusation of prudery too far to worry about being naked in front of a cat. But he still looked over his shoulder when he reached the dressing room. The grey eyes were still on him.

Trust the Sinclair cat to be as unnerving as possible.

Edge found Sam in a large south-facing parlour and though she must have heard him enter she did not look up from her sketching.

'Good morning, Sam.'

'Good morning, my lord.'

He grimaced. It was perhaps too much to expect last night would erase her anger. She took a crayon from the box of drawing implements and her dark hair fell forward like a curtain between them. The urge to slip it back behind her ear so he could see her was so strong he put the table between them. It was not smart to manhandle his wife again within moments of being alone with her. He wasn't desperate, for God's sake.

'Lucas and Olivia are leaving today. For her brother's wedding in Yorkshire.'

'I see.'

He searched for a safe topic of conversation and found none so he shoved his hands into his pockets and inspected the portrait that hung on the wall behind her. It was of a bewigged and ruffled man with a wicked gleam in his pale eyes. Though Sam and her brothers favoured the darker Venetian side of her family, there was a definite likeness to this specimen of the Sinful Sinclairs.

'That was one of the worst Sinclairs,' Sam said without looking up. 'Lucas keeps it to remind us whence we came.'

'I think I can remember well enough without having the likeness of my father glaring down at me. No doubt once Rafe takes possession of Greybourne he will toss my father's portrait in the fire.'

She finally looked up.

'I dreamt about him.'

'About Rafe?'

'No. Your father. Or rather of a great big bear with matted fur and red eyes looming over me and trying to push me into a shaft, like the ones in tombs.'

'God, Sam... I'm so sorry. I didn't mean...' He reached for her but she moved away.

'It is not your fault. My dreams have always

been vivid; it helps my drawings. You and your brother were in the pit with me. You were playing spillikins.'

'Spillikins?'

'Yes, that rather ruins the horror, doesn't it? You were losing, too.'

'Rafe was probably cheating, then.'

Her mouth curved upwards and fell, as if the weight of the smile was too much. There were shadows under her eyes he had not seen last night in the dark. Guilt twisted his stomach.

'Sam…'

'Your mother was in a pit next to us,' she continued, not looking up. 'She said you may have another Dora if you won. I dare say she would have preferred someone like her rather than a Sinful Sinclair.'

He shrugged, uncomfortable. That was close enough to his mother's words. *'My dear Edward, naturally I am glad you have wed again, especially since poor Rafael is unlikely to, but must it have been into that dreadful family?'*

'Her opinion hardly matters.'

'Doesn't it? Did you ever ask her why she sent you away?'

Edge was having difficulty keeping up with Sam's mercurial shifts, but he didn't want her to stop talking with him so he tried for honesty.

'No. I always thought it had something to do with my health.'

Sam straightened, more present now in her curiosity.

'How strange. Janet used to say you were the only one she dared allow help her when families brought their ailing children to Bab el-Nur because you rarely fell ill for more than the length of a day, even as a child. I doubt she would have subjected you to risk if your health had been poor.'

He rubbed his left arm, frowning.

'I broke my arm once.'

Her eyes lit, tightening at the corners with suppressed laughter.

'Were you climbing something? No wonder you are such a namby-pamby about my mountain-goat tendencies. But that would hardly be a reason to send a child away.'

'I have no idea what namby-pamby means but, no, I wasn't climbing anything. I...' Pain shivered along his arm and he shook it. 'I cannot remember. I must have been six, before I went with Poppy and Janet. It was the last time I saw snow for many years.'

He stared at her drawing, uncomfortable with the memory and with the worry in her winter-sea eyes. The drawing was of a rising sandstorm behind a shadowy figure standing on Senusret's temple, his robes billowing about him as if he was conjuring the storm by sheer will. It was beautiful and powerful, but there was something very wrong with it—hidden in that storm was something evil and the man had no defence against it. It would be utterly perfect for a scene in the next *Desert Boy* book. He should be pleased, but he felt almost…invaded.

Sam slipped her hand through his arm and he looked away from the drawing. A hard fist of pressure was lodged in his chest again and without thinking he pressed her hand to the insistent thud under his vest. It was like walking into a brand—an aching heat spread outwards, a flush of fever spreading over his skin.

'What frightened you just now?' she asked quietly and he dropped her hand.

'Nothing.'

To distract her and himself he reached for the leather-bound drawing case on the table, but she moved past him and took it.

'These aren't ready.'

'I don't mind, I merely wished to see…'

'I mind.' She slid them into a drawer, leaning back against the dark wood. 'My uncle is coming this morning. I dare say he will be here soon.'

He stepped back as well, tucking away his hurt at her rejection. If she didn't want to share her drawings with him, then fine.

'You spoke to him?'

'No. I promised I wouldn't, but Lucas said he

would if you didn't return before he left. I never expected you to be absent so long.'

'Believe me, I derived no joy from spending days and nights riding hired hacks the length of England. You knew full well this was my priority.'

'Full well, my lord.'

'Don't snarl, Sam.'

'You started it.'

He rolled his shoulders, trying to pull back. 'So I did. I apologise. I should have at least told you where I was going and how long it might take.'

'Blast you, Edge. I hate when you pull the rug out from under me.'

'That was very ungallant of me, I know. Shall I apologise for that as well?'

'Pray don't bother; your apologies only make me feel guilty. Will you speak to my uncle, though? As long as Rafe isn't threatening to undermine Parliament I give you my word Oswald shan't harm him. He would even have protected Ricki had I asked and he detested him.'

Edge leaned against the table. She never mentioned her husband and he'd never asked. He searched her face for some indication of her feelings and saw nothing. Sam of old could never have kept so much of herself hidden.

'Detested is a strong word. Why?'

'Ricki belonged to a fast set. My uncle was afraid he would not change his habits when we married.'

'Did he?'

'For a while.'

'And then?'

'It hardly matters now. Will you speak with him?'

'Yes, blast it.' He shoved his hands into his pockets and turned to face the leering portrait of her ancestor.

'Have you hoarded all your curses over the past couple of weeks, or is it the Sinclair influence?'

He didn't turn to see the smile he heard in her voice. There was something useful about the old Lord Sinclair's leer—it was an antidote to his own lechery.

'Edge.' Her hand slipped over his and into his pocket, proving him utterly wrong. Every inch of him went on alert. 'We *will* find him.'

'I know we will.' His voice was far too rough, but it wasn't anger or dismissal. It was the sensation of her fingers slipping between his, their tips trailing fabric over his thigh. Just a little to the left... He opened his mouth to make the suggestion when the door opened.

'Hello, Edge.'

There was a smile and a warning in Lucas's voice and Edge returned the smile stiffly as Sam moved away.

'Where is Olivia?' Sam asked as she sat on the sofa, hands clasped with pointed propriety.

'Overseeing the packing and trying to find

Inky before we leave. Well, Edge. It has been a while.'

'Yes. Lisbon.'

'During the war?' Sam asked.

'No, on my way to Brazil.'

'Four years ago. Your brother was busy there.'

'As I remember so was yours.'

'Oh, do kiss and make up, you two,' Sam said. 'I thought you were friends!'

Edge smiled at the concern beneath her annoyance.

'We are. Your brother is merely voicing his objection to the unorthodox manner of our marriage in his own inimitable way.'

'That is one way of putting it,' Lucas said. 'If it were anyone else I would take them outside and deliver my warning in a rather more direct manner.'

Edge shook his head.

'We were always too evenly matched. I don't think both of us sporting a black eye or a bloody nose would quite make your point.'

'Learn some tricks in Brazil?'

'There is this fascinating method of combat called capoeira.'

Lucas's dark eyes brightened with interest. 'I have heard of that. You must show me some time. We've turned the great hall downstairs into a boxing and fencing saloon and I've been teaching Olivia how to fence…'

Sam straightened.

'Lucas! I asked you dozens of times and you never agreed.'

'That is because I trust Olivia not to run me through when she's annoyed at me.'

'I am twenty-six, not six, you know.'

'It's not a question of knowing. It's a question of accepting,' Edge interjected, watching the silent battle in Lucas as he almost visibly unravelled the bonds of responsibility over Sam's fate. No doubt he would have to go through the same circling and sniffing when Chase arrived. 'It is good to see you again, Lucas.'

Lucas sighed.

'I'm glad you're back, Edge. As long as you are good to Sam, I will remain glad.'

Sir Oswald Sinclair was a man of about fifty, more slightly built than Lucas, with grey-streaked brown hair and the face of a contemplative monk. His eyes were either grey or a pale brown, it was hard to tell the way he kept his gaze veiled.

'Sam.' He placed his hands on Sam's shoulders after the introductions were complete and looked her over and almost smiled. 'That is better.'

He turned to inspect Edge.

'So. You are Greybourne's son.'

'I am afraid so.'

'Yes. I never met your sire, but your brother

expressed a similar sentiment towards him when we met.'

'You met Rafe? When?'

'The first time was some ten years ago in Paris. The last time was a year ago in London while he was between…occupations.'

'There, you see? I told you it was best to speak with Oswald.'

'My dear Sam,' Oswald interjected, 'I do not believe it is wise to begin wedded life by wielding the phrase "I told you so". Not so, Lucas?'

'Let's just say I would suggest making that point more diplomatically,' Lucas replied. 'But this is Sam, after all. Her idea of diplomacy used to be "once more unto the breach". I'm happy to see you still have your lance and sword on you, Sam. Give Edge hell.'

'Thank you, Lucas,' Edge said.

'Enough, you two. Now, Lord Edward, I would like you to tell me everything you know about your brother's activities and then I shall tell you what I myself have heard.'

Edge straightened.

'You have news of him? How…?'

'You needn't look at Sam like that, Lord Edward, she said not a word to me on this issue since her arrival in London. But my people track persons of interest entering our ports and your brother is even more distinctive now than he was before his scars, a fact which undoubtedly makes his occupation rather more challenging than usual. Add to that the fact that he arrived aboard a vessel manned by a captain known for making unreported stops along his routes. Now, we shall begin by telling each other what we know. You begin, if you please.'

Edge hesitated, but with a look at Sam he put his cards on the table and told Sir Oswald the little he knew.

'If you know of my brother, Sir Oswald, then you know he is not concerned with formalities. I am worried he might have become embroiled in something not quite…above board.'

'Your brother is no fool, Lord Edward. Though his antipathy for your father has propelled him into a rather colourful existence, it is his skill and inclination which kept him there. To my knowledge he has never yet done anything counter to the interests of King and Country. As far as I can ascertain, whatever took him to Egypt and beyond has thus far not had international repercussions barring the message regarding his death which was clearly a forgery. If he is settled in London, I shall no doubt hear of it. A man of your brother's physique and connections is unlikely to go unnoticed here.'

'He might not have returned to London after Cumbria.'

'True. However, he will have left a trail. Everyone does, even the best of us. Leave the matter with me.'

'I cannot sit and do nothing,' Edge objected.

'Naturally not. Surely you have other matters to attend to after so many years abroad?'

Sir Oswald's gaze rested briefly on Sam and Edge's jaw clenched at the subtle emphasis, but he refused to be manipulated.

'Nothing more immediately pressing than finding my brother.'

'Commendable, I am sure. However, I prefer you grant me a day or so to do just that before you muddy the water. I will be leaving for Paris by the end of the week so make use of my resources while you can. Come, Lord Edward... Edge, you are by nature a patient man. If I cannot secure any information in two days, you may rampage through town like a stuck bull if you wish. Meanwhile there is surely something you can think of doing in this great city?'

Sam smiled, assessing Edge.

'Yes, there is. I have an errand to run.'

Chapter Eleven

'Open it,' Leila said.
Gabriel obeyed, a little wary. Opening
strange boxes led to peculiar outcomes in
the Hidden City.
   This one didn't suck him into Jephteh's
dungeons, but into another world and for a
brief, beautiful moment he was home.
                    —*Treasures of Siwa,*
                    Desert Boy Book Five

'I keep forgetting how noisy London is,' Edge
said as he helped Sam descend from the carriage
into the orderly chaos of Piccadilly. 'I think I've
missed it. A little.'

Sam's hand tightened on his arm and he looked
down. Her eyes were smiling and with a peculiar pang he realised he'd spent far too much of
their short married life avoiding her, chasing his
brother, or sulking. That time could have been

spent so much more enjoyably. Once they ran this errand he would start rectifying matters—first by taking her back to that wonderfully soft bed so he could unfurl her hair into a dark, fragrant waterfall over her body...

Not suitable thoughts while standing in the middle of Piccadilly.

'We had best get this over with. What is this errand, anyway?'

'I need a new wardrobe and you shall help me choose fabrics.'

His horror must have shown on his face because she burst out laughing.

'You look like a toddler being dragged to have a tooth pulled. This is Hatchard's, silly, not Madame Fanchot's. I need a new set of *Desert Boy* books. I usually read the manuscripts Mr Durham sends me and rarely read them after they are published, because I am too scared to discover that my illustrations are all wrong for the final version, so when my copy of *The Treasures of Siwa* arrived I gave it to Ellie before I even read it. But now it is officially published I do wish to have a copy, especially since the manuscript Mr Durham originally sent me wasn't complete.' Her hand tightened a little on his arm as she stared at the damp pavement. 'I tried to visit Mr Durham to ask him if he knows whether Mr Bunny is writing a new book, but he is in Boston commissioning new authors. His son is at the helm during his absence and I did not stay to speak with him—he is rather an unctuous young man, not at all like his father. I hate not knowing. I always worry I shall learn that something happened to Mr Bunny or perhaps…perhaps he no longer needs my illustrations.'

Edge was also a little worried. More than a little. After a particularly memorable occasion of childish evasion years ago, Janet had pointed out lies by omission can be just as poisonous as lies by commission. How had he managed to forget this issue still lay between them? How had he not admitted to Sam that he was Mr Bunny, as she insisted on calling the author of the *Desert Boy* books?

'Sam…'

'Oh, no, it is beginning to rain. Hurry, there is no escape now.'

No escape.

Edge followed her inside, his mind tossing arguments back and forth as they were swept into a kaleidoscope of pelisses and bonnets and the rumble of the street was replaced by the buzz of people.

Edge clenched his teeth. This was neither the time nor the place for a crisis of conscience. He would consider the issue later when he could think it through carefully. Perhaps if he told her while they were more…intimate…it might be less of a shock. He could have told her last night while she was lying half on him, with her leg over his, her hand stroking his chest while his shaped that wonderful curve of her hip, up and over...

'Edge?'

He breathed in, taking his time.

'Let's buy those books and leave. This place sounds like the camel market at Imbaba and with all these perfumes it smells almost as bad.'

She laughed and stroked his arm. A woman with a bonnet three times the size of her head managed to both glare at them and look away in disgust. Sam immediately dropped his arm, surprising him. He glanced down at her.

'What is it?'

She shrugged and turned to the closest bookshelves.

'Nothing. I don't like being stared at.'

'Pure envy. Ignore them.'

The corners of her mouth picked up.

'Are you saying they envy me my handsome husband? I never suspected you of vanity, Edge.'

'Don't be coy, Sam. You know I was referring to you.'

'Do I? I don't even know if you think I am moderately attractive.'

'You don't...you cannot be serious! What on earth do you think last night was about?'

'I have been told females are practically interchangeable when men need their physical needs assuaged.'

'This is hardly the place for such a discussion, but who on earth was the idiot who told you such nonsense? Not your brothers, I'd warrant. And it certainly does not apply to me. Look at me, Sam.'

She shook her head, a sharp flush colouring her cheeks.

'Not here. Everyone is staring.'

All at once his own discomfort was gone. He didn't like seeing Sam pull herself inward like that.

'You were never concerned with appearances in the past.'

'My debut in Venice taught me otherwise. It might be the Capital of Sin, but it is brutal to women who don't play be the rules. After we married, Ricki mocked all my missteps and did his best to civilise me. I'm afraid he didn't succeed any more than you did.'

'I never mocked you, Sam. Ever.'

'No, that is true. It is not in your nature.'

'Nor did I want to change you, I merely wanted…' He searched for the right words. 'I merely wanted you to be safe.'

It wasn't a lie, but it felt inadequate. He'd never understood the urge to protect Sam—she might have been a madcap, but she was, as he'd told her so indelicately, alarmingly sturdy. Not to mention her brothers were already perfectly adequate guardians. There'd been no role for him, but he'd forced his way in none the less.

She'd always brought out the best and worst in him.

'Let's go, Edge. I hate this. I shall ask Tubbs to buy the books.' Her gaze was flickering around the room and not with the avid curiosity that sometimes exasperated him, but with uncustomary dread. He wanted nothing more than to leave, but he drew her hand through his arm, turning her back towards the bookshelves.

'They might just as well be staring at me. After all, we are serving up a surfeit of scandals. Between Rafe's disappearance, my reappearance, our wedding abroad and the Sinful Sinclair family name it is hardly surprising we excite curiosity. I would be more concerned if we drew no attention. Clearly that would mean something so horrific had happened civilisation itself was under threat.'

She laughed, leaning her shoulder against his arm for a moment. It was such a small thing but it shrank his lungs. He'd never been tactile, not like her, but the need to touch Sam was an underskin itch—constant, irritating, undeniable. He almost wished she would do something impetuous like climb the footstool the clerks used to reach the upper shelves so he would have an excuse to steady her...he could already feel the pliancy of her hips under his fingers, her warmth.

The urge to make a fool of himself was so strong he took a random book from the shelves and opened it. Sam leaned closer to read the title page.

'*Guilty or Not Guilty. A Lesson for Husbands* by Ann of Swansea. *"Husband, I knew this not of you…"*,' she read aloud with a muffled laugh, before Edge snapped it shut and shoved it back into place. He would have done better to have encouraged her to keep reading because her tension returned immediately.

'They are still whispering behind us, you know. I am certain I heard your name mentioned.'

'They're like vultures circling a carcase; show some spirit and they'll be off to search for a more amenable target.'

'That is a gruesome metaphor.'

'It is a simile, not a metaphor.'

Sam rolled her eyes and he couldn't help smiling.

'Come now, where is the Sam Sinclair who took on Khalidi's troops and scaled the pyramids?'

'Weren't you the one who thought that Sam was a wild hoyden in need of proper schooling?'

'I was wrong.'

'I beg your pardon?'

'It does happen. Not about the wild hoyden part, which you were, but about the proper schooling. It would not suit you in the least to be like any of the tittering lace-and-frill-wrapped confections surrounding us. Come, we shall buy your books and go…' He almost said home until he realised there was no such place. That was something he should rectify. Soon.

'Oh, goodness, it *is* you. Lord Edward!' A voice trilled behind them. 'Come along, Phoebe, it is Lord Edward Edgerton, the Duchess of Grey-bourne's son. My dear, *dear* Lord Edward!'

Edge set his teeth.

'Be nice,' Sam murmured beside him and he tried hard for a smile and turned to face two women approaching them like ships of the line. He recognised them from the year he'd married Dora, but could not for the life of him remember their names. Luckily they presented their colours immediately.

'I was just telling Mrs Murchison we hope your dear mama shall come to town now the year of mourning is over. Did I not, Mrs Murchison?'

'You certainly did, Lady Buckley. And now this! Why, when we read the *Morning Tattler* you could have knocked us both over with a feather.'

Sam shifted back a little, as if contemplating escape. He tightened his hold on her arm. They were in this together, for better or worse.

'I had no idea how or why the news appeared in the *Morning*…whatever…but I wasn't aware matrimony still had such an impact on anyone in town. May I introduce my wife, Lady Edward?'

The excitement faded from the two elderly women's faces, replaced by bewilderment and then a totally different look—something very much like greed. Edge hadn't realised quite how private the Sinclairs managed to remain because clearly by some miracle the news of their marriage had not yet spread throughout the *ton*. Until this moment. Only the two matrons were looking at them directly, but he could feel the crowd's interest as oppressively as a *hamsin* wind.

'Your *wife*! Dear me, what a pleasure of course, Lady Edward. We did not know...'

'Had not heard...'

'Since we only returned to England recently, that is not surprising. Which reminds me, we must be going. A commission for the Duchess, you see,' he explained broadly and their heads bobbed like the little parrots that used to perch on his veranda in Brazil hoping for treats. 'Thank you for your good wishes.'

'Of course, of course, but perhaps before you go we might yet convince you to do a *reading* for us at our salon. A most exclusive grouping... And of course, Lady Edward, you must come as well.'

Sam finally spoke.

'Reading?'

Lady Buckley nodded vigorously, lining up her guns.

'*The Treasures of Siwa*, Lord Edward's latest book.'

Everyone within hailing distance of Lady Buckley's flute-like voice rustled a few inches closer. Before Edge could shift his guns about, Sam spoke, her voice a little hoarse.

'You must be mistaken, Lady Buckley.'

'Oh, have you not seen the morning edition? That was precisely what we thought, but the *Tattler* quotes Mr Ewan Durham's words quite clearly, did it not? He was asked about the *Treasures of Siwa* already being sent for a third printing and he said he expects this will be the most successful of the *Desert Boy* books yet and that the author is none other than the younger son of the late departed Duke of Greybourne. At first we wondered whether this might be the new Duke, but it distinctly said *younger* son. Did it not, Mrs Murchison?'

'It most certainly did, Lady Buckley.'

'And then I remembered you have lived in all manner of outlandish places and I said—why, yes, it might very well be true! My words precisely, were they not, Mrs Murchison?'

'Precisely, my dear Lady Buckley.'

This time the silence that followed this assault was absolute, as if a church's dome had dropped down upon the room. Edge forced a smile, tucking Sam's nerveless hand around his arm. He didn't know if he was anchoring her or himself. She wore no expression, as if she'd stepped away and left her body propped by his side. He kept his voice pitched as low as possible when he replied, hoping Lady Buckley would lower hers.

'You do know you cannot rely on anything titled *Tattler* for veracity, Lady Buckley. Such rags thrive on innuendo and invention.'

'But it was printed as clear as day! Why, we could speak of little else at Mrs Felsham's at-home hour. In fact, I just dashed a note off to your mama to enquire if it is true…'

'I am certain my mother will be delighted to hear from you, Lady Buckley. Now, my wife and I really must be going, we are already quite late to…' He groped helplessly for something, anything, and failed. 'Good day.'

The few yards between the shelves and the door felt longer than the path from Zarqa and Qetara and far less hospitable. Not that he was concerned about the people around him. His only concern was Sam. He was about to suffer the lashings of hell and he deserved every one.

He risked another look at her and looked away again, but this time because it hurt. He'd never seen Sam look so shocked, not even when the ground fell out from under her when she tumbled through the roof of the tomb in Saqqara and ended up spread-eagled on a heap of rubble. But just like at that moment his heartbeat flew ahead like a bolting horse and he finally realised what he'd done.

* * *

Once inside Sinclair House he followed her upstairs to the private parlour adjoining their bedrooms. She placed her hand on the wooden table, as if trying to overcome a wave of giddiness. He waited, every muscle and tendon in his body clenched.

'Sam…'

She shook her head.

'It is a jest, yes?'

'No. Sam…' His voice was so hoarse he had to clear it.

'You're *Bunny*?' Her own voice rose into a squeaky whisper and he groped for humour.

'I'm most definitely not Bunny, but I am the author. I meant to tell you, but…'

'You *meant* to tell me,' she repeated.

'Yes, I…'

'When?'

She no longer looked shocked. She looked as cold as ice, her skin leached of colour, just two sharp streaks of fire marking her cheekbones like war paint.

'I beg your pardon?'

'*When* did you mean to tell me? When did you mean to tell me you were the author who for the past six years I have been working for? Who I am now married to. When?'

'You don't understand. I never meant to tell *anyone*.'

'I am not *anyone*, Edge. I am, for better, and at the moment for much worse, your wife. I am your...your partner in this. *When* would you have told me?'

'Sam, it isn't that simple...' He floundered again. He needed time to think this through. He needed time to answer the question for himself before he answered it for her.

'I don't think you meant to tell me at all. Ever. Did you?' Sam demanded and he felt the heat crawl up his face and her eyes widened. 'You. Are. *Mad*. Mad! And *blindingly* stupid. As blind as a mole popping out of the ground under the noonday sun, Edge! Did it not occur to you it would be a matter of time before I discovered the truth? At some point I would have come across something that gave you away. Or perhaps you intended for us to live apart? Or to do all your writing in some secret *pied-à-terre*? Or have a locked room and warn me away from it with all manner of dire warnings in good Gothic novel tradition?'

'Sam, calm down.'

'I will *not* calm down. You didn't trust me! You let me hang from the gibbet of my uncertainty every year, wondering if there would ever be another commission, if perhaps Bun...the author didn't want my services any longer or...or had died and it was over. And all the time... Why would you do that to me? Did you think I would reveal your great secret? Have you so little faith in me?'

'I thought you wouldn't agree to illustrate them if you knew I was the author.'

'Why on earth would you think that?'

'After what happened in Egypt back then… I thought you would misinterpret…'

Her laugh was harsh, dismissive.

'I know I made a fool of myself then, but surely you could not have imagined I didn't understand your rejection. That was my fault, not yours. I would have been delighted to know you didn't despise me after that.'

'Of course I didn't despise you and that is not what I meant, blast it. Hell, I know I should have…'

She sat abruptly, her shoulders slumping, and the ache in his chest expanded, pressing hard against his ribs.

'I didn't think. Sam. No, that's not true. I considered telling you in Egypt, but I didn't want anyone to know, not even you. Especially not you. This is a part of my life I keep apart. It is somewhere I escape to. Bringing it out into the open… I hate it.'

She began pulling off her gloves and did not appear to be listening to him, so he pulled the reins on his own confusion. He looked about the room. The parlour was decorated in colours of wood and sky. It suited Sam so much better than

Greybourne's heavy colours. They would not suit Sam in the least. *He* did not suit her in the least.

It wasn't his fault. She'd inserted herself into his life and he had hardly any time to consider the benefits or the costs of marrying her. He'd acted on pure impulse. Greed.

Lust.

Need.

Eight years of bottled-up, unsatisfied, unspoken, hardly admitted lust and a need he didn't even understand.

He'd wanted her eight years ago and that want tainted his marriage from the very beginning. And he'd wanted her again the moment he saw her howling at the skies above Bab el-Nur.

And that was all he'd thought when he accepted her proposal. Little more than: *'Finally!'*

Impulse. Nothing good happened when he acted on impulse.

He'd offered for Dora on impulse, because she'd represented a world that was the opposite of the war-ravaged hell he'd been desperate to put behind him—Dora had been light-hearted, carefree, she'd grasped pleasure with both hands and pushed aside unpleasantness. She'd been everything he thought he wanted to become. But it was precisely those characteristics he'd come to resent, and when they hurt Jacob, he'd come to hate them and Dora.

Now he'd married Sam on impulse as well

because…because he wanted her. Because the moment the possibility of her marrying someone else was raised every nerve and muscle in his body protested at the thought of another man having her. It had been as fierce as grief and it scared him enough to say yes without thinking it through and now he was paying the price, but what was worse—so was Sam. He hated seeing her like this, hated being the cause of it.

'Sam…'

'You lied to me, Edge.'

'I didn't lie…'

She held up her hand and it was more powerful than a blast of wrath because he would have preferred that she be Sam and yell at him.

'You lied. I thought…of all the people, I thought I could trust you, Edge. I always knew there were limits to this union, but I never thought I would not be able to trust your word.'

'*Sam.*'

'Leave me be. Go talk to your lawyers and see if they have learned anything more about Rafe. That is what matters most now, no? We can talk… later. I'm tired.'

She sounded exhausted and he felt it. He felt beaten.

He turned and left as he was bid.

Chapter Twelve

The temple gates groaned and heaved like a wounded beast trying to rise.

Khonsu placed a hand between Gabriel's shoulder blades and shoved him forward. 'Don't believe anything you see inside, young Gabriel. Remember Seth tricked Osiris himself. A dung beetle stands a better chance than you.'

—Lost in the Valley of the Moon,
Desert Boy Book Three

Sam turned over in the darkness, wishing she could sleep, but her thoughts were pounding away like Ayisha smashing chickpeas and sorghum in her pestle. *Smash, smash, smash.* The same thoughts over and over and going nowhere, catapulting her between fury and despair.

She didn't know where Edge had gone or when he would return. *If* he would return. Perhaps she should not have sent him away. Twice.

But his lie burned and burned.

Edge is Mr Bunny.

Edge is a liar. By omission, but a liar. The worst kind of liar—a stupid liar who didn't even have enough respect for her to realise she would find out. She almost wished she had discovered he had a mistress...

She turned over again, grinding her teeth. No, that wasn't true. But it felt equally a betrayal.

The bastard! The son of a flea-bitten, mangy cur of a... No that wasn't fair. Dogs were far more reliable and faithful.

And loving.

What a fool she was to trust him—fool that she was, she'd read into his quiet and calm all manner of depths that he did not possess in the least. She'd truly believed Edge would never betray her. Her world had always stood on shaky ground. Growing up, she'd never known where they might be the next year, whether her mother would succeed in pushing back the veil of pain or whether she and her brothers would be mostly left to their own devices.

Like the desert of ever-changing dunes, she could never know from year to year what the landscape would look like, but even in a world built upon shifting sands there were some constants. Or so she'd thought. Her sense of stability should not depend on him, but losing that bedrock that was Edge... It left her adrift. Threw her back years and years to when they'd been plucked from England without explanation and then not long after she began to understand Venice they'd been plucked up again and taken to Egypt like so many sheep. She and her brothers and Edge had come together in that unpredictable adult world.

She'd believed without question that Lucas and Chase would defend her up to and through the very gates of hell. She believed Edge would take her seriously even when he wanted to strangle her, would watch over her even when they wished each other at the devil and would never ever lie to her, even when she'd wanted him to. Ever since she could think rationally she'd concluded he and her brothers were the only beings on this earth she truly trusted.

Had trusted.

She'd *needed* to trust him and he'd taken that away from her as well. She didn't know where that left her world.

She could kick herself for being such a fool. No. She'd rather kick him. He was a sneaksby, a coward, an inconsiderate lump of cloddish muck you scraped from a camel's hoof. She wished she could push him off a thousand temple roofs and he would land on a bed of spiky *sabaar*...

She froze as the connecting door between their rooms opened slowly and the wall glowed with candlelight from the dressing room.

She had not even heard him return, damn the man for moving so stealthily.

She closed her eyes very slowly, as if the mere motion of her eyelids could be detected. There was nothing she could do to relax the tension in her body without being obvious, but she hoped he understood the silent message and went away. If he thought he could waltz into her bedroom as if he'd done nothing worse than returning late from his club...

Did Edge belong to any clubs before he left London? She didn't even know. There were so many things she didn't know about him...

She stiffened further as she sensed rather than heard him move towards the bed.

Blast it, she couldn't keep up the pretence of being asleep. Her whole body was itching to jump up and yell at him.

The bed sank under his weight as he sat and his fingers rested gently on her shoulder. A wail of hurt welled up in her and the words burst from her.

'I don't want you here.'

'I'm so sorry, Sam.' He withdrew his hand and his voice was flat, utterly Edge, but she thought she heard true regret there, though perhaps it was merely because he wished to put this confrontation behind him. She wished she could tell.

'So am I, Edge.'

'I was wrong.'

'I'm tired, Edge.'

'You cannot ignore me for ever, Sam. We are married.'

'So we are.' She turned her back to him, pulling the cover higher.

'Damn it, get angry, throw something. This isn't like you!'

'I've changed. You always wanted me to change, didn't you? You should be happy. Now go away.'

'No. Turn around and talk to me.'

'No. Go away.'

'What are you most angry at—that I am the author of that I did not tell you?'

'That you didn't *trust* me.'

He fell silent. She could hear the strain of his breath and the image of that looming bear rose over her again and she spoke before she thought. 'I'm scared.'

'Scared?'

'I had two things in my life—my brothers and my...*your* books. And now this marriage and you. Except now you *are* the books and I don't... I haven't... I'm not making any sense, am I?'

'I...a little?'

'Everything has always moved in my life. There was no home, I never knew where we would be next year or the year after that. My father disappeared before I even truly remembered him. One moment he was the most wonderful man and the next he was a terrible one. I never knew if my mother would be happy when I woke in the morning or back on her island of grief, betrayed and abandoned. When I met Ricki I thought…at least he was so open, so present, there would be no horrible surprises, but then I discovered he had a daughter no one ever mentioned.'

His indrawn breath was a hiss like water striking the fire. She tensed as well and almost stopped. Discussing children was clearly dangerous territory for Edge and discussing Maria… But she didn't want Edge to believe she'd resented another man's child. She rubbed her forehead and forced herself forward.

'I wouldn't have cared if he'd told me. Maria was the most marvellous little girl you could imagine, I would… I *did* welcome her into our home. Even if she was not mine, she would be our children's big sister and I wanted her to be part of the family we would have. I didn't even have to try to be kind to her—she made it so easy to love her…'

Her voice cracked and his hand curved around her arm, and she could feel her pulse leaping against his fingertips.

'Perhaps…perhaps he was afraid of disappointing you?' he asked. His voice was as tentative as his touch.

'No, Edge. I would have understood and forgiven that, believe me. It wasn't it at all—Ricki just never thought it was important enough to tell me. He had paid off her mother and forgotten all about her. At least until he wanted to use her against me.'

'God, Sam…that is…despicable. Surely you cannot believe…there is no comparison between his secret and mine. And I would never use this against you.'

'I know that, Edge. I asked you to marry me because you are nothing like him, because I trust… I *trusted* you wholly. But can't you see? It wasn't the essence of Ricki's lie, but the way it peeled everything back—it showed me…both of us. We were too different to be happy together. I know you aren't like him; you would never, ever use a child to try to coerce or hurt anyone. But… I'm afraid. What else don't I know about you? I never had a home so I don't know how one builds a foundation for one, but I thought trusting you was almost as good, and I'd hoped you trusted me enough to… Oh, I can't explain!'

She thumped the mattress and his hand tightened on her arm.

'Sam, turn to me. Please.'

'No. I don't know what to do if there is no trust between us, Edge. How can we build anything on that?'

He let her go and there was a rasp and groan, as if he'd scraped his hands over his face, and her eyes burned in the dark. She was driving him even further away. She began to turn to him, but he spoke first.

'I failed you, Sam, but it isn't because I don't trust you. I don't trust myself. I feel safer in… compartments. It seems mad now, but I honestly thought I could keep everything separate. Clean. I've forgotten how to think of other people in my life. If I ever knew.'

She wasn't imagining the bleak viciousness in his voice and her resentment stumbled. She groped in the dark and found his hand, braced on the bed.

'You did. You do. But you're not just in my life, I'm in yours now. Even if this isn't a marriage that began…like yours with Dora, we must live together. And work together, it seems. I don't expect you to tell me everything, Edge. But this… Being the author of those books is at the heart of who you are. Who *we* are.'

'I know that. That is the problem, Sam.'

'Tell me how. *Talk* to me, Edge.'

His hand was tense under hers, then it turned, skimming up her arm, sliding under the thin cotton of her nightgown. Her body lit like a firefly, so hot and ready she had to stop herself from jerking away from his touch.

'Those books are all I have left. A man in the middle of the ocean on a dinghy doesn't risk his one safe haven to go for a swim.'

All I have left...

His words sheared through her as viciously as the heat.

You have me *now.*

She was so tempted to say the words, but did not want them handed back to her, by word or by deed. She was too lonely to weather that rejection.

She also wanted to throw it back at him—those books were all *I* had left of myself, too. They were the one corner of the world that was mine and filled with pleasure and anticipation and vivid life, and now...

And now I don't know what to think.

She was torn between turning her back on him and holding him to her so fiercely he couldn't try to keep secrets from her. But those desires were from old Sam and older Sam. She didn't want to be either at the moment.

So she turned over her arm, laying it open to his caressing fingers. It amazed her how lightly he could touch and how potently. As if all those years treating precious antiquities under Poppy's tutelage were embedded in his hands. Ricki had been rough and boisterous, his hands everywhere at once, his body heavy on hers. But Edge could send her body heavenwards merely by exploring her arm.

A shiver ran through her, her legs stretching under its force. She reached for him, but he caught her wrists, pressing them down by her head, his thumbs brushing the sensitive cores of her palms. He bent and pressed his mouth to the crook of her elbow, his breath warm, his touch like moonlight on water, but his next words were rough and angry.

'I don't like *needing* anything.'

More of her anger faded into mist at this admission. This was Edge—poor Edge, whom she'd manoeuvred into marrying her. And he was trying to be honest.

'I'm scared, too, but we are tied together now, Edge.'

Tied together. For life.

He waited for panic and felt only regret that he'd already tarnished what they'd barely begun to build. Again and again. He'd punished her on the *Lark*, abandoned her at Sinclair House with hardly a word and now this, the worst blow of all. He'd acted on lust and a barely understood impulse when he accepted her proposal, but that did not excuse his behaviour since.

'I am so sorry I hurt you, Sam.'

'I know you are.' It didn't sound like forgiveness, it sounded like defeat and he couldn't bear it. He needed her to understand, but he didn't understand it himself.

'Trust is…hard.' He put the words out like a

chess piece. He could almost hear the click of ivory on ivory.

'Do you trust anyone at all, Edge?'

A hand closed on his throat, a great, burning giant's hand. It was an effort to breathe past it and words weren't even an option.

'Do you trust Poppy and Janet?'

He closed his eyes. He owed them an affirmative. Nothing came.

Her hand shifted and touched his.

'Do you know they would give their lives for you?'

He shook his head, not denying, but not accepting.

'They lived in as much uncertainty as I did all those years,' he said. 'There weren't many letters from Greybourne, but every time one came I saw them prepare. Maybe this time I would be summoned back and there was nothing any of us could do about it. The worst was I never knew what I wanted.' A sharp pain speared his temple, just above his brow, and he touched his palm to it. It was a warning, but he knew he had to explain to her so she would know the fault lay in him, not her. 'Each time I realised it wasn't happening I would be as relieved as hell, but at the same time I would think—they have Rafe so they don't need me. But what I knew was that if one day that letter came and said I was to return, perhaps if they lost Rafe and needed to replace him,

Poppy and Janet would have no choice. So, no, I don't know they would give their lives for me, nor would I have expected it. It wasn't the way the world worked. The only person I ever trusted absolutely was Jacob, but I certainly never expected him to trust me. Which was proven correct. I couldn't protect him—not from illness or pain or death or even from a mother who was afraid to love him or his grandparents who were terrified of his imperfections. You are right not to trust me, Sam. It is safer that way. You see? I am only hurting you as well...'

Her hand tucked under his so that his weight was on it, pressing it into the softness of the mattress. The fist was coiled tight around his throat and ribs, that ragged, matted giant bear wrapped around him and squeezing...

'I was too young to see any of that when we came to Egypt,' Sam said. 'All I saw was a very serious, very smart boy who I wished would like me, as I knew he liked Lucas and Chase. I wish I'd understood you better.'

'You were a child. You weren't meant to understand. *I* didn't understand. And none of this excuses how I've treated you.'

She sighed, slipping her fingers through his.

'I'm not looking for excuses, Edge. I may not understand you, but I know you. I know you aren't cruel. I only need you to try to trust me a little.'

'I do trust you,' he said the words before he

even thought them through and if he could have snatched them back he would have. They hung in the darkness like a sword hovering above his exposed neck and he waited for her to expose them for the lie they were.

But she merely squeezed his hand.

'You look tired.'

He almost dismissed her words, but decided to try out his new resolution of honesty.

'I'm exhausted.'

'Lie down. We can talk tomorrow.'

His disappointment was so severe he pushed to his feet so swiftly he almost stumbled.

'Edge? Where are you going?'

'You said…we should sleep.'

She twitched back the blanket.

'I said you should lie down. And soon—it is cold in here. I had forgotten how un-spring-like English spring can be.'

He lay down carefully and her mouth lost some of its tension as she tugged at his sleeve.

'You needn't live up to your name by clinging to the edge. This isn't the cot on the *Lark*. There is plenty of room.'

He smiled in the dark, thanking the gods Sam didn't know how to hold a grudge, no matter how justified. He moved closer to her warmth, still feeling peculiarly tentative despite the banked fire in his body. He laid a hand on her shoulder and realised with dismay that she was shaking.

'Sam?'

'Oh, no. I just realised!'

'What is it? Sam, are you cry—? Are you *laughing*?'

'Bunny!'

She *was* laughing.

'My sweet, fluffy *bunny*,' she cooed, her hand feathering down his chest, his nerves leaping in its wake.

'Don't call me that…' Ending on a groan, it wasn't quite the pre-emptory statement he'd wanted to make.

'Bunny…' she murmured again, pressing kisses to his throat, her laughing breath spreading over his skin like sun-warmed silk. 'Warm. Cuddly. Bunny.'

How the devil did she make something so humiliating sound so erotic?

'Stop it, Sam.'

He was filling with unbearable fire, any second now he would go up in flames like a paper lantern.

'Should I, Edge? Should I stop?' She dropped her hands to her sides, brushing them over the bed instead, the fabric hissing under her fingertips.

'Damn it, call me whatever you want, just don't stop.'

She laughed and turned back to him, her fingers curling into the fabric of his shirt as she pulled it upwards.

'Anything you say, my adorable, fluffy bunny…'

* * *

'Wake up! Goodness, you sleep like a log.'

Edge groaned, trying to cling to the image of Sam dancing in the middle of a lush garden, her scarves floating away one by one as she came closer... He reached for her. She could at least atone for interrupting such a promising beginning.

'Wake up or I shall have Inky wake you!'

That shattered the marvellous dream.

'Don't you dare!'

She laughed, bouncing on the side of the bed. He opened his eyes and smiled at her. Her bouncing once annoyed him to no end. Right now he didn't mind in the least if she would only bounce a little closer.

'I'm awake. Now make it worth my while to remain awake.'

'My uncle sent a note.'

He sat up so abruptly he cracked his skull on the headboard.

'Blast. What does it say?'

'It is addressed to you. I do not open other people's correspondence,' she said primly. He reached for the sealed paper she held, but then thought better of it. Trust.

'Read it.'

Her bouncing stilled. After a moment she broke the seal and read aloud.

'"*You are in luck, Lord Edward. A man resembling the description of your brother, accompa-*

*nied by a younger man, was spotted at the Ship
and Kettle in Shoreditch, speaking with a Mr
Geoffrey Pettifer two mornings ago.*

*"Not a reliable person, Pettifer owns Pettifer's
World of Wonders on Piccadilly, which is apparently a museum of curios with a strong emphasis
on the Egyptian and the Oriental. Currently his
most successful crowd-pleasers are Mummy Un-
wrappings—he acquired a shipment of moulder-
ing mummies lately from Egypt, and the hoi polloi
pay a princely sum to witness him unpeel them.*

*"At the time our viewer was not aware of our
interest in your brother and only made note of
the discussion because the trio struck him as out
of place in the Ship and Kettle. Since then he has
been told to be aware and report. I have also requested someone keep a watch on Mr Pettifer.
Discreetly.*

*"I am hopeful other avenues will produce
something rather more conclusive, but for the
moment this is the most tangible trail".'*

She held out the note.

'He never signs his notes, though one could
never mistake his handwriting for anyone else's.
This is good news, isn't it? In a way? At least you
know he has recently been in London. Have you
ever heard of this Pettifer?'

'No. Nor do I particularly wish to. *Damn* Rafe!
I beg your pardon.'

'For heaven's sake, Edge. I learned to curse before you did.'

'Sometimes I think you were born cursing, Sam. At least you have moderated a little.'

'So have you. A little. There is, perhaps, hope for you yet.'

She smiled. The sky was as clear a blue outside the window as the Egyptian sky in winter. Her eyes had that colour in them, caught between a darker blue rim and Atlantic grey. He wanted very much to trust that this current would take him somewhere safe. Or drown him. He had no idea any longer.

'Shall we visit Mr Pettifer?' She laid her hand palm up on the bed, more a question than a request, and he took it. He wanted to ask again if he was truly forgiven, but he still had enough sense to keep quiet.

'Good. Now, what does one wear to visit a World of Wonders on Piccadilly?'

Chapter Thirteen

*'You must turn back Gabriel's ship!' Leila
cried, but Khonsu shook his head.
'It cannot be done. His dreams are tangled in the flow of Anuket's river like a fish-
ing net among the reeds.'*
—Temple of the River God,
Desert Boy Book Two

Mr Pettifer was not quite what Sam had expected.

Or rather, not quite what the advertisement outside the halls of *Mr Pettifer's World of Wonders*
depicted. Unlike the impressive figure clasping
a writhing dragon by the throat in one hand and
a diamond the size of a small child in the other,
Mr Pettifer stood only a couple of inches over five
feet, with soft brown hair and even softer brown
eyes filled with childlike wonder that enhanced
rather than detracted from his impact.

He was speaking to a dour man who scuttled

off as they approached, rather in the manner of a publican hurrying to hide his stores of smuggled brandy upon the entrance of an excise officer.

Mr Pettifer on the other hand assessed their clothes with a swift glance that showed both interest and caution, but when his gaze moved from Sam to Edge his eyes widened, giving his round face the look of a startled but still appealing sheep.

'Goodness!' he exclaimed.

'You look discomfited, Mr Pettifer,' Edge said and Mr Pettifer's downy face reddened, but already Sam could see him recover his balance, a wide, welcoming, and wholly practised smile of invitation taking front and centre stage.

'Not at all, not at all. I was merely momentarily struck by your resemblance to a man I once met, sir. You know what they say. Everyone has a twin somewhere and in my occupation I meet a great many people.'

'Indeed. You find me curious, Mr Pettifer. Tell me about this twin of mine.'

But Pettifer was not to be pressed into a corner by so direct an approach.

'Dear me, dear me, there is nothing to tell, sir. A mere acquaintance. A passing one at that. I'm afraid you have strayed a little—the theatre is down that corridor and the unwrapping does not begin for half an hour. You are more than welcome to visit the exhibits while you wait. I particularly recommend the Burmese Dragon and the Angel of Kathmandu—our most sought-after attractions and utterly unique.'

'We are not interested in your attempts to defraud the gullible public, Pettifer. We are here for information.'

Pettifer held firm to his smile, his gaze slithering past them down the empty corridor. But then he gave a little sigh.

'Naturally I shall be happy to assist you if at all possible, Mr…?'

Edge ignored the prompt.

'Good, then you can begin by informing me where and under what circumstances you met this doppelgänger of mine?'

'This…what?'

'The man who looks like me.'

'But, my very dear sir, there is nothing to tell. We merely chanced to share a table and a tankard of ale at a crowded public house, talked of the unseasonably cool weather and then each went about our business.'

'I'm afraid not, Mr Pettifer. You see, the man you speak of does not care for ale.'

Mr Pettifer appeared even more thrown by this statement than by Edge's resemblance to his drinking companion.

'He does not?'

'No. When you choose to lie, try not to lie about matters of no consequence, they tend to undermine your credibility regarding more serious matters.'

Sam pressed her lips together. Sometimes Edge's pedantry was useful. Mr Pettifer's doe-like brown eyes darted about the room.

'It was whisky, then.'

'Thank you. Was it only the two of you?'

Edge sighed and raised his hand as Pettifer's lips parted. 'You are about to lie. Please do not. There was another person there as well.'

Pettifer cleared his throat.

'Yes, there was a, ah, young man with him.'

'Good. Now, what did you discuss? The truth, please. I do not wish to cause trouble, but I will be delighted to recommend excise officers have a closer look at the next shipments you receive.'

Mr Pettifer's brows and hands danced up and down.

'No need, no need for that. Not that there is anything at all of interest to the excise officers, I assure you, nothing at all. But still, the bother, you see. So tedious. There is nothing much to tell you, after all. Mr Grey—'

'Mr Grey?'

'That was the name he gave. As I said, he and the, ah, young man wanted news of Mr Osbourne, the fellow who arranged the shipment of my marvellous mummies. Unfortunately, the last I had heard of him was the note accompanying the mummies assuring me he was in the process of procuring a treasure that would secure his fortune. I'm afraid I did not set much store by his promise as Mr Osbourne was not always reliable. Why, once I did not hear from him for two whole years and then up he pops with the most fascinating specimen of a primordial dragon you could have hoped for. It is still one of my most popular displays. That is, until the mummies began arriving. I am unwrapping one in half an hour. Did you see the crowd gathering? At three shillings per person…and then there are the restoratives on sale for those who faint…' His gaze sailed away into far pleasanter scenery of shillings and pounds and he sighed happily. 'Do stay and watch. I am hoping at least for some scarab amulets wrapped into the linen. The ladies are particularly fond of them.'

Sam touched Edge's sleeve at the audible creak as he ground his teeth and he breathed in and out very slowly.

'Did he say how to contact him should you hear news of Mr Osbourne?'

'He did, sir. In such an eventuality, I am to place an advertisement in *The Times* requesting Mr G. contact Mr P. and then watch the advertisements the following day for instructions. A very straightforward man, Mr Grey.'

'And do you intend to comply with his request?'

'Ah, were that it was merely a request. It was

rather more in the nature of a royal decree. He is a big man, your Mr Grey. I would see he has an inch or so on you and you are a most formidable fellow yourself, sir. I am a peaceable man and prefer not to antagonise giants. Naturally should Mr Osbourne appear I will insert said advertisement.'

Edge nodded and took a strip of paper from the desk, scrawling a direction on it.

'Should you hear of anything—Osbourne, Mr Grey…anything—send word to this solicitor's office. And should you breathe a word of this to anyone I will tear this vulgar little circus down about your ears. Understood?'

Pettifer's eyes widened, an appreciative look brightening his gaze, as if the dramatic image of Edge singlehandedly toppling his kingdom, rather like an enraged Samson, appealed to him.

'My understanding is excellent, I assure you, sir.'

'Good, we're done here. For now.'

He strode towards the door, but Sam turned to Pettifer.

'Why did you keep emphasising the words "young man"?'

Mr Pettifer smiled. 'I see you are a lady of insight. You might think me a fraud, but I am merely a man who knows how to provide a good show and I know when I am watching one. That was no young man—she might have some experience acting as one, but she is past the age where she can do so credibly. And the resemblance, though not marked, is there. Unless I am very much mistaken your…ah… Mr Grey was in the company of Osbourne's daughter. Now I must rush or the masses will become restive and that is not good for the accounts. Do stay. I shall even waive your cost of admission.'

With that Parthian shot he hurried off. Edge's glare following him as he took Sam's arm.

'Little weasel. Come, let's go.'

'Not yet. I wish to see the unwrapping.'

'Good God, you cannot be serious!'

'I am most serious. I am curious about this man and I want to see him at his trade, as he put it. At the moment he is the only link to your brother and his peculiar activities. The most sensible thing is to examine him as minutely as if he were one of Poppy's antiquarian finds or one of Huxley's embalmed monstrosities.'

'He might be a snake, but I have no wish to dissect him, nor do I want to spend the afternoon crushed between fainting matrons and gaping layabouts while someone's body is desecrated for their base entertainment.'

'Poppy has unwrapped mummies.'

'To my knowledge he only did so twice and has long since desisted. I told him at the time I thought it thoroughly disrespectful of a culture we otherwise esteem. If someone went around the English countryside digging up graves and pulling out bodies…'

Sam had never seen that look on Edge's face before. The hard, handsome carapace cracked for the briefest moment, vivid pain turning his eyes from ice to molten lead. It slashed through her and without thinking she pressed her palm to his cheeks, but he drew back just as swiftly.

'Don't. I don't want your pity.'

'It isn't pity, Edge…'

'I said *don't*! If you wish to stay, stay. I'll be in the carriage.'

Sam wanted to rush after him and hug him. Or rush after him and kick him. Well, she wouldn't rush after him at all. As devastating as that glimpse of his pain was as he thought of his dead son, she was tired of having every gesture of affection or empathy that did not suit his particular mood flung back in her face.

If he wished to suffer alone, then let him suffer alone.

Not twenty minutes later Sam was regretting her stubbornness. Not that she would tell him so, but she *really* didn't want to watch this.

The exhibition rooms were large and airy, painted in improbable pink and green and gold, and filled to the brim with exhibits that ranged from absurd to oddly impressive. But the theatre resembled paintings she had seen of a medical theatre, benches encircling a stage dominated by a long wooden table surrounded by smoking torches. A body lay on the table under a sheet, a landscape of white peaks and planes. It might have been deceased for hundreds of years, but there was something about this which was…wrong.

The crowd, however, evidently found the spectacle the peak of titillation. Mr Pettifer was, as he would be the first to admit, an expert at pacing his 'Grand Reveal'. Despite her own distaste, Sam wished Edge was there after all because Pettifer's presentation of Egyptian culture was so fantastical Sam found it hard not to laugh even as she squirmed at the thought of what was to come.

'No wonder people swoon in here,' a voice grumbled just beside her and Sam managed to just barely choke the small exclamation of relief at Edge's appearance. It wouldn't do to show him how grateful she was he'd relented.

Pettifer reached a pitch in his presentation, clasping the sheet shrouding the mummy and with a practised flourish unveiled 'The Horror'. The communal gasp was punctuated by a few highly satisfied shrieks, the benches creaking as people craned for a better view. Sam leaned back to allow a portly couple to shuffle down to gain a better view and Edge's arm went about her waist, holding her against him.

'Careful,' he muttered, but he did not let her go and she remained there, her hip pressed against him, his hand on her waist. His voice was abrupt, but his hands were gentle, his hold as natural as if they did this every day, with just a quiver of tension as if he, too, was holding back from pulling her more firmly to him.

More likely it was just indignation about to boil over as Mr Pettifer launched into a reverberating speech about the dangers of the 'Mummy's Curse' as he peeled away frayed strips of greyish-brown cloth. The crowd was quivering, too, though from a different kind of passion.

'Look at them. It's like feeding time in a barnyard,' Edge grumbled, but his hand slipped further around her and she wondered if he was even aware of it. Probably not.

'When was the last time you were in a barnyard? I think you're just worried about the curse.'

'If I believed in curses, I would wish it on the charlatan about to desecrate that poor mummy. I am more worried *I* will start cursing. Imagine anyone walking into your family's crypt, taking out one of your ancestors and de-coffining him in front of a titillated audience. It's obscene!'

The contrast between his words now and his reaction earlier in the corridor made her heart sink a little. He was determined to show her his emotional wall would not be breached again. Well, she could stick to form, too.

'True. Though most Sinclairs were obscene even before they were buried. In fact, dying was probably their most valued contribution to the world.'

Another quiver ran through him, this time of suppressed laughter, and she relaxed a little, leaning more firmly against him. She wished Pettifer would get on with it—she was suddenly quite anxious to leave.

Edge felt the familiar mix of amusement and exasperation with Sam overtake his annoyance at the tittering crowd. Coupled with the feel of her body against him it made a potent brew—they gathered into a sensation almost of giddiness as warmth flowed upwards like the first signs of heatstroke. It was probably merely the smoke, the crowd, the shifting wood of the benches as people alternately craned and cowered. He didn't like the thought that merely by pressing herself against him Sam could make him feel like the ground was quivering beneath his feet.

As if aware of his annoyance with himself, Sam glanced over her shoulder and her smile—half-roguish, half-commiserating—sent the heat the rest of the way to his head, staining the inside of his skin as if he, too, were encased in stiff wrappings that were beginning to curl and flake away in the heat. There was a stinging sensation along his cheekbones and instinctively he brushed at it, his palm catching on the roughness of stubble. He remembered he had done a poor job shaving this morning because he'd woken so late. And he remembered why…

The crowd rocked on its feet as Pettifer gave a cry of alarm, extracting a small black object tucked beneath the linen strips binding the chest.

'Behold! The Sacred Scarab! Bearer of Life and Death! Messenger of the Gods!'

'What twaddle,' Edge growled under the oohs and ahhs of the spectators and Sam's laugh rubbed against him, stifling his breath and contracting all his muscles like a closing fist.

'Can you not stop fidgeting?'

'Is that what I'm doing?' Sam murmured, her behind settling against his thigh as she leaned forward. 'I'm merely trying to get a better look. What do you think he is about to do with those peculiar scissors?'

I don't care, Edge almost said aloud. Her behind was perfectly positioned now and the blasted woman knew it. He hadn't even noticed he was holding both of her hips. In the unlikely event that anyone looked around, they would see a spectacle quite as titillating as the desiccated relic of a man being unveiled on the table.

He truly no longer cared, not about mummies being desecrated or about frauds and barely about his idiot of a brother at the moment. Right now all of his concentration was on keeping his breathing even, which was ludicrous. One shouldn't have to concentrate on breathing. It was almost as natural an action as the beating of one's heart, but both those animal functions were proving faulty at the moment, out of step and rhythm.

His other animal functions were running rampant as well. It was absurd and embarrassing. Just last night they had more than amply satisfied their carnal needs in bed. He shouldn't be desperate to get her back there so soon; or at least not so fiercely.

Damn Sam.

His hands tightened on her hips, he wasn't certain whether he meant to hold her there or move her away, but she merely pressed back further, her fingers sliding between his for the briefest of moments, leaving the skin between them raw with longing. He wanted to lace his hands with hers so that when he moved her against him it would be *their* motion, not just his.

For a brief moment she rested her head back against his shoulder, her hair brushing against his jaw and her orange-blossom perfume enveloping him, crowding out the familiar scents of the mummy—beeswax and myrrh and the higher note of juniper from the berries that had probably been added to the wrappings. He bent his head, allowing his lips to brush her hair, breathing her in.

'Behold! The arm of a great king!' Pettifer intoned in an impressive alto as he peeled away a layer of stained linen and exposed a withered limb as dark as lacquered wood. A wave of his own arm set the light of the torches next to him dancing. 'See the gold upon his nails? A sign of royalty! A sign of greatness! Of a direct link to the ancient gods!'

'That is nonsense. Many of the mummies have painted fingernails. Poppy conjectured it was meant to protect the nails during the mummification process,' Edge growled, relieved to have something to focus on other than Sam's gyrations.

'Fascinating…' Sam replied and with another sweep of her hips regained lost ground and more.

'Sam, stop,' he groaned.

'Stop what? I am merely keeping to the Egyptian theme and practising my *ghawazi* dance.'

'What do you know about *ghawazi* dancing?'

'I once followed you and Lucas and Chase to that place in Khan el-Khalili. It was so… enthralling…'

She drew out the word and he bit down another groan, his voice cracking a little as he spoke.

'That was a supremely foolish thing to do.'

'I was the foolish one? The three of you looked like a row of village idiots, staring at those dancers like manna from heaven.'

There was a snap of disdain in her voice and at least she stopped torturing him, shifting away. Contrarily he held on to her and after a moment of resistance she let him pull her back against him. He breathed in and out, slowly. He was in agony, but she felt so good, soft and warm and…

'Sam.' He couldn't stop that single word and the answer shivered through her, like a silver ripple on the surface of the Nile. 'Let's go home.'

Home. He hadn't meant to use that word. The only home he could remember aside from Poppy's was the home he'd temporarily created for Jacob. Too short and too bittersweet for him to even realise that was what it was until death destroyed it. He'd never expected to have one again. But Sam deserved the home she so obviously yearned for.

'We need a house of our own,' he murmured against her hair.

She began to turn, her morning-sea eyes searching his, but he moved her towards the exit. He didn't want to talk. Right now all he cared about was getting her into bed. He could even make do without the bed.

Inside the carriage he watched the streets flow past, trying to think about his next move regarding Rafe and not the way his hands itched to pull Sam to him. He'd set out on this journey to find Rafe, not a wife. If he'd been a little swifter he might even have come across Rafe in Meroe and would have put an end to this uncertainty. But then he would not have found himself in Qetara. Or met Sam again. None of this would have happened. He might have found Rafe, but still been lost himself in a world without an ounce of passion.

Until he'd reached Qetara he'd hardly paid attention to his passage through Egypt. He'd not stopped for a moment to sink into the world he'd known better than any other, as if stopping to smell the camel dung and the almost-cinnamon scent of the desert dust would act on him like laudanum on an opium fiend. Like quicksand. He'd felt nothing but duty and fear. At least until he came to Bab el-Nur and found Sam yelling at the skies like a *houri* and she'd begun to subvert his life once more.

Then his rusty innards were kicked into motion. Annoyance and exasperation were feelings, too, weren't they? And lust. At the moment it felt more like cataclysmic earthquake. No—earthquakes didn't burn like this. A volcano, perhaps.

Sam. His own Vesuvius simmering away under the surface and threatening to upend everything.

'Did Pettifer make you less worried about Rafe?' Sam's question broke through his thoughts and he turned to her, grateful for the distraction.

'I don't know… No, he didn't. Rafe is a law unto himself, but his actions are always rational. Right now I can't make sense of them and that worries me—more than worries me. Rafe cut off all ties with our parents when he was practically still a boy and other than his valet Birdie I may be the only person who cares what happens to him. He stood by me through the worst days of my life, but he would never expect anything of me and that is precisely why I need to see him, to hear directly from him that all is well. I know it might appear…obsessive or even quixotic to you, but if there is even a chance that he is in trouble and needs me…'

Sam took his hand, squeezing it between hers.

'It doesn't appear obsessive to me at all, Edge. I think especially for you knowing something is wrong but not being able to put your finger on it is worse than knowing precisely what is wrong. At least if you knew that, you could take action.'

'Yes.' He sighed with relief that she understood. 'So I cannot stop until I am certain he doesn't need me, Sam.'

'I would never ask you to, Edge. You always call me stubborn, but you are by far the stubbornest man I know. And loyal. And infuriating.'

Laughter made her eyes shine like the dawn sun on a winter sea. He wished he could take her hair down right now, sink his hands into its dark warmth. Sink in to her…

'You're doing it again.' Her smile faded. 'Going away.'

'I'm right here.'

'No. Not truly. So shall we ask my uncle to enquire about this Mr Osbourne?'

'I already have.'

'What? When?'

'While you were inside I sent the footman, Tubbs's son, to your uncle with a message.'

'So that was why you were gone so long. And here I thought I had won a battle of wills with you.'

'Are you keeping a tally? You needn't bother, the odds are clearly in your favour.'

She tilted her head to one side, capturing her lower lip with her teeth. His thumb brushed across the upholstered seat, imagining that warm, damp surface…

'I may win more small ones, but you win the large ones, Edge.'

'Do you think so? I am not so certain. You certainly won the battle to distract me from that charlatan's mummy unwrapping. I was far more engrossed in thoughts of unwrapping you.'

Sam laughed, but her cheeks flushed sunset red. 'Those are very sacrilegious thoughts in such a solemn setting, my lord.'

'Since your posterior is as close to divine perfection as I can imagine, calling my thoughts sacrilegious is sacrilegious in itself. Ah, thank God.'

'Thank God?'

'We've finally reached Sinclair House. First thing tomorrow I will ask the lawyers to begin searching for a house for us to lease. No, buy. Even with your brother in Yorkshire, there is something daunting about making love to my wife in the afternoon in his house.'

'Is that…is that what you are about to do?'

'That is what *we* are about to do. Since you set

this in motion I expect you to accept your share of the responsibility for our breach of etiquette.'

Her smile kept growing. Any moment she'd start shimmering like an approaching star. It felt good. Yesterday he'd been afraid she'd never smile at him again, that he'd ruined what had barely begun. He looked out the window, waiting out this bout of pressure somewhere between his stomach and his chest. She was becoming too important too fast, pulling him along. He felt like a fool placed backwards on a horse, unsure where to grasp to stop himself from being thrown. A horse's ass. Sam would probably like the image.

'What is so funny?' Sam plucked at his sleeve and he rested his hand on hers.

'Nothing. We're here. Come and finish what you started.'

Chapter Fourteen

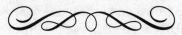

*'And, most importantly, do not walk along
the river after dark, boy,' the Jackal warned.*

*Gabriel hesitated mid-step. 'There are
crocodiles?'*

*'No. Worse. Others of your kind. They
might actually wish to talk.'*

—Captives of the Hidden City,
Desert Boy Book Four

Lincoln Inn's Fields was dark, but beyond a
clump of trees the windows of a rather dull row of
houses sparkled invitingly. They didn't look like
they might harbour anyone connected to Edge's
secretive brother, but the message they received
from Oswald only an hour ago had been quite
clear. A Miss Cleopatra Osbourne, daughter of
and sister to noted explorers John Osbourne and
Dashford Osbourne, had recently been engaged
as companion to Mrs Phillips, a relative of the

illustrious Mr John Soane and currently resid-
ing at his home.

It was a quiet area of town, both simpler and
more dignified than Curzon Street. They left
the carriage at Holborn and it was a strange and
pleasant sensation to walk arm in arm with Edge
through the evening darkness. So very…normal.

By the frown on his brow she doubted Edge
was similarly appreciative of the experience.

'Which house is it?'

'That one.' Edge pointed to the most brightly
lit house with a classically pale façade between
more stoic dark brick buildings. Three tall arched
windows were separated only by gilded column
capitals that seemed to hover unsupported by anything but air. It was a peculiar touch and she rather
liked it.

'I didn't realise this was a dangerous part of
town,' she said.

'It isn't, there are too many solicitors about.
Why?'

'Someone stole his columns,' she whispered
and Edge shook his head.

'Behave yourself in there.'

'I shall do my best.' She watched a carriage pull
up in front of the entrance and Edge tensed, but
a footman jumped down from the perch behind
and helped out two elderly couples. Edge whistled
under his breath. 'What is it, Edge?'

'That was Viscount Gordon of the Society

of Antiquaries, and I think the other man is Mr Planta from the British Museum. Blast, Soane must be entertaining.'

'Perhaps we should have sent word.'

'No, I didn't want to alert them if there was anything at all peculiar...'

Another carriage pulled up, depositing three middle-aged men.

'What shall we do? Should we return tomorrow?'

'No. I came here with Poppy years ago and I doubt I shall be turned away if I come presenting his compliments.'

'You? What of me? Shall I hide out here among the trees while you enjoy yourself drinking port and discussing antiquities?'

'Don't be foolish, Sam. But do try not to frighten them off with your Sinclair sense of humour.'

'Better than putting him to sleep with the Greybourne version, my lord. *Oomph*... Edge, put me down!'

'*Do* I put you to sleep, you aggravating little mountain goat?'

'Only in the best possible way, Bunny. Careful of that branch, I cannot go in there covered in moss...'

She was quite certain she heard her cape rip against the tree bark as he raised her on to a protruding branch, but lost all interest in sartorial matters as Edge covered her mouth with his. His body was warm against her in the chill air. The puckered seams of his leather gloves rubbed against her jaw and neck and her skin prickled. What would it feel like if they pushed under the layers of clothing that separated them, over her bare skin, here in the empty darkness of a city square when any moment someone might pass by...

The same thought appeared to occur to Edge as well. Even as his hands slipped beneath her cloak, moulding over her body, he drew back, his breathing as shallow as hers.

'Damnation, Sam. You make me do things I never thought...and, no, that is not a compliment so do not look so smug.'

'You cannot possibly see what I look like in this darkness.'

'I can feel your smugness. Hell, let's get this over with. And when I find Rafe I'm going to beat him within an inch of his life for making me waste my time like this.'

'I am rather enjoying myself.'

'That is what I'm afraid of. Remember, Mr Soane is a good friend of Poppy's and one of the premier collectors of antiquities as well as the architect of the Bank of England.'

'Good for him. What is your point?'

He gave a strangled huff.

'Behave. No climbing on *anything*.'

'Is there anything to climb on?'

'Actually there is. The whole house is a warren of rooms and antiquities, including a most exquisite bust thought to be of Nefertari and—'

'I think *you* are the one in danger of losing your concentration in there, Edge. Never mind, I shall remind you discreetly if you forget yourself, never fear.' She shook out her cape and set off across the garden towards the house, but Edge caught her arm, pulling her to a halt.

'What is it, Edge?'

'It just occurred to me... Do you think they might have heard about...the books? People like them aren't likely to have read them, are they?'

Even in the dark she saw the alarm on his face and actually considered lying.

'Of course they are likely to have read them. Edge, your books are as successful and anticipated as Scott's and Byron's poems.'

'Don't be ridiculous, Sam. There are no points of comparison. They are *novels*. These people are serious scholars.'

'All the more reason for them to read them, then. Think of Cousin Huxley—he was fascinated with how accurate they were and convinced they must have been the work of a scholar and one well acquainted with Egypt and its culture. But even if they weren't, how many people can create a door into another world that people want to visit again and again judging by the number of editions? Your books are brilliant.'

'You are not an impartial party here, Sam.'

'I am far more impartial than you, Bunny. I dare say you wouldn't be as white as a bleached bone if you'd written some boring old pamphlet about irregularities in the succession in the Middle Kingdom dynasties.'

His mouth curved, but he flattened it again.

'I only want to go in, find out what we can, and leave. I don't want… Damn Durham's son. I should have ignored you and forced him to print a retraction. And wrung his neck.'

'After the blistering lecture you heaped on that dolt's head he won't be speaking your name again in this century, but you know full well denial only feeds gossip. But that is not the point. The point is that despite being furious at you for hiding the truth from me I am so proud of you I would have the words "I am married to the author of the *Desert Boy* books" embroidered on my dress.'

'For God's sake, Sam!'

'Well, I *am* burstingly proud. I always knew you were brilliant, but this is in a class of its own. I refuse to allow you to be ashamed of writing what anyone else would give his soul to the devil to create.'

'Hell, it feels like I have at the moment and he's about to exact payment.'

Sam fisted her hands in his coat and raised

herself on tiptoe, brushing a butterfly-wing kiss to his tense mouth.

'Brilliant, Edge. Magical. You make people happy. Revel in it.'

He groaned and hauled her against him, his mouth capturing hers in a kiss that coaxed out her soul all over again. For a long moment afterwards they stood in the dark, their breathing slowing, his hands moving gently on her back. The words in her heart hovered inside her, but she held back. Edge had enough on his mind at the moment. Finally he pressed a light kiss to her lips and stepped back.

'So you won't mind if I tell them you are the illustrator?'

Her heart hiccoughed and she laughed.

'I said I am proud of *your* work. I'm dreadfully embarrassed about mine. What a hypocrite I am.'

'So you are. You are lucky you are adorable. And talented.'

'But we needn't say anything about me. After all, no one knows…'

'True, but the fact remains that though you keep referring to them as my books, they are *our* creation. I refuse to stand there taking either all the credit or the blame. We shall face our fate together.'

Sam nodded, her throat too tight for words.

In the end it was so much easier than they anticipated. The moment Edge gave his name at the door Mr John Soane, a grey-haired man with a long face and dark, sleepy eyes, strode forward with evident pleasure as if there was nothing at all irregular in appearing uninvited at his soirée.

This was no small intimate evening and no regular town house. At least two dozen people were milling about a series of connecting rooms, talking, admiring and basking in the hundreds and hundreds of artefacts and works of art and architectural oddities that made this much more museum than home. Most congregated in a domed room which stood at a crossroads between entrance, drawing rooms and exhibition rooms. It was called the breakfast room, but had nothing to do with breakfast as far as Sam could see.

She saw and knew Edge did, too, the moment his name registered with the guests Mr Soane introduced them to—the shift from politeness to dazed realisation and then avid interest. At least on the surface Edge remained far calmer than she did once he introduced her and her role in the books. At first she turned as red as the wall hangings and mute as a landed fish, but then she realised she'd been right—even these stuffy scholars loved Edge's books.

Her own discomfort eased as she watched accredited scholars try to remain stoic while expressing their enjoyment of the books. Soon Edge was deep in a discussion with a group of antiquarians about his use of local mythologies and the interweaving of the new scholarship on Egyptian history and language. The more detailed the discussion became, the more Edge appeared to relax and once he even smiled at a comment by a distinguished-looking woman with greying hair and kind brown eyes comparing his High Priest Jephteh with Imhotep.

Half Sam's pleasure was watching Edge in his element. Here, surrounded by intelligent discussion and men and women who valued the same things he did, she remembered how he had been back in Egypt. Bab el-Nur and the Carmichaels' home in Cairo were often full of visiting antiquarians and scholars and she'd always envied Edge the ease with which people gravitated to him, despite or perhaps because of his reserve.

They would listen to him and wait upon his opinions and simply shine when he showed any sign of approbation. She thought it was because there was nothing feigned about his generosity— Edge always managed to pinpoint that achievement or characteristic which made a person stand out from the crowd.

She'd been convinced he'd done that for everyone but her, but of course she'd been wrong— he'd been protective but always appreciative of her drawing skills and he'd never belittled her intelligence. She'd wanted more, but that had been wholly her fault.

She still wanted more. She wanted Edge to trust

her, to want to share himself with her. To care for her. Far more than care…

It was too soon and too complicated to expect anything more from him. She would have to watch herself and her greediness. Step by step. First—help him find Rafe. Then, perhaps a house. A life in common…

She watched as he lowered his head towards the woman, still smiling as he listened. He could be so attentive when he wished, make you feel utterly visible. Utterly real. If they found a trace of Rafe here or not she was so glad they came. She wanted more of this for him—friends with shared interests, Edge relaxed and smiling and alive. Even if she could not give him everything he needed herself, she wanted to see him like this with others.

Mr Soane leaned towards her suddenly.

'Come, Lady Edward. There is something here I think a talented illustrator like yourself will appreciate. Do you mind if I steal your wife for a moment, Lord Edward?'

Edge's gaze caught hers, shifting immediately from his interest in the conversation to the protective awareness she'd never valued in the past. She smiled at him and followed Mr Soane into the exhibition rooms. She had barely time to absorb the dizzying abundance of artefacts on walls and stands when they entered a smaller room at the end which was filled floor to ceiling with prints and paintings. Her mouth fell open as Mr Soane unlatched a fastening on the wall to reveal a cupboard that opened like pages of a book, each one covered with dozens of framed prints.

'This…this is marvellous!'

'I didn't have room for them all, as you can see, but I could not bear not having them on display. A fine compromise, don't you think, Lady Edward?'

'A brilliant compromise. Oh, look at this one of the Parthenon…'

'Ah, if you like that, then you will appreciate the one of Meteora by the same artist…'

Sam utterly forgot her discomfort as Mr Soane shared his treasures with her. When he was called away by another guest she remained in the room, happily imagining one of her sketches, perhaps of the Citadel of Cairo or the temples of Karnak, gracing these walls.

'It is spectacular, isn't it?'

Sam turned at the voice. A pretty young woman in a pale lavender gown, her unfashionably short hair dressed even more simply than Sam's, stood in the doorway. 'You are Lady Edward Edgerton, are you not?'

Sam's nerves danced back into attendance and she wished Edge had come with her after all.

'Yes. I'm afraid you have the advantage of me, Miss…?'

'Miss Osbourne.'

Sam also wished she possessed Edge's ability

to keep his face an utter blank. She could feel her features vainly struggle not to reflect anything of what she was feeling. It was hopeless. The woman's intelligent hazel eyes were fixed on her and she gave a little nod that Sam felt did not bode well for Edge's plans to extract information from her about Rafe.

'Are you here because of me?'

'I beg your pardon?'

She sighed. 'I knew the moment I saw Lord Edward that he must be closely related to Mr Grey. He did mention a brother and if that is the nature of their relation I conclude he did not see fit to share his true name with me. But that is hardly the point. If you are here by coincidence, I apologise, but if you are here on my account, pray tell him to stop interfering. I do not need to be watched like a newborn lamb. He has done enough already.'

Sam fingered the latch on the fantastical cupboard and counted out her breath, registering facts. The woman's skin still had the warm colour of prolonged exposure to the sun and she looked to be Sam's age or little older.

'The Greybournes are a stubborn lot. They mean well, though,' Sam said.

'So I have noticed on both counts. Truly I am grateful for his help thus far, but there is nothing more to be done at this point. And if he is indeed that... Disappearing Duke everyone is gossiping about, clearly he has his own affairs to see to.'

A sour note entered her voice and her brows drew together and Sam gathered the soft-spoken Miss Osbourne had a temper. Good. Sam hoped Rafe had received a lashing from it. She very carefully stepped out on to the quivering ice.

'I find that Edge… Lord Edward has a fixation with seeing things through. Perhaps his brother suffers from the same weakness?'

Miss Osbourne snorted indelicately.

'That is putting it very mildly, but I made it clear to him I am not proceeding in my search. I am grateful for his help—I know I might not have succeeded in returning to England without him and I certainly would not have succeeded in convincing that unctuous Mr Pettifer to honour his debt to my father on my own. But I could have found a companion's position without his interference. Mrs Phillips might have agreed to employ me as a favour to Mr Soane, but she might very well yet decide to find someone who is not accosted on the streets at night by a giant with no manners and a dubious sense of humour. She almost saw him speak to me in the square the other day.'

Sam took another careful step.

'Are you quite certain there is nothing more to be done?'

'Since I believe my brother suffered the same fate as my father and I do not believe in the occult, then, yes, dead is dead.'

Miss Osbourne's gaze fell from hers for the

first time. She was fiddling with the cupboard's other latch and she set it swinging, like a little golden pendulum.

'Would you or your husband please try to impress upon him that there is nothing more to be done? Now Papa's debts are settled, any further digging into my brother's activities risks doing more harm than good. Now I had best return to Mrs Phillips before her argument with Mr Thorpe regarding the true nature of Medusa comes to blows.'

Sam searched for something, anything that might yet keep her, but it was Miss Osbourne who stopped at the doorway.

'I do hope he keeps out of trouble. He was very kind and helped me, though I was nothing but trouble for him. I hope to repay the favour some day, though I cannot see how.' She hesitated and rushed forward again. 'I dare say you will think it forward of me to say so, but I do hope you and Lord Edward are working on another book. I cannot tell you the pleasure they gave me while... Never mind. Thank you for listening to me, Lady Edward.'

Sam resisted the urge to stop her and went to find Edge instead.

'What did Miss Osbourne tell you?'

Sam gave a squeak of alarm, her hand fisting against her chest as Edge spoke behind her.

'Edge! How on earth does someone your size tread so stealthily?'

'I don't. You were lost in thought. That was Miss Osbourne, wasn't it? I heard you talking and decided not to interfere.'

'Very clever of you. Yes, she—'

'Not here. Come with me.'

Just outside the room he led her up a spiral stone stairway with barely enough room to accommodate his shoulders. On the upper floor she stopped short at the sight of a full-size statue of a man with his arms outstretched, draped in nothing more than a robe and a clearly contrived fig leaf drawing attention to, rather than distracting from, his nether regions.

Edge glanced back at her, frowning as he saw what she was staring at.

'Stop gawking at Apollo. Over here.'

'I will gawk if I want to. I am merely comparing points of interest. He doesn't look as strong as you and you are far more handsome and larger... but he is passable.'

Edge took her arm, his frown fading and more than just a shade of smugness about his mouth. Once past the statue Sam gave a gasp of delight as they looked down into the open space of the Sepulchral Chamber below. It was even more impressive from above, though the sheer number of statues, urns and architectural elements was dizzying, allowing the eye no rest. Above them was another domed skylight and she leaned on the railing, looking up into the night sky. Except it wasn't the sky—the indigo velvet of night and the golden stars were just reflections of the candles along the walls, an illusion of openness.

'Careful.' Edge moved towards her swiftly, his hand resting on hers, warm and firm. 'I don't know how sturdy the railing is.'

'It *would* be embarrassing if I landed in a heap in the middle of all the antiquities, wouldn't it?'

'It would be...memorable. Come along.'

'Do you know where you are going?'

'I think so. He said it was directly above...ah.'

The buzz of voices from below muted as he closed the door behind them. This room wasn't crammed with statues, but with temples. A central structure supported dozens of models of Greek and Roman temples in wood or plaster or stone. The walls were covered in glass-fronted bookcases and even the windows were decorated with odd-shaped panes reflecting the quivering gold of the candles and for a moment Sam was flung back to that night in the desert, standing on her rock with Edge beside her.

God, she wanted to be back there, with him.

Edge remained just inside the doorway, watching her.

'Well? What did she say about Rafe?'

Of course. Rafe was all that mattered.

She repeated Miss Osbourne's words as best she could and watched him assimilate them.

'So they were searching for her brother. Interesting. Anything else?'

'No. I don't believe she was lying about not knowing anything about Rafe's whereabouts. She is quite nice. I like her.'

He gave a little snort of derision, as if liking someone was a ludicrous proposition at this juncture.

'No one else here appears to know anything about Rafe. They are naturally curious about the Disappearing Duke, but no one showed the slightest sign of guile when his name arose. As for Miss Osbourne, I can easily see Rafe offering his assistance if she found herself separated from her rather eccentric relations in Egypt. But if what you said is correct, whatever Miss Osbourne's connection with Rafe, it might now be over.'

He went to the window, tracing a rounded pane of glass with this finger. She stood beside him and traced the other rounded pane, stopping when she realised she was copying him. Not that he noticed.

'At least you know he is alive and well. Perhaps you should trust him about the rest. It sounds like he has never failed you yet.'

'I am not worried about him failing me. I merely wish…' His lips compressed further.

'Stop being so Edge-ish and keeping everything inside. What do you wish?'

He turned his head and smiled, but it lasted only a moment, slowly fading away as his eyes settled on hers. The room shrank to the size of those miniatures, her skin tight and tingling, she could even feel her breasts firming, readying. Her lips parted because there wasn't enough air. How did this happen so quickly? Each time it struck faster, harder. If it became any more acute she would start melting in the middle of the street if he merely took her arm.

'We should leave.' His voice was rough, or the pulse thudding in her ears made it sound so.

Yes, she wanted to say. Yes, we should leave and go into that tiny copse in the cold night air and you will pull up my skirt, your warm, rough and soft hands on my thighs. His hands pressed on her cheeks now, his fingers hard against her temples and cheekbone.

'Sam. You can't look at me like that and...'

'And what?'

'God, this isn't the place. Outside in the square wasn't the place, the blasted Pettifer hall of horrors wasn't the place. What the devil is wrong with me?'

'I am, evidently.' She tried to make light of it, but though his grip slackened, his fingertips moving gently along the curve of her cheek, the heat in his eyes was still mostly angry. She licked her lips and with something between a growl and a groan he turned away, wandering from miniature to miniature as he moved safely behind his battlement again. Eventually he stopped, picking up a statue of a horse and balancing it in his palm.

'Rafe gave Jacob a horse just like this. He told me it was in recompense for the one he took from my room after I was sent to Egypt with Poppy. Guilt is a strange beast.'

Sam reached for the opening he offered.

'You and Rafe became close after your marriage?'

'Very. He said we were very close before I was sent away, but I can't remember. When he returned from school that year and was told I was gone he was furious with me, as if I'd left him behind on purpose. In his mind I was living his explorer's dream while he remained trapped in a life of prohibitions and punishments. It took him years to realise I had had no say in the matter. We both presumed the other was the lucky one. When he paid a duty call at Chesham after Jacob was born we were both prepared to thoroughly dislike each other, but it was as if we'd never been apart. In the end he stayed most of the next two years with us.'

'Does he know why you were sent away?'

He shook his head, still focused on the horse.

'No. He said no one spoke of it, or of anything much at Greybourne for that matter. Absurd that we both envied the other, isn't it?'

She slipped her hand into his. 'I never would have given my child away, no matter what.' She flushed a little at the childishness of her words, waiting for him to toss them out with the rest of her gestures, but after a moment of stillness his fingers threaded through hers, slowly rubbing the back of her hand. Then he raised her hand, brushing his mouth along the base of her palm.

'I know you wouldn't. You are like...' He dropped her hand immediately as if he'd been stung and she glanced at the doorway, thinking he'd heard someone approach, but there was nothing.

'What is it?'

'Nothing. Nothing. Time to leave.'

The transition from the sparkling clutter of Mr Soane's house to the dark silence of the square was disorienting. Sam held her cloak about her and shivered though it was not cold. Edge was a dark monolith moving by her side, his profile silvered by the gas lamps lining the road.

'That went better than expected, no?'

He laughed, a warm sound in the darkness.

'Is that your version of *I told you so*?'

'No. I'm merely glad. Edge... I noticed you evaded their questions about whether you plan to write another book...'

Her own question trailed away and he stopped.

'I evaded their questions because it was none of their concern. It is yours. If you wished to know, why didn't you ask me?'

'Of course I wish to know. How could I not?'

'Then why not ask?'

'I am scared.' She tried to laugh, but it sounded like a crow's croak. He touched her cheek.

'Of what, Sam?'

'I told you. There are three things that matter in my world and you are now at the centre of two of them. I've lived with uncertainty all my life, but somehow I hoped my mythical Mr Bunny would always need my little contributions to his world. But I can no longer play that game. I've lost a...a crutch and I'm afraid to reach for another because it may not be there.'

She rushed the words out before the gates of her good sense closed.

'Sam. Even if I did not write another word—which I hope is not the case because I seem to need to write—your talent is undisputed. On the strength of those books alone you could secure enough commissions to keep you busy until you are a hundred. I kept expecting to hear from Durham you'd been tempted away by another author. As for me, I can no longer imagine my worlds without your images. I feed off them. From the first book you made Gabriel and Leila's worlds more real to me than my own words. I wrote the second book imagining which parts would come to life for you, trying to see what you would, and if I didn't feel there was anything there to give you, that part withered and died. I'm not certain

I can enter Gabriel and Leila's world without your drawings any longer.'

He took off his gloves, cupping her face in the warmth of his palms.

'I wrote the first chapter watching Jacob sleep,' he continued. 'He was all of three months old, but he would fall asleep staring at the drawing you sent with your mother's letter congratulating me on his birth. Do you remember it?'

She nodded. Of course she did. That drawing had cost her. The news of Jacob's birth had been an even worse agony than Edge's marriage. Only a horrible person would wish a child unborn. But while the wounded core of her crawled deeper, the part of her that cared for Edge beyond herself and wanted him to be happy drew a kitten seated on a stoic camel as they made their way through the desert.

'He liked it?'

'He loved it. He would babble at it long before he babbled at me. So I told him a story about two friends lost in the desert trying to find their homes and Rafe told me I should write it down for Jacob so I did. Then I couldn't stop and by the time it was done it was a book. Rafe convinced me to send it to a publisher for Jacob's sake. By that point Jacob had been ill and I knew his life would be marked by suffering. I wanted the book to be a gift for him, for him to know he'd inspired them. I wrote it for him, but I wrote it with your vivid world in my mind. I didn't ask Durham to contact you because I was being kind, I did it because it was the most natural thing in the world, however hard it was knowing… I felt it best you did not know I was the author.' His hands stilled, withdrew, like a flower furling as night fell.

'Thank you, Edge.' Her voice sounded as though she'd crushed it into the gravel path. She wanted to wrap herself around his words, capture them like fireflies in a glass jar so she could warm herself by their light when she was alone.

'You have nothing to thank me for. Quite the opposite.' He was back to Edge now, the vivid music of his words leached away. He was nervous, she realised. As afraid as she by this strange bond that was connected yet separate from their marriage. She touched her fingers to his chest.

'I'm glad it's you. Frightened but glad. I don't want to ruin it. For either of us.'

His chest rose and fell, her fingers with it.

'Well, that's both of us, then. I still wish other people didn't know. It would be nice to find a house away from…people. I didn't tell you, but one of the guests in there told me his wife is hoping their next child is a boy so they can name him Gabriel. I could do without any more such confidences.'

She laughed, moving closer. 'Poor Edge. I shall have to build you a castle with a moat and fend off the hordes.'

'If you bellow at them from the battlements as you did from the Howling Cliffs, I doubt they will make any effort to invade.'

'You see? My madcap ways may prove useful after all.'

'Yes.' His hands slid under her cloak, over her waist and hips and down over her behind, holding her as he stepped in and shaped her against him. His breathing changed. 'We need to find this castle soon. I'm tired of chasing Rafe.'

'You don't really mean that.'

'I needed to know he is alive and Miss Osbourne's words prove he is obviously well. He must know I'm worried and if he can't be bothered to send me word then devil take him. I have more pressing matters to see to.'

Since one of them was pressing against her right then Sam found it hard to think, let alone object, but she knew Edge.

'Tomorrow you will change your mind. I know you cannot let it go without at least trying that advertisement in *The Times*.'

'Tomorrow. Come, let's find the carriage. I need to warm you before we reach the bedroom.'

'We could warm up in a nice hot bath.'

'I will reach a boil before the water does. You are a very bad influence on me, Sam.'

Chapter Fifteen

Sobek wrapped his thick tail about Gabriel's legs, scales rasping against his skin. 'Two kinds of people cross this river. Those searching for something and those escaping something. Which one are you, Servant of the Sprite Queen?'

—*Temple of the River God,*
Desert Boy Book Two

The cool air wrapped about his naked body as he let the curtain fall back and Sam snuggled deeper under the covers, as if even in sleep she could feel the cold skittering over his skin.

For someone with such an impetuous streak she was far too attuned to others. Or perhaps it was just to a few. She had a disconcerting knack of seeing where he was going and cutting around him, like a *djinn* popping up in front of him when he least expected her. Like Leila the sprite—always a little ahead of Gabriel, always prepared to sacrifice more, do more for those under her care.

He believed Sam—she would beat off the hordes if she thought they threatened him. That should be *his* role. It *was* his role, but he couldn't deny he liked the image of her as his warrior queen.

He'd told her part of the truth, but not all of it. It wasn't only her illustrations that inspired him.

How had he not realised Leila was a portrait of her? Loyal and impetuous, passionate but private. She brought out the best and worst in Gabriel, who plodded along trying to do what was right, sometimes in the worst possible way.

This was a perfect example of that—he hadn't only lusted after her for eight years, he'd written about her, and it wasn't until she'd forced his hand that he'd realised it.

Like Gabriel, the only time he shone was when he was focused on Leila—the real and the fictional.

He came to stand by the bed and again she did that little sigh and snuggle, her fingers sliding under his pillow with a hiss that travelled over his skin. Even in sleep she refused to stay on her side, she had to keep invading, testing, pushing and prodding... And giving.

He breathed in and out, trying to will his body into quiescence, but it was useless. He wanted her with an ache that had nothing to do with sexual gratification. He wanted to be inside her not so he could climax but so he could be as close as life and physics permitted.

So they could be parts of the same story.

He should have looked for her eons ago. He should have been a man and admitted to Dora it was a mistake eight years ago when he returned to London and realised he had proposed to her for all the wrong reasons…except then he would not have had those years with Jacob and no matter how horrible losing him was, it felt infinitely worse thinking he might never had had him. He could never wish away that gift.

He sat on the side of the bed and her eyelids fluttered, her fingers withdrawing from under the pillow. He moved his thigh until they rested against it. Foolish things like this. This was what he wanted. Little raindrops of joy, one by one, gathering into a mighty ocean.

I will never let you go, Sam. Ever.

He could almost hear the words, shoving through him like spikes. Ripping and shredding as they went until they pierced so deep inside a viscous heat began spilling from his core.

'You're mine,' he whispered and her lips moved again, an echo without sound, but she didn't wake. He slipped under the cover, her legs and hips warm and soft against his chilled skin. That woke her, the remnants of the firelight turning her eyes a deep endless grey.

'Why are you so cold?'

'I was thinking,' he answered and her mouth curved.

'Night's for dreams, not thinking,' she murmured, her eyelids fluttering closed again. She wrapped her arm around his torso, snuggling against him.

It felt so good. So *right*. So utterly foreign and right.

She was right, night was for dreams, not thinking—and for now he could dream she was utterly his and wanted him wholly for himself and that is how the world would always be. His Leila.

'Leila.'

Leila.

That single word pushed back the pleasant warmth flowing between their bodies. She'd been sleepily revelling in the perfect fit of her body against his, the velvet-soft skin over hard surfaces. But that word shook her and she didn't know why. She raised herself on her elbow to try to make out his features in the darkness. He'd unplaited her hair and it flowed over her shoulder on to his chest like a pool of dark blood. She tried to push it back, but his hand tangled in it, holding her there.

'I like it on me. I feel I'm drowning in you.'

'That doesn't sound good.'

'It's heaven.'

It looked like Edge, and sounded and felt and

smelt like Edge, but this could not be Edge. Even in the stuttering of the embers she could still make out his expression—he was always different when they made love, but this was different still. He looked…mesmerised. His hand was toying with her hair and his eyes with her face, moving over it as if he'd seen her for the first time.

'Edge, have you been drinking?'

He shook his head.

'Thinking.'

'About?'

'Leila.'

Oh. So that was what inspiration looked like. He was probably far away and any moment now he would be out of bed, searching for pen and paper. A small sigh of disappointment escaped her before she could call it back.

'You always were a fierce little warrior.' His fingers were as soft as the words as they skimmed her lower lip. 'God, what a fool I am.'

'You're not a fool,' she said instinctively, a little crossly, because she didn't quite understand what he meant. He smiled, the mesmerised look replaced by laughter.

'You can't help defending me, even when you don't know from what.'

'Defend first, reason later, that is my motto.' She smiled back. He looked so beautiful, leaning against the pillows in the dark. 'Are you glad you accepted my proposal?' she blurted out.

His fingers threaded through her hair, tucking it behind her ear and coming back to cup her face. It was like the way he'd touched her in the darkened square, but different. She had no idea what to make of all this.

'I was just congratulating myself on my good sense.' His hands tightened, his smile faltering. She almost cried out her objection—don't go away yet. Stay with me.

'Are *you* glad I accepted your proposal?' His voice was turning tentative, losing its dreamy warmth. 'I know these weeks haven't been easy. *I* haven't been easy...'

'Yes, yes, I am... I think proposing to you is quite the smartest thing I have done.'

He wrapped his arms around her and she sank into them. Not that it was easy to sink into rock, even warm rock. He was so tense. She kneaded the arm closest to her and it softened just a little. She breathed him in, deep, so deep a whole world came to life in her mind—that forest cocooning her, the wood warmed by the sun, and him all around her, as though she'd come to live inside him. Safe, alive, happy.

Home.

Edge.

In her mind her arms opened wide because the truth was too enormous to hold.

I love you, Edge. Love you. I always have. You were always mine and never were.

She lost the image, surfacing because her eyes and face were burning with knowledge and hurt.

'Sam?' The whisper fluttered the hair at her temple and she shook her head, burrowing against him. His arms softened as they gathered her closer, his breath warm against her hair, his hand caressing her back in that way that made her want to purr.

It should be enough, she told herself. *This. He* does *care*. Maybe not the way she wanted him to, but perhaps as much as he can right now. Maybe with time it would grow. Or not.

She *needed* it to grow.

She touched her mouth to the soft skin below his ear, letting the words swirl inside her, but keeping them close so they didn't escape. Patience. She needed patience. It was little more than a month and a half since he'd scared the devil out of her on the Howling Cliffs and already he'd changed…no, not changed, just opened the door for her a little, each time a little more.

Patience.

'It feels like you are about to grab someone by the throat and throttle them, Sam. Out with it.'

'I'm happy.'

He tensed, his hand stilling between her shoulder blades, and she closed her eyes and teeth tight. She'd hoped that was mild enough, but evidently it was still too much.

His hand resumed the slow sweep downwards,

just feathering over her bottom, his leg shifting to bring her closer.

'Good. That *is* good, isn't it?'

'Yes. Very good. And that is very good, too. Don't stop.'

'Do you like it?' Edge's words bounced off the uncarpeted floor and empty walls, amplifying the worry in his voice.

Sam stood in the open garden doors, her hands clasped to her chest, looking across the sloping lawn to the willow trees scratching the green water with their spiky hair. The full view of the river was blocked by an elongated tree-covered island, shielding them from the world. This green cocoon was only broken by a blue rowboat with a yellow rim attached to a wooden jetty and a great shade tree with branches that rose out of each other like a drunk candelabra standing in the middle of the lawn. She imagined them sitting beneath it in the golden light of late afternoon; reaching out to touch him.

Their home.

She was in love. Again.

'I… Edge… This is… Oh.'

'If you can't find words, I assume you like it.'

'I shan't move from here. I shall hold the fort and ward off all other potential purchasers while you battle with the lawyers. Just leave me a sword.

Oh, I wish I had Inky with me. She could be my dragon.'

'I'll be your dragon,' Edge growled, wrapping his arms around her and she leaned into their warmth, their strength. For the past hour they'd behaved like utterly civilised man and wife, but with each room they'd entered and stair they climbed she'd imagined him as anything but civilised—in her mind he'd touched her, pressed her against the wall, his mouth warm and insistent on hers, on her neck, under her clothes… Making this house theirs, utterly theirs…

He could not know what she was thinking, but his hands tightened around her and she could feel that quivering tension, like a drawn bowstring, that came before he unravelled her.

'As long as you like it.'

'I *love* it. I feel…this is foolish…'

'Tell me.'

'I feel I belong here. I didn't feel that in any of the other houses we saw. Not even in any of the houses I've lived in over the years. It feels *right*. Our own little island.'

His mouth brushed lightly over her temple and rested briefly on her cheekbone before he straightened again.

'You wanted a moat. The river will have to do. That toy boat can be our armada though I doubt it can hold my weight.'

'We will name it Sobek after the crocodile god and chase off invaders from the water.'

'Excellent idea. You can paint a toothy grin on it.'

'No, that will frighten the children...'

His hands stuttered on her, dropped to her abdomen for a second and then withdrew abruptly. Sam closed her eyes and cursed herself. When would she learn to think before she spoke? She needed to have the word 'patience' stitched on to her pillow so she could memorise it morning and night.

His hands returned, settling on her hips, but the moment was gone.

'I'll tell Mr Grafton we will be relieving him of this property. Wait for me in the carriage.'

Sam settled in the carriage, cursing herself and him.

One word. One simple word and a world of meaning.

You knew *I wanted a family*, she wanted to rail at him. *I told you when I proposed, you said you wished for one as well. Why must any mention of it send you running for the hills?*

The words rumbled inside her head, but for once came nowhere near her mouth. Every tumble off a cliff was a lesson in staying away from the edge. She smiled a little sourly at how aptly she'd named him all those years ago. He was her boundary line and now controlled both sides of it.

The carriage door opened and Edge came to sit beside her.

'It's done, Sam. Congratulations on our new home.' His voice was so suspiciously bland she wondered if he'd rehearsed that line. Well, she knew how to knock a few bricks from his walls.

'I know which room I want for my drawing,' she challenged and he turned from his contemplation of the passing countryside.

'Hmm. It is probably the one I wanted for my writing.'

'If it is, I shall fight you for it.'

'You will likely win. I had best concede in advance.'

'No need. You want the one on the corner, with the view of the river, correct?'

'That isn't the one you wanted?'

'No, that is perfect for you. Mine is next to the drawing room, facing south.'

'Are you only saying that to please me?'

'Is that likely?'

He smiled.

'You might, but I don't think you are. Why did you and your husband have no children?'

Her skin blazed and she stared at him, almost certain she'd misheard. He looked calm and only mildly interested, not at all like someone who'd shoved her off the cliff more effectively than she ever tossed herself off one.

'If you don't wish to answer, you needn't.' He looked away. 'I didn't mean to pry.'

'You aren't…that is…the truth is… Oh.' She breathed in, gathering herself for the truth. 'Ricki and I were not…intimate for long. A few months only.'

'But…you were married for four years.'

'Yes, but we lived together for less than a year. Less even than you and Dora.'

'I don't understand.'

'It is a long story.'

'Was he not capable…was he wounded?'

'No, not in body. I did wound him, though. I was young and so, so stupid.'

'There was another man.' Edge's voice was as cold as only he could make it. It sent cracks along her skin like veins forming in the ice. Any moment now the truth would spill out and she still had not the faintest clue what Edge would do with it. And that terrified her.

'Yes.'

The silence went on and on and she still didn't know if it was right to tell him. She only knew she was terrified she might chase him away.

'You were young,' he said finally. 'Impetuous. Was that why you left him? For another man?'

'No, I left him because he killed his daughter, but it was my fault.'

'What?'

She held out her hands and they were shaking. Edge shook his head, the fury replaced by shock.

'I don't believe that. Sam, I know you—you would never ever…' He touched her face, his fingers sliding down a trail of tears. She was crying and hadn't even realised. 'Tell me what happened. Whatever it was, I know you. You would not wilfully hurt anyone, Sam.'

She grabbed his hand. Maybe if she held on hard enough his certainty would counter her guilt.

'Not wilfully, but because I was wilful. I never, ever should have married him, but I was so *lonely*.' The words shook out of her. 'It's no excuse, but it is the truth. That year… I have never felt so alone.'

He put his arm around her, very gently, even though her fingers were digging into his hand. Her body shook against the length of his arm, the words rising out of her like bubbles in water.

'I *meant* to care for him. But I was never a good actress and when it became…intimate I couldn't lie. I began hating it and he would become angry and I didn't know what to do.'

'He hurt you.' His arm stiffened, his body going from cocooning to looming. She shook her head. She wanted cocooning back, she needed it.

'No, not like that. In every other way, though. He was jealous of the other men I had…flirted with, though I told him he had no reason to be.

When he asked me directly why I married him I did the worst thing ever. I told him the truth.'

'What was the truth?'

She closed her eyes, blocking out even the sight of his chest. She'd accused Edge of lying by omission about the books and she was about to do the same, but it could not be helped.

'That I did not love him, that I married him because I wanted a family, a home.'

Edge flinched as if she'd jabbed him with a pin. Ricki had done the same.

'Did you tell him…about the other man?'

'I told him everything, it spilled out of me and I could not stop. I was *horrible*, Edge, but he paid me back. From that moment he brought courtesans to the palazzo, telling me they were real women and I was nothing but a stupid child, which I was. When that didn't work he brought Maria.'

'The little girl you told me about? His daughter?'

Sam nodded. 'She was barely three. She wasn't pretty—she looked like a little owl with enormous dark eyes and cheeks that were always a patchy red, but she had a smile that could…melt you. He moved her into the palazzo and said that I would never have a child of my own until I told him I loved him and meant it.'

'That is ludicrous. Cruel.'

'It was sad and pointless. He was often out with

his friends and I spent all my time with Maria which only made him more jealous. She even slept in my room, but one night I woke and she was gone and I heard Ricki shouting beneath my window. He was in the gondola. Drunk. Holding her in the air and telling me to come get her if I wanted her. By the time I reached the jetty people were shouting and I realised something was terribly wrong. He tried to tell me later he hadn't meant to drop her, that she'd wriggled out of his arms. I jumped into the water and so did a few others, but we couldn't find her. They dragged me out in the end, but I don't remember. I left Venice as soon as I recovered. Ricki drowned three years later when he fell off a bridge during *Carnevale*.'

The silence this time was different. Halfway through her tale he'd pulled her on to his lap, his hands moving soothingly on her arms, his breath warm against her hair. But she could feel the distance between them. Edge was with her but far away, watching her battle from his moated castle.

'Did you go to…the other?'

She shivered, the words piercing her like a rapier.

'No, I returned to live with my mother until she died and then I went to Sinclair Hall. But there was never a question of that. He was married and did not love me. It was all my own foolishness. I told Ricki that, but it made no odds.'

314   *The Lord's Inconvenient Vow*

He breathed in very slowly and even more slowly out, as if consciously arranging his words.

'The pain of discovering you are second best doesn't fade because the other party isn't interested in being first. It is a pain that is wholly personal.'

The sting of his thrust was all the sharper because she could hear the echoes of his own pain. He might love Rafe, but the almost-lifelong belief his brother was better loved and valued would never be uprooted by facts.

'I meant to make him happy. I truly thought I could.'

'I'm sorry, Sam.'

'I don't deserve your compassion. Maria—'

'Yes, you do,' he interrupted. 'We all make mistakes, some of them terrible, but you loved that girl and I don't doubt she felt it. You aren't responsible for everything, Sam. You can't *fix* everything. You Sinclairs are always trying to arrange the world. It must be exhausting.'

She hiccupped back the tangle of tears burning in her throat.

'You are the one who is chasing Rafe like he is the holy grail.'

'True. Sometimes I don't understand it myself except that when I was at the ebb point in my life he stood by me and dragged me out of my pit. For a long time he was the mirror reminding me I still existed. There was nothing else. When I received the letter he was dead… I need to hear he is well from his own lips. I need to know I tried everything to protect him if he needs it. We may not have grown up together, but we both are shaped by the same forces. He is part of me. Still, if the advertisement doesn't elicit a response in a week, I'll concede defeat and wait until he deigns to remember he has a brother who is worried for him.'

His face was still stern, but there was also sadness in his eyes and it deepened hers. If she could only make him happy. Right now that felt impossible—she was not enough. She might never be enough.

He touched the tip of his finger to the aching spot between her brows.

'Don't look so worried. I know my limits. I see I shall have to help you brush the sand dunes off yours.'

Sam tucked herself into his shoulder, leaking slowly into his coat while he held her.

Edge watched London form around them. She'd stopped crying, but remained in his arms and for once the lust that buzzed every time he touched her wasn't there. No, it *was* there, but held at bay by a wall of ice. He could feel the cold creeping through him, dousing candle after candle.

Finally, he was beginning to understand what had happened to madcap Sam—her loneliness and need and the almost desperate act of her proposal.

He must have been a fool to believe it was only because she wanted a home to atone for the one she'd never truly had. That restless, vivid soul of hers was twisting and turning, trying to fill the pit created by her one-sided love for some Venetian fool. She'd spoken of her love for that other man with an intensity and fatalism that didn't sound like a love long faded—it sounded alive, with hooks deep in her flesh. She'd turned to her first husband to fill that pit, then to Maria. And now to him.

He could feel the ice spreading again, just like it had after Jacob's death. But then he'd been numb and had hardly felt it until much later. Now it ripped and stung as it crept through him, like frost crawling over buds and destroying them.

He was tempted to send her to the devil. To give her this house and bid her joy of it. To leave her in the same limbo she was shoving him into. It was contemptible, but he could understand Ricki. Not his actions, but his anger, the need to wound... He wouldn't do any of that. To walk away was simply not an option. He knew all about living with disappointment, but at least this time there would be the consolation of having Sam in his life and his bed even if he could not be in her heart.

He closed his eyes, tight, waiting out the sharpness of the pain. He very much hoped this was the beginning of a megrim, but it felt deeper than that. It felt as though he was breaking.

Chapter Sixteen

Jephteh's smile was a crescent moon in the darkness of the tomb. Gabriel could smell his smugness—it reeked of mouldy papyrus and river sludge.

'Being noble is a bitter brew, is it not, boy?' the Priest cackled as he raised his staff for the blow.

—*Lost in the Valley of the Moon,*
Desert Boy Book Three

Edge tossed *The Times* on to the breakfast table with disgust.

'It has only been three days.' Sam felt as though she was watching a tiger pacing its cage—the beast might be confined, but the sense of peril leaked through the bars.

'I know that,' Edge snapped and then changed the subject with obvious effort. 'I must meet with the lawyers this morning, but afterwards we may go to Richmond if you wish. The furniture is arriving today.'

His voice was utterly flat, even that momentary sign of impatience called back. For the past few days this had been their pattern. Every morning he'd glanced at the advertisements, his mouth a straight line, and then put it aside and set about the business of preparing their new home with a single-minded concentration that pushed everything else out of the way, including her.

No, that wasn't true.

At night in the shared darkness of their bedroom they were still close. At least their bodies were. It was almost a race—every night they honed their skill at making the other moan and beg before joining in release. Every morning he made a conscious effort to be attentive and to anticipate her wishes about the house. But the chasm between them grew.

Since she'd told him the truth about Ricki and Maria a fragile layer of tenderness she'd come to depend on had been packed away and she didn't understand why. She didn't know whether it was because of what she'd told him about using Ricki to escape her broken heart or about her role in Maria's death.

She'd been quite certain he would realise he had been the 'other man', but Edge seemed to have no vanity where she was concerned. She wondered if it would be better or worse to confess it all—that she had been in love with him eight years ago and though she'd not fully admitted it to herself, she'd only proposed in Bahariya because she'd never recovered from that heartbreak. Because she'd hoped he would come to love her as well.

She wanted so badly to tell him, spit it all out and have him judge her or condemn her on this truth, but she was terrified and didn't even understand why. Every new admission felt as though it drove this wedge deeper between them. She was sinking back into timid, tame Sam and she hated it, resented him and despised herself.

Patience.

She kept repeating that one word. Patience. This is Edge. Give him time, give him space and hope he will reward you by sharing his concerns once he has worked them through.

Patience.

She had no patience, none. Only fear that what had barely begun was dying and there was nothing she could do.

She looked across the table at her husband and wished she was brave enough to demand the truth and face it.

Instead she folded the newspaper. 'Are you placing another advertisement tomorrow?' she asked.

'Yes. Though there is hardly any point—no

doubt he's guessed it is I, blast him. I hate that he is one step ahead of me at all times.'

'Only one?' With an almost conscious act of will she tried to recapture some of the teasing that had existed so easily between them.

'You aren't helping, Sam.' He looked so disgruntled she had an almost overpowering urge to walk around the table and hug him. But disgruntled was better than cold so she poured fresh coffee into his cup and continued.

'Fuming won't help either, Edge. You used to be such a calm, staid fellow, Bunny. What happened to you?'

'*You* happened to me. And kindly stop calling me by that ridiculous name.'

'I *like* Edge. It is very…edgy—all sharp angles you can cut yourself on if you're not careful.'

'I didn't mean that, I meant… You *know* which name I meant. It is demeaning.'

'No, it isn't, it is adorable. And perfect. You are Edge on the outside but inside there is that little fluffy, darling Bunny…'

'Oh, for heaven's sake,' Edge pushed away his coffee, but his gaze moved over her with that shade of tenderness she missed, his mouth softening. It was such a small thing, but her heart felt like it was bleeding with relief. She reached across the table.

'Edge, I—'

The door opened abruptly and Tubbs entered.

'A gentleman to see you, my lord. He goes by the name of Mr Grey.'

Edge was out the door before the name even registered on Sam.

'Tubbs? Is it him?'

'Unless I am very much mistaken, it is, Miss Sam. In a rather disreputable state. I shall go prepare a bath, I think.'

Edge had seen his brother in various states over the years, but rarely so unkempt. He wore a grimy serge coat and was half-seated, half-prone on a *chaise longue*, the beginnings of a beard only partially covering the scars along his jaw.

'Good God, Rafe. You look like hell. Are you ill?'

Rafe's laugh ended on a wince.

'Always blunt, Edge. No, I had a little altercation with a cutpurse and his cronies. My mistake, I wasn't paying attention and one of them stabbed me in the leg. I'm too old for this nonsense.'

'Do you think so?' Edge held himself firmly against the need to drag his brother into an embrace. The relief was so overpowering he wanted to break something. He wanted Sam here with him. He pushed that thought away just as he'd pushed away most of this thoughts about Sam these past few days.

Rafe. Concentrate on Rafe.

'You need a doctor.'

Rafe sighed and nodded.

'I hoped to get by without a blasted surgeon, but that was probably optimistic.'

Tubbs appeared promptly at Edge's summons, glancing past him towards the newcomer.

'We will need a doctor, Tubbs…'

'I know just the one. What shall I tell Miss Sam? She is worried.'

Edge rubbed his hand over his knuckles.

'Ask her to wait.'

'Not your run-of-the-mill servant,' Rafe commented when the door closed behind Tubbs. 'I've heard the Sinclairs have their little battalion of efficient minions.'

'Yes. And knowing him that doctor will be here in moments so I suggest you take that time to explain why you have put me through hell these past months. I thought you were dead, Rafe.'

'Don't look like that, Edge. Damn this leg. I knew it would take something drastic to drag you back into the land of the living. Every time I told you to return to Egypt you told me to jump off a cliff. So I did, figuratively. A contact of mine forged that letter from the embassy. I knew you might not believe it, but you couldn't ignore it. I planned to leave clues along the way and wait for you in Luxor and have you finally show me this precious Egypt of yours.'

'You amaze me. So what happened to that charming little plan?'

Rafe shifted his leg with both hands and wiped his forehead.

'I came across someone who'd become separated from her family in a very inhospitable corner of the world.'

'Miss Osbourne.'

Rafe looked up with a grimace.

'I was wondering about that advertisement. I knew it wasn't that unctuous little worm Pettifer. How did you figure it out, by the way?'

'We had some help. But what has that to do with being stabbed?'

'That was purely my foolishness. I thought I had a lead on finding her brother.'

'Brothers appear to be disappearing at an alarming rate recently.'

'As amusing as ever, I see. I never really disappeared. I always knew where I was.'

'As *annoying* as ever, I see. You do realise you are now Duke of Greybourne and have been back in England for almost a month and have not yet even contacted the lawyers let alone the brother who you led to believe was now about to assume your title?'

'I planned to do so once I resolved this little issue. Unfortunately, I'm afraid I shall have to admit defeat. If Dashford Osbourne is alive, he is likely long gone from England. And I made sure that fellow you paid to look out for me in Cairo followed me to Alexandria so you would know I was alive and well and on my way to England.'

'I would have appreciated a note to that effect. The fact that you disappeared again once you disembarked was not precisely encouraging.'

'Yes, well, I was distracted. I needed to arrange some matters.'

'Yes, meeting with fraudsters and convincing them to pay debts they'd never considered paying and then securing a companion's position for Miss Osbourne while making her think she'd done it herself. I can see why your only brother's peace of mind would rank below those.'

Rafe grinned. He was sweating now, his cheeks sallow beneath the ragged beard, and Edge knew he should pull back at his anger, but it was like trying to hold a team of four frightened, bolting horses. He set to pacing the room instead, following the geometric design of the rug.

'I'm sorry, Edge. If it's any consolation, you dealt me quite a shock when I heard you had somehow managed to marry your Sam while chasing me down. Good for you. I don't know quite how, but I feel I ought to receive some credit.'

Edge continued his pacing. There was too much to say and too much he didn't even understand himself... No, he understood it, he just didn't want to.

'That is good, isn't it, Edge?' Rafe's voice shifted into uncertainty. 'I mean, you've wanted her for ever, as far as I could tell. We've never talked about it but, devil take it, man, I would have had to be blind and dumb not to realise how important she was to you. The only times I've ever seen you light up were around Jacob or when you received the drawings she made for your books. And when I came to haul you out of Chesham after the funeral you were quite voluble about—'

'I was drunk,' Edge snapped, not stopping. Trust Rafe to throw every weakness and tragedy in his face in a couple of sentences.

'*In vino veritas*, as they say. When I heard she was widowed as well I thought…if Edge had an ounce of sense he'd go see the lay of the land. But, no, he stays stuck in Brazil like a barnacle. So I decided to scrape you off and see what happened. You can only write love letters so long, brother mine.'

'I've never written a love letter in my life.'

'No? I've read four of them so far and so have thousands of other adoring readers. Damn long ones, too, but at least there's some adventure and excitement and history along the way while we all wait for Gabriel and Leila to come to their senses. That's why this last book has everyone swooning, from what I hear. I've been damn busy these past few weeks, but even I've heard the raving. I mean everyone has been waiting for Gabriel and Leila to admit they are batty about each other. I managed to leaf through someone else's copy and

those last lines, on the cliff? *It was only ever you.*
Damn romantic. No wonder Sam agreed to marry
you. She finally discovered the romantic pudding
under that dour exterior.'

Edge shook his head, trying to form the words
to dismiss Rafe's ridiculous interpretation.

They weren't love letters. Only stories. He'd
begun writing them for Jacob.

Had he written those words?

It was only ever you.

Heat spread through him and he sat, as shaky
as his brother looked.

He couldn't stop this final rearrangement of
his internal map of constellations. At the Howling Cliffs he'd known Sam still held his body in
thrall. In Bahariya he'd admitted he wanted her
in his life. Now he had to face the fact that he'd
always kept her there, at the centre of his being.
Not Najimat al-Layl, star of the night, unreachable and tantalising. Not just inspiration for his
stories because she'd unconsciously set them in
motion and given him something to cling to when
Jacob died, but the sun—warming him while he
revolved around her. She, gleaming hot, while he
remained a barren planet in his predictable, empty
orbit. Writing love letters.

He was blind. Blind, stupid and hopeless.

While Sam had been falling in love with some
Venetian fool who couldn't or wouldn't love her
and escaping her disappointment by marrying a

man who would drive her to guilt and despair and solitude, he'd been writing her stories, tying her to him and talking to her in the only way he knew.

Like a juvenile admirer sending anonymous love poems.

'My God, I'm pathetic.'

Rafe shifted in alarm.

'Damn it, Edge, that's not what I meant. Any woman would kill to have someone write masterpieces about her and for her. Don't tell me Sam doesn't appreciate them—her illustrations are a work of love in themselves.'

'Not to me. She had no idea I was the author. That is just the way she is.'

'But…you told her, didn't you?'

'She found out a week ago. In a bookstore.'

'Oh. Well, that must have been…uncomfortable.'

Edge shoved his hands through his hair.

'Yes.'

'Do you mean to say you proposed to her, but didn't think of telling her?'

'I didn't propose. She did.'

At least that silenced Rafe. His sigh, though, was eloquent.

'I told you I am pathetic.'

'No. Stubborn. Wary. And luckier than you deserve. What is wrong, then? You should be in seventh heaven.'

Edge laughed.

'I was on fourth and climbing, but I've fallen a few rungs. I knew from the beginning Sam wanted to marry me because she wanted a family and a home and I was willing to make that devil's bargain. This shouldn't make a difference, but it does.'

'What shouldn't?'

Edge wished the doctor would come. He didn't want to talk about this, even with Rafe. He wanted to push it underground as he'd been trying to ever since her revelations in Richmond. To be patient and woo Sam and hope he'd win her warm loving core. But he knew he was pulling away from her and he couldn't seem to stop.

Rafe was right about him. He took his pain into a cave and hid. He didn't want to be second best with her. Another Ricki—filling a void created by someone else. It was like living with a thorn lodged deep into his chest, gouging at him every time she smiled or touched him. He was greedy—he wanted to be at her centre as much as she was at his. He wanted to reach into her and rip out the bastard that had left her trying to patch her life around him.

He sank his hands into his hair again and told Rafe everything.

Sam stood outside the parlour door, trying to rally her courage. She staked her impatience to the ground and dropped a pyramid atop it, but it still had her by the throat.

She knew the doctor had come and gone, that Tubbs and Edge had moved Rafe to a guest room. She'd watched the various members of the Tubbs family come and go—with clothes and towels and food and shaving implements. Tubbs had taken pity on her and told her the doctor had cleaned and dressed the wound and given his opinion that it would heal well now. But other than that she'd asked no questions and made no demands aside from a pot of tea which was now cold.

She kept waiting for Edge to come tell her something…anything. That everything would be all right now. His brother was safe. Now he was free to…to what? With a strange sense of panic she realised she did not know what he wanted from her. The only thing she knew, with a clarity that ranked alongside a Cartesian certainty, was that she loved Edge. Everything else felt flimsy, like a set upon a stage. She thought she'd wanted a home, children, but she was no longer certain. Of anything.

Except Edge.

And he was fading away again.

She closed her eyes and knocked on the door.

Patience, patience, patience.

'Sam?'

She opened her eyes. Edge stood in the door-way. He was in his shirtsleeves and had taken off his cravat and waistcoat. Just as he had looked on the *Lark*—beautiful but distant. Her heart squeezed; she wanted so desperately to reach for him, but of course she didn't.

'How is he?'

He glanced over his shoulder towards the open door of the bedroom.

'Asleep. A little feverish, but the doctor believes that is more loss of blood than infection. He says he needs rest and feeding. I would like him to stay here a few days if you don't object.'

'Of course I don't object, Edge. I am so happy for you…'

She stood like a fool, waiting for him to touch her, to ask her in or to take her to their rooms. Anything but stand there.

'Did he explain? About disappearing and Miss Osbourne and everything.'

'Yes. It is…complicated. Nothing that need concern you.'

She breathed in, her temper finally snapping into life.

'Under the circumstances I believe it does concern me.'

He straightened further and she had to tilt her head back to hold his gaze. Sometimes she wished he was shorter.

'If you are concerned about his presence at Sinclair House, I assure you…'

'Don't be an ass, Edge. I am only too happy for

him to be here, but I won't have you talking to me as if I were a stranger. I am your wife.'

'Yes. I am aware of that.'

'What on earth does that mean?'

'Never mind. I must change now and leave for Greybourne.'

'Edge, won't you tell me what is wrong? Is there something wrong with your brother?'

'Nothing but his own particular brand of imbecility. Once he is settled at Greybourne I will return to oversee the house at Richmond. It will probably be ready for us in a couple of weeks.'

'Edge. Please *talk* to me.'

He took a step forward and she realised she wasn't the only one who was angry. 'About what, Sam? You wanted a tame spouse so you could go ahead with your nice little dream of a family to replace what you really wanted. Very well. I'm here, aren't I? But, by God, Sam. Don't push me—I am in no mood at the moment to be told how wanting I am in that role. I am telling you as clearly as I am capable without breaking something that you, too, must honour your side of this devil's bargain! Right now I intend to see that Rafe is well and back at Greybourne. After that you can play cat's paw with me to your heart's content as you try to fill the hole left by the man you could not have.'

'Edge, that's not true...you don't understand...' Sam reached for him, but he shook off her hand.

'I don't wish to understand. *Any* of it. I'm sick and tired of understanding.'

He strode past her, leaving the air thick and clanging with his anger.

Tame spouse… He could *not* believe that was how she thought of him. He was about as tame as a desert lion. No, it was his anger at being trapped. And she *had* trapped him. He'd been vulnerable, worried, alone, and she'd sunk her talons into him and not let go.

What would he do if she told him he was the man who'd left this hole in her? Right now he would probably fling that away as well. It would be one more shackle around his neck…

'Ho, there! Sam.' The voice, deep and rusty, barely reached her. 'Sam Sinclair. In here. I'd come introduce myself, but this leg of mine…'

Sam moved through the parlour a little blindly and stopped in the bedroom doorway. Rafe did look like Edge, even with his ragged hair and the scars twisting the skin along the side of his jaw and throat into milky rivulets. Under his swarthy colour he was pale and his pupils were dilated, making it hard to determine the colour of his eyes.

'I've been wanting to meet you for a while. I'm Rafe.'

'Yes. Hello, Rafe. I am Sam.'

His brows rose at her flat voice.

'Yes, well. I was just dozing when I heard my

brother's bark. I can't remember the last time he let slip his dogs of war.'

Sam tried and failed to make sense of what he was saying. Her mind was locked on the image of Edge's face. His fury and disgust.

'Not a fan of the bard, are you? Never mind. What did you do to make him so angry?'

'Forced him to marry me.'

'No one forces Edge. Well, I did once. Dragged his carcase to Cumbria, but he was unconscious at the time. Stubborn lug. Don't look like that.'

'Like what?'

'Like your heart's breaking.'

She touched her forehead, her cheek. Her eyes were dry as dust. How could they show this crashing storm inside her?

'Come inside. You need some whisky, girl.'

Edge stood by the bed. Sam lay with her back to him, curled into a ball around a pillow. Inky was also curled into a ball, back to back with Sam, but the feline was awake and glaring at him as if she knew he'd been a fool.

Worse—cruel, childish, jealous. Sam had been honest with him from the start. It was not her fault he was finding it so hard to live with her terms.

The familiar burst of pain struck in his chest. Every few hours it happened, like water slowly filling a vessel and then spilling over on to flames, setting everything hissing. It was absurd and he hated it. He was becoming something he despised—resentful, maudlin…desperate.

He wanted to take her to the house they'd found and start over—wipe everything away and tell her the truth.

That he needed her.

And worse—he needed her to love him.

A thousand questions snapped at him like rats in the dark, only chased off when they were together in her bed and even then they burrowed under his skin, wondering if when she closed her eyes that man was there, a memory, a wish, a need…invisible but between them.

He'd married her knowing she was dangerous, knowing she was the only woman who'd ever reached past his defences. He'd married her without knowing where it would take them. And he had no reason to complain—she was giving so much of herself. She was passionate and compassionate and trying so hard to accommodate him, but it only made him more desperate. He didn't want her to make an effort. He wanted her to love him, need him. Not the children or the home he could give her.

Him.

Inky hissed and hopped off the bed. Sam whimpered, wrapping her arms more securely around the pillow, and heat hit him like a pugilist's blow to the sternum. He wanted to wake her, turn her to him, have her reach out to him as she did at night when weariness overcame his scruples and he gave in to the need to love her, holding the words so deeply inside him it was like swallowing a mace—every move made the spikes grind and gouge.

Instead he left the room and went down the corridor to see if his fool of a brother was still alive.

'How was your visit to the ancestral pile?' Rafe asked, putting down the book he'd been reading as Edge entered the room. With a grimace he realised it was *Treasures of Siwa*.

'Depressing as always. Mother will be arriving tomorrow morning.'

Rafe groaned.

'You are punishing me, aren't you? Why the devil couldn't she wait until I came to Greybourne?'

'I told her. To which she responded, not without cause, that she was not at all convinced you *would* come. Perhaps now that the tyrant has expired she's remembering her motherly instincts. Rather late in the game.'

Rafe sighed and smoothed the page he was reading.

'Sam gave this to me.'

Edge straightened his back.

'She came to see you?'

'No, she came to see you and you lambasted

her and stalked out, remember? I called her in and tried to soothe her, poor thing.'

'Why don't you give the knife another twist, damn you?' Edge's voice grated in his own ears.

'I imagine you've been doing nothing but twisting it since you left. And before. You hurt her deeply, Edge.'

Edge could do nothing about his visceral satisfaction at those words. *Good—because she is destroying me.* He wasn't proud of it, but it was there, like a starving hyena, grinning and waiting for its chance at the carcase because it was not strong enough to win its own prey.

'You are right. I have no excuse. I will apologise tomorrow.'

'I don't think an apology will cut it.'

'Why the devil did you have to interfere in my life in the first place? I was finally beginning to settle into…'

'Into what? Into your comfortable little hole in Brazil? Doing nothing but writing books?' Rafe waved the open book in front of him. 'This is damn good, I grant you, but it was never meant to be everything. Deuce take you, you should be on your knees thanking me! You have the one person you have wanted in your life more than anyone else outside of Jacob and you are cursing me for pushing you into her arms. The best *you* could do was tie her to you with those books. You're not only ungrateful, you're a coward.'

Rafe could always unravel him. One of the very few people who could. He didn't want to be unravelled because he was not certain he could gather himself together again. He dug his hands into his hair, tugging until it hurt, until his eyes burned. He could feel Rafe's gaze on him. Probably pitying him.

'I'm so tired, Rafe.'

'I can see. I meant well, Edge. Everything you said about me is right. I never should have interfered.'

Edge shook his head.

'I wouldn't change it. It's not enough, but it might have to be. I just need to…accept that and hope that with time her affections will grow. It was only… I didn't know she had been in love with someone else so much that she gave up hope of loving anyone else. I don't know why that hurt even worse than thinking of her with her husband. I'm trying to be sensible, but I can't and it's killing me.'

'Why don't you talk to her?'

Edge shoved his hands deeper into his hair. He wanted to be with Sam.

'And tell her what? Dear Sam, I have been in love with you from the moment you fell on top of me eight years ago and wasn't brave enough to admit it and spare either myself or my poor spoilt wife from an unhappy marriage that suited neither of us. I wove you into my life through those damn books because I couldn't have you and the moment I saw you again I wanted you so badly I thought I was hallucinating when you proposed marriage.'

'That will do to begin with. Don't forget to mention you are a coward. That might clarify some things to her.'

'God knows why I never strangled you, Rafe.'

'Because you love me, little brother. You're the only one who does.' He yawned and put down the book. 'I'm exhausted. God knows I have enough troubles of my own at the moment. What a mess we've both made. Go sleep. We'll need our strength to face Mother tomorrow.'

Chapter Seventeen

Isis raised her Ankh high above Gabriel's head, catching the sun in its eye. 'With tears, anger and love I wove Osiris's body together. But what is resurrected will never be what was—what is lost remains lost.'
—*Captives of the Hidden City,*
Desert Boy Book Four

Sam stared at the door to the drawing room. She could hear voices insides, but not the words. Edge's deep voice—calm. And a woman's voice—calmer. Her mama-in-law.

Her hands fisted. Edge had not come to tell her. He'd left it to Tubbs to inform her.

She didn't want to go in. She didn't want the first time she saw Edge after his anger to be like this. She took a deep breath and entered none the less. Edge might be angry at her, but he would need her now, whether he admitted it or not. She would show him precisely how proper and patient she could be.

The woman in a dove-grey dress seated on the sofa looked very much like her sons—the same high cheekbones, thin lips and cold eyes. The archetypal Duchess.

Edge rose to his feet, his face even more than usually expressionless. He looked like a bored stranger accompanying his mother on a morning call.

'Mother, may I introduce Lady Edward, my wife.'

Sam had an absurd urge to curtsy. Instead she murmured a polite greeting and turned to Edge.

'How is your brother this morning?'

'A little feverish, but better, thank you. I will see if he is ready for you to visit with him, Mother.'

Sam quelled the urge to grab at his sleeve as he passed. That or pick up the porcelain figure of a sphinx on the table and hurl it at him. Instead she tightened her jaw into a smile and wondered what did one say to one's mother-in-law when she was regarding you like something a rag shop wouldn't deign to sell?

'I am happy to finally make your acquaintance, Your Grace. You must be delighted to have your sons back in England.'

'Naturally. I would have preferred it to happen under less…irregular circumstances.'

'I see. I presume by irregular you mean our marriage? Would you care for some tea, Your Grace?'

'No, I thank you. I was referring to that, yes. Naturally I would have hoped Edge would respect the family name by marrying at the Greybourne chapel as he did with poor, dear Dora.'

Poor, dear Dora. Flame mixed with ice in a viscous dance inside Sam's chest. She pressed her hands to her thighs and noticed they were damp and shaking.

'We felt it best to marry in Cairo at the embassy. It was perfectly respectable, I assure you. My brother was married there.'

'Ah, yes. Your brother. Lord Sinclair or the other one?'

'The other one.'

'Nevertheless. Such a hasty marriage and then that nonsensical gossip that Edward might have written those books. Naturally I denied it, but thanks to rumours surrounding the marriage it fell on fertile ground.'

'Denied it?'

'Of course. Greybournes do not pen *novels.*'

Sam's jaw was beginning to ache. She drew 'patience' in big block letters in her mind.

'Did you not ask Edge about it?'

'Naturally not. *Edward* might have had his moments of weakness after the boy's death and I will always regret that he chose to leave rather than follow dear Dora to Bath and attempt a reconciliation, but he would never stoop so low as to sully the Greybourne name by penning pamphlets.'

Patience be damned.

'They are not pamphlets. They are novels and they are brilliant! Why, even your own friend— what was her name? Lady Buckston or Munchinson or something?—adores them. You should be bursting with pride Edge has created something so marvellous, so unique...'

'My dear... Lady Edward. You obviously belong to a younger, looser crowd than *Edward* is used to associating with, but I assure you—'

'Edge.' Sam bit out the word. 'He might have resented it when I forced that name on him as a child, but I do know he *hates* being called Edward. I don't even call him Edward when I wish to annoy him, which is often.'

'Nonsense. The Dukes of Greybourne have named their sons Rafael and Edward for the past two hundred years.'

'Edge didn't. He named his son after Poppy, your brother. Jacob Phillip after Phillip Jacob Carmichael. Not an Edward or a Rafael in the list. I dare say the Duke was not happy with that.'

The pale eyes, very like Rafe's, Sam realised, were now fixed on her with a totally different quality. But then they went utterly flat. Edge might have been sent away young, but he must have absorbed certain skills at a very young age.

'No, he was not happy. The Duke said the child's death was ordained thanks to Edward's disrespect to the Edgerton name.'

Sam gasped in shock.

'He did not. He *could* not have said such a thing.'

The Duchess didn't answer.

'He said that…to Edge? To his face?'

'Yes.'

Sam leaned forward, then sat back. She could not sit still.

'I have never heard anything so cruel, so ignorant…so *brutal*. To say something like that when they had just lost their child.'

'They?'

'Edge and Dora. It is too cruel. They must have been devastated.'

'Dora was not at the burial, naturally. She had been ill and was with her mother in Bath for some months. The child was very poorly that last year. He never did recover after the rheumatic fever struck him and the doctors did not give out much hope the child would live to adulthood, you see. He could hardly even crawl. So naturally they recommended Dora not expose herself to the worry of her son's ailments given her delicate constitution. The Duke felt that, too, was a sign. He felt it best to place the child in the care of a woman on one of our lesser properties. Once that was arranged Dora's mother would naturally have considered advising her to return to Chesham so they could begin again.'

Sam shook her head. Edge had shared only the barest bones of this tragedy and it had still been devastating. She had never realised how alone he had been in his love for his son.

'You keep saying "naturally",' she said. 'I see nothing natural about any of this other than Edge's love for his son. Do you mean to say that for the whole year between Jacob's illness and death Dora was coddling her nerves in Bath, being manipulated by her mother into punishing and threatening Edge, while his own father proclaimed it an act of God that a baby suffer and die? And you stood by and didn't howl to the heavens at how wrong this was?'

The Duchess plucked at some lint on her grey wool gown. She opened her mouth to speak, but Sam could not bear another word. She stood and realised her legs were shaking.

'I am sorry, Your Grace, but you must excuse me for a moment. I… No, I am not sorry. I am so very, very grateful to you. You will never know how much.'

She had finally succeeded in exciting an emotion other than disdain from the woman, if surprise could be considered an emotion.

'Grateful?'

'Yes, grateful. I did not understand how you could have given away your child, a boy of six, but it was the very best thing you could have done. Poppy and Janet loved him with all their enormous hearts, unconditionally. They helped make him the marvellous, unique man he is. Someone any *natural* parent would be so proud of they would likely purchase a hundred copies of his novels and force all their friends to read them, but would fight tooth and nail to protect his privacy if he so wished it. It broke their hearts when your…when *their* grandson died. It broke their hearts when Edge went even further away and they had to let him go and hope he would return. I saw their faces when he arrived in Qetara. *That* is love. And I guarantee you that they are probably even now filled with happiness at the thought that they will see him again when they reach England. That is why Edge will always turn to them when he needs to see what he is really like. Not to you.'

'Yes. I know. And now to you. What *do* you call him when you wish to annoy him?' the Duchess asked.

Sam felt very much as if she'd run off a cliff. Her breath was still choppy, her heart beating faster than a horse at a gallop, but she'd lost her ground. The Duchess wasn't even looking at her, but over her shoulder, and with a shiver of premonition Sam turned. Edge and Rafe were standing just outside the open door. Edge was holding Rafe's arm, whether to support him or anchor himself was unclear. Rafe was leaning on a cane and he moved forward awkwardly.

'Yes, Sam. What do you call this lug when you wish to annoy him? I could use some leverage. Hello, Mother. I admit you have succeeded in surprising me.'

'I dare say I have. You are not looking well, Rafael. These past two years have not dealt kindly with you. Do sit down before you fall down.' She patted the sofa by her, but Rafe managed to ease himself into an armchair opposite her. Sam wavered and found herself pressed back down on to the sofa by Edge. He sat within reach but unreachable, his gaze on the Duchess.

'What game were you playing just now, Mother?'

'Game?' Sam demanded, still trying to steady herself.

'I do not indulge in games, Edw... Edge. I was curious about your wife, that is all. She is nothing like Dora.'

'No. Thank God.'

'Yes. Dora was a charming girl, full of light and laughter as long as the sun shone, but not built for hardship. A delightful lapdog to your current lioness.'

'You were *testing* me?' Sam demanded, but the Duchess turned to her sons.

'I am aware my choices when you were young mean I will always have but limited access to you and I have accepted that. I still believe it was the best decision under the circumstances after the effects of your father's accident became apparent. Now that Rafe has little choice but to assume the responsibilities of his title—' she glanced at Rafe as he shifted in the armchair '—I will remove to the Lancashire property. I have only remained until now to ensure Greybourne does not fall into disrepair and I hope I have not done too ill a job. I know neither of you will voluntarily seek my company in future so naturally I wished to take what is likely to be a singular opportunity to see if this woman will make you a good wife. I see that she shall and I was wrong to worry.'

Sam's eyes moved between the three of them. The resemblance was almost comically marked at the moment, each more rigid than the next as if afraid to turn over the stone the Duchess had tossed into their midst. Sam had no patience for circumspection at this point.

'What accident? And what has it to do with sending Edge away?'

'I am surprised you have no memory of this, Rafael. You were, after all, seven years old at the time. The Duke was thrown from his horse and suffered a severe injury to the head. For a long time we thought he would not survive and though he did he was no longer the same man. He became most pious and intolerant and…occasionally violent. After the incident when he broke your arm,

Edw... Edge, Dr Parracombe and I decided it was judicious we limit his access to the children since there was no question of having the Duke confined. That scandal would have stained the Greybourne name beyond repair.'

Edge clasped his left arm.

'He broke it? My father broke it? How?'

For the first time Sam saw true emotion in the woman's eyes—but the fear and pain were tucked swiftly away; only a faint tremor remained in the Duchess's next words.

'That day...you were reading to me from a book. Even then you had the most marvellous voice and nothing gave me greater pleasure than to hear you read. But Greybourne walked in and tried to take the book from you. You were always stubborn, my boy, and unfortunately you held on. Before I could even think he threw you against the wall. By the time Dr Parracombe came and treated you and sedated him I had made a pact with myself. I would protect my children by whatever means possible and that meant removing you from danger and ensuring no one but I and the doctor knew the truth. By luck Poppy was still in London and I asked if he would take you for a spell.' She smoothed her dress again, but as no one broke the silence she continued. 'As time passed I realised you would be infinitely happier with them than at Greybourne. I could hardly expect the Duke to condone sending his heir to Egypt, but I ensured you spent most of the year at school, Rafe, and the girls with the governess in their own wing. Naturally we could allow no taint of madness to cling to the Greybourne name and as far as I know there have never been rumours. Rigid religious beliefs served as a fine excuse for his spells. Now he is dead we need no longer be concerned with discovery. Doctor Parracombe is completely trustworthy.'

'Trustworthy… Mother, why did you never say a word of this? We have not been children for a while. We *deserved* to know.'

'I thought it the best course of action.' She turned to Rafe. 'Greybourne is your cross to bear now, Rafe. I do hope you find someone to share it with who will make it a happier place.'

Her gaze moved over Rafe's face and her fingers reached out and hovered within reach of his scarred jaw.

'I hope…no more of this for a while?'

He shook his head, looking as bemused as Edge.

'Good,' the Duchess said. 'I have promised to visit with some friends while I am in town and then I must prepare for my departure to Lancashire now I have seen all is well. Do ring for my carriage to be brought round.'

Sam sensed Edge enter the room and placed the drawing she held face down on the table.

'Has she gone?'

He nodded. He was watching her as warily as he had watched his mother.

'And Rafe?'

'Sleeping. He is still weaker than he wishes to believe.'

'He has been busy.'

Edge's mouth picked up at the corners. His first true smile for her for days. Her sad little heart stretched itself at his feet like a panting puppy.

Oh, Edge. I am trying so hard to do what is right and I keep ruining it.

'So have you, Sam. That was quite an attack.'

'You heard it?'

He nodded.

'How much of it?'

'Most of it. Rafe was already in the corridor when I went to fetch him, but once we reached the door we heard you… I wanted to go in and stop her, but he said…' Edge spread out his hands as if trying to explain the unexplainable. 'He said to trust you. I'm sorry.'

'You're sorry?'

'I should have protected you, not the other way around.'

'I was a vicious shrew.'

'Not vicious. Protective. A lioness, as my mother said. No, a warrior queen on the rampage. Boadicea. Hatshepsut. Cleopatra. Nike…'

'Nike is mythical, not real.'

'Many myths are based on reality. Besides, I don't need comparison. You were magnificent, Sam. Thank you.'

'You're not angry?'

'My manly pride is a trifle trampled at having been rescued from the dragon by the damsel, but I find I rather like the experience.'

'You look…strange.'

'I'm smiling.'

She smiled as well.

'That is not what I mean.'

'I know. I think I am…in shock. A little. All these years I thought I wasn't…important enough to keep. Or worse—that there was something so objectionable about me I was best kept far away. Even Dora's pulling away when she became with child felt like proof—I tried to tell myself it was foolish, but there was a part of me that believed the taint was showing through. When Jacob fell ill… I didn't believe my father's vicious rant about judgement, but I couldn't shake it off. When your life is built around a gaping pit it's easy to populate it with monsters. So I decided to place a lid on it and ignore it as best I could. Until I met you again and you kept shoving me in. And now this… Strange how it never occurred to me it might be the other way around. Now I feel guilty I hated my mother.'

She took his hand.

'She made her choice, Edge. I know what she said, but she *should* have told you.'

'Yes. But we become stuck in our ways. With our choices.'

Before she could stop him he reached out and turned over her sketch. It was an absent motion, but as soon as he saw the drawing his gaze focused, colour staining his cheeks. Her heart sank. Just when he was softening towards her. He would probably see this as another offence.

'Sam…'

'You cannot expect me not to draw you. That is not fair. I keep them all safely in a case so you needn't worry anyone will see them…'

'There are more?'

He followed her glance towards the leather-bound case on the table and something between a whimper and a groan escaped her. She didn't try to stop him as he opened it and looked through them. There was no hiding it now. All her drawings of him on the *Lark*, the endless drawings she'd made during his two-week absence and those of him in their bed…

He took the one of him leaning back in the bath, looking beautiful and weary and worried.

'I can't help drawing you.' The words burst out of her and he finally put them down.

'You are so damnably gifted, Sam,' he said quietly. 'I don't deserve you.'

'Edge…'

'No, please listen. I know I have been... unbearable these past days. I will do better.'

'Can you not tell me what is bothering you? I would rather know the worst than imagine it. Even if you are regretting this marriage. Just *tell* me.'

He planted his hand on the case and took a deep breath.

'Marrying you was the best thing I have ever done, Sam. Remember in *The Curse of the Valley of the Moon* when the dragon warns Gabriel not to use his wish to find Leila, that being granted your heart's desire too easily can poison the gift? Well, I was wiser than I realised when I wrote that because it is true. Out of nowhere you offered me what I wanted most in the world, though I barely admitted it to myself. I knew there would be a price, but I was willing to pay it. I still am, but I can't deny it hurts like the devil to know I am a compromise, Sam.'

'A *compromise*?'

'Until you told me about the man you loved I was beginning to hope you were learning to love me a little, too—I mean not as a friend but as the person you need more than anyone else. Perhaps that was why it hit me so hard, to be pushed back like that. I wanted to wrap my hands around his throat and squeeze and watch him empty of life as if I could drain him out of you like a poison. It was a foolish, juvenile reaction and I vented my fear and disappointment on you though you are not to blame for loving him. It is what it is. I hope that with time you will come to care for me in the same manner as I care for you, but even if you don't I will never regret this.'

His eyes were a very clear green as they searched hers. 'I've scared you. I didn't mean to do that, but you wanted to know the worst. And I suppose the worst is that I love you. You will no doubt think me a fool and a cad and you would be quite right, but I fell in love with you eight years ago and I didn't even understand it. I made a terrible mistake with Dora and she paid the price, poor girl. She could have been happy with someone else. She deserved to be. Dora was what I thought I wished to be after I escaped that hellish war, but with you I was completely myself—good, bad and boring.'

'You were never boring,' Sam managed to say, trying to cling to something in this foreign landscape. Beautiful but foreign, like a dream.

He smiled again.

'Yes, I was, rigid, boring, trying to herd you into a corner where you wouldn't threaten me. But I couldn't and I didn't really want to. If I had, I wouldn't have followed you around everywhere those weeks, scolding like a pathetic mother hen. I employed every excuse I could to be around you and not once did it occur to me why until you fell on top of me and knocked some sense into me when it was far too late. That moment shifted my life on its axis, Sam. I never admitted it, but from that moment onwards the only time you weren't at its centre was when Jacob was born. For a while I had him and I was so happy...'

He looked down again and she risked her dream by taking his hand and threading their fingers together. He closed his eyes.

'I wish... I wish he had met you. I wish he were here with us.'

Sam wrapped herself around him, her face against his chest.

'I would have loved him and loved him and loved him.' She spoke the words to his heart, her lips reverberating with its beat. His hand smoothed her hair, gently pulling the pins out of it.

'I know that, little mountain goat. I told him all about you, everything I could remember. I wrote my first book for him, but you inspired it like a madcap Don Quixote, tilting at pyramids and ambitious priests and wrathful gods. I don't know if he liked my stories, but I know he loved your drawings.'

'I want you to tell me all about him, everything and anything you wish. I'm so afraid to ask and have you push me away again, but I'm tired of being afraid with you. And you are such an idiot, Edge. It's my fault, but you *are* an idiot. Do you really believe I would have made the same mistake *twice*? I only married Ricki because you were married to Dora.'

'You don't mean…you were very young, iso-lated…' He shook his head and the warmth was already being furled back in, but she held on to his hand, ready to weather this wave as well.

'I know that is how you thought of me, but I wasn't being madcap Sam when I kissed you eight years ago, Edge. When you told me about Dora that day you smashed a world I'd hardly even re-alised existed. I was miserable and lonely and it was even worse when Mama and I returned to Venice. I needed so desperately to be loved and I made a horrible mistake. I told you I wanted a family, but that wasn't why I proposed to you. I may not have admitted to myself I still…cared for you, but within two days of seeing you at Qetara I knew I couldn't bear for you to disappear, not again. I had to try…'

His hand jerked in hers and the battle for and against believing her was evident in the tension that deepened the lines about his mouth. She clasped her hands tighter around his. She needed him to believe her. If he were to trust her, to open to her, he had to believe her.

'I was young, but not a child, eight years ago, Edge. It wasn't an infatuation, no matter how handsome you were and how peculiar my up-bringing. Because even then I knew you, Edge. Down to my core and down to yours. That hasn't changed. I never thought of it, but I could always feel who you were behind those mile-high walls you erected and I think you always knew it, too, even if it didn't affect you as it did me. When you left I was determined to overcome you, but I never did, Edge. I'm so glad you were brave enough to tell me you love me because the words have been burning inside me for weeks and weeks, but I was terrified of chasing you away again and I'm exhausted with being patient. I love you so much. You are the only man I have ever loved.'

'Sam... God, Sam, I *need* this to be true.'

'Of course it is true, Edge. Can you not see it? It is in every one of these drawings I have been hoarding and hiding from you. Lucas was right when he said that I'd drawn you into my illustrations for your books even before I knew you were the author. I wove you into my life the only way I could. I don't need you to give me a home or children. *You* are my home. I need to be with you because I am utterly myself with you, even when you are impossible. And I am beginning to believe it is the same for you, so it is good Rafe and Lucas and Chase interfered in our lives. What do people do without big brothers?'

She was babbling and she could see him teetering on the verge of his wary need to shore up the battlements. True to form.

She grabbed his shirt in her hands.

'I love you, Edge. I dare you to believe me and step off that cliff with me.'

'You always did enjoy tossing out dares, Sam.' His mouth softened into the smile that melted her each time, but she was lost in the sea green of his eyes.

'I dare you,' she repeated and his hands swept down her back, moulding to her backside as he raised her towards him.

'I love your posterior, Sam. Every lush inch of it.'

'You shan't distract me. I dare you to step off the ledge, Edge, and trust me to catch you.'

'I'll crush you. You nearly broke every bone in my body when you jumped off that temple. And you definitely broke my heart.'

She heard the catch in his voice, the need, the fear, the yearning.

'You broke mine, so we're even. *Trust* me.' She brushed her mouth over his, fitting their lips together as perfectly as she had that first time so long ago. God, he tasted like heaven, like honey cakes and bliss and eternity.

'Sam, I adore you…'

'I dare you, love of my life. Jump…'

So he did.

Epilogue

The sound of hammering followed Edge as he crossed the lawn towards where Sam was standing beneath the willows, the rowboat shifting lazily on the water beside her. Her hair was loose over her shoulder and he brushed it aside to kiss her nape, breathing in the scent of another world.

His chosen, perfectly imperfect world.

His hand skimmed downwards, hesitating before coming to rest on the rise of her abdomen where their child was growing. She placed her hand on his, their fingers interlacing. He knew the heartbeat he felt was hers, not the child's, but his breathing tightened anyway—with fear, with love, some more fear and finally with hope. He wanted this, with Sam, so badly. He was so much luckier than he deserved.

If he'd learned anything in these past months with Sam, it was that they were good for each other. Even when they fought he felt himself grow, open up to her, resting each time more easily on this trust he'd never trusted. On Sam. He had no idea how he'd survived for so long in his loneliness when being with her felt so natural. It was into this world, this reality they would bring their child…their children. It felt so right his heart cracked each time he allowed the realisation to settle.

Each time he let himself love her a little more.

'Love of my life,' he murmured against her skin and she sighed and took his hand, pulling him towards the wide wicker chair under the willows.

'I knew not even you could write with all that noise. At least this time the nursery won't take as long as the rest of the house did.'

'It wasn't the noise that distracted me. It was the sight of you through the window. We need a larger chair. Better yet, sit on me, you two.'

'I'm beginning to feel like two. At least I no longer feel seasick. Perhaps our little girl was practising for all the voyages we shall take her on.'

He pulled her on to his lap, touching his lips to her forehead and breathing her in.

'Or boy,' he murmured against her skin and she took his hand, but he could feel that quiver of tension that came over her when she worried memories of Jacob were hurting him. 'Whatever it is, Sam, I'm so happy I was clever enough to accept your proposal.'

'Occasionally even you have bursts of intelligence.' She snuggled more deeply against him and picked up the book that was resting on the arm of the chair. 'Like this one. I never asked you, Edge, but now that I've read *Treasures of Siwa* again I couldn't help wondering…' She opened the book and he tensed as her fingers rested below a particular passage. 'I wondered why Durham only sent a partial manuscript of this one and when I discovered you were the author I was so upset I forgot to ask you why. Was it because of this?'

He glanced at the page. Strange that he had not thought much about it when he wrote it almost two years ago in Brazil. It had just…come. Now it looked like a premonition.

Leila knew love was never intended for her kind and she had no such expectations. So when love came she hid it deep inside the caverns of her soul and turned her back on it, though it blazed hotter than the August sun.

But even the best hiding places must eventually be abandoned or they become graves. And so, when she stood at Gabriel's side above the valley and felt his pain strike sharper and deeper than the swords that decimated her family and dreams, she finally said the words that would bring either damnation or release.

'It was only ever you, Gabriel, my one and only love.'

Her finger rested below the word 'love' and he took her hand, raising it to press a kiss to the heart of her palm.

'I didn't think about it at the time. I only felt... unnerved and as usual I did my foolish best not to consider why. But, yes, I put those words on Leila's lips because I needed to hear them, Sam. Even if it was only in my mind. They were true for me even if I was too great an idiot to realise it. Rafe told me the *Desert Boy* books were one long love letter and he was right. They were always my love letters to you, Sam.'

Sam touched his cheek and smiled and his world filled once more.

'I'm glad you wrote them, Edge. Because it was only ever you, my one and only love.'

* * * * *

MILLS & BOON

Coming next month

CONTRACTED AS HIS COUNTESS
Louise Allen

He was dangerous, reports said, but they were hazy about who he was a danger to, other than the aforementioned blackmailers, presumably. The judgement was that he was ruthless, but honest. Stubborn, difficult and self-contained.

No one had reported on Jack Ransome's looks, on that straight nose, on that firm, rather pointed, jaw that gave him a slightly feline look. Certainly there had been no mention of a mouth that held the only hint of sensuous indulgence in that entire severe countenance. Other than those faint laughter lines…

So far, so…acceptable.

'You show no curiosity about why I have engaged your services, Lord… Mr Ransome.'

'No doubt you will inform me in your own good time. Whether you decide to employ me or not, I will present your man of business with my fee for today and for the time I will spend travelling to and from Newmarket and for my expenses incurred en route. If you wish to expend that money on chit-chat, that is your prerogative, Miss Aylmer.'

Very cool. Very professional, I suppose.

She stood, glad of the table edge to steady herself, and he rose, too, a good head taller than she, despite her height. 'Please. Sit.' The lid of the coffer creaked open until it was stopped by a retaining chain, standing as a screen between Mr Ransome and its contents. Madelyn lifted out the rolls and bundles of paper and parchment that it contained and placed them on the table in a pile at her left hand, except for one which she partly opened out. She kept her right hand on that as she sat again.

'What I require, Mr Ransome, is a husband.' She had rehearsed this and now her voice hardly shook at all. In some strange way this situation went beyond shocking and frightening into a nightmare and nightmares were not real. Father had left careful and exact instructions and she had always obeyed him, as she did now. Even so, she kept her gaze on the parchment that crackled under her palm.

'Then I fear you have approached the wrong man. I do not act as a marriage broker.' When she looked up Mr Ransome shifted on the carved wooden chair as though to stand again.

'You do not understand, of course. I have not made myself plain. I do not require you to find me a husband. I wish you to marry me. Yourself,' she added, just in case that was not clear enough.

Continue reading
CONTRACTED AS HIS COUNTESS
Louise Allen

Available next month
www.millsandboon.co.uk